A Historical Western Pioneer Romance

Alice's Journey West
Finding Her Way

Katherine St. Clair

ISBN: 9781725149977

Printed in the United States

Chapter One

April 5, 1876
Augusta, Georgia

Alice Cleary was wearing her best dress, a hand-me-down blue cotton frock that had once belonged to her cousin. Her long, thick hair was braided and pinned in the latest style, making her head ache from the weight of it. Her feet hurt from the tight-laced shoes that were, like the dress, slightly too small, and the corset her aunt had insisted she wear for the occasion was pinching. It was laced tight, to make her waist as tiny as her cousin's, so this fancy dress would fit. The weather was unseasonably warm for April, which only contributed to her discomfort. But her physical complaints were soon forgotten as she listened with a growing sense of dread to the older man who was seated in her aunt's sparsely furnished parlor.

"Miss Alice," he said as he gazed at her in a way that made her skin crawl, "You are looking lovely this afternoon."

Jackson Chandler, or *the colonel* as he was known in Augusta, led the militia in town and was widely respected. He owned a large plantation on the outskirts of the town, which he somehow managed to keep despite the high taxes and the lean years after the war, when money – like everything else – was scarce. He was as old as Alice's uncle, although he appeared to be much older. But if Alice was honest, it wasn't his age that bothered her, it was everything else.

Colonel Chandler was a widower, twice. His first wife had died in childbirth years before the war. His second wife fell from the top of the stairs in his enormous house. Her death was an accident (too much laudanum, it was said) but Alice wasn't so sure. There was something about the colonel that made her wish he had never noticed her. It wasn't his red, jowled face or his thick meaty hands, or even his bloated belly. To focus on his physical detractions was vanity and she'd been taught not to judge on the sake of appearance.

No, it wasn't his looks that made Alice want to run away from the man, it was the sense of wickedness that surrounded him. The war had happened when she was a little girl; she barely remembered her life before her parents died and their farmhouse was destroyed by the Yankees. Maybe that was why she disliked the colonel. For a man who led the militia, he seemed to have suffered no consequences. His own palatial home, a grand place with enormous white columns and marble floors, was left intact. Other people starved when food was scarce or too expensive, but he ate well and grew fat. Alice's friend Daisy whispered rumors that Colonel Chandler was cruel to his servants and to his only son.

As Alice tried to ignore the way the old man looked at her, she thought of his son. He was a man in his thirties who was pale, weak, and prone to drink. This was not a family she wished to marry into, especially not when she thought about sharing a bed with the colonel. Alice shuddered involuntarily as her aunt Helen, a demure but kind woman, set her teacup down on the small wooden table at the side of her plain chair.

"Alice, are you unwell? Is there a draft? We can lay the fire on," the frail, thin-faced woman asked as she frowned in Alice's direction.

Alice knew that there wasn't much firewood left. There wasn't much of anything left. So much had been sold for money to try to pay the crushing taxes her uncle owed on the house and farm.

"No, don't worry about me. I'm well; it's plenty warm in here. There is no need for a fire."

The colonel wiped his round face with a silk handkerchief. "It's hotter than Sherman's march through Georgia. Miss Alice, I know what you need, you need some good fresh air. Come and sit a spell with me on the porch."

Alice looked at her aunt. She was desperate to be away from this man, not alone with him on the porch.

Her aunt looked away as she said, "Yes, Alice, you should go outside with the colonel and take in the air. It will do you good. I'll be along with some lemonade."

"Thank you, Mrs. Cleary. Lemonade would be a fine drink on a warm day," the colonel said as he rose with a great deal of effort out of the chair he was occupying. The chair creaked as though a great weight had been lifted. He offered his fleshy arm to Alice, and she had no choice but to accept it. She had no wish to lay her hand, (even encased in a lace glove) on his arm, but she must do what was expected.

"My aunt needs my help in the kitchen, but I can sit for a spell," Alice said, trying to give herself a reason for a shortened visit.

"I can manage. You sit with the colonel," her aunt said.

Alice's spirits flagged. Now there would be no escape from this great hulk of a man. She shuddered again to think of how he may try to steal a kiss from her if given a chance.

As if he sensed what she was thinking he smiled at her, except to Alice it was less than a smile and more of a leer. She grimaced.

"Miss Alice, I do hope you will share a seat in the swing with me," he suggested.

Alice raised her gloved hand to her mouth, and faked a cough just below her aunt's hearing. Whispering, she said, "Forgive me, I have been feeling under the weather these past few days. I do not wish to alarm my aunt; she has much to trouble her. I have to decline sharing the swing with you, perhaps another time?"

Undeterred, he shrugged. "You don't have to worry about getting me sick with your little cough. I'm healthy as a horse. Don't you worry about me. You come right along and have a seat beside me. I have something I want to give you."

Sighing, Alice could not think of a way out of this man's insufferable company. Walking out onto the porch, she was greeted by a beautiful early spring day. Birds sang in the treetops, and the blue hydrangea bush bloomed by the front steps. She took a deep breath. She longed to be out of the corset and free of her shoes and the heavy dress. If she could unpin her hair and let her braid fall to her waist, she would slip on her old worn out muslin house dress. Then she would be happy.

Instead, she was trussed up like a roast chicken, stuffed inside layers of clothes that were itchy and too hot. Everything from her feet to her chest hurt. She could barely breathe, and when she did she was certain she caught the scent of whisky on the colonel's breath.

He sat down in the swing, his prodigious girth giving her little room to accompany him. Since her coughing hadn't worked, or her bid to help her aunt in the kitchen, she decided that modesty was her only defense. She chose a rocking chair beside the swing.

The colonel patted the seat beside him. "Come on over here, Miss Alice; I don't bite. I have something pretty I want to give to you."

"Thank you, Colonel, but it wouldn't be proper," she said as she made herself comfortable in the chair.

"Your aunt and uncle don't mind. Why would they? If it weren't for me they would have lost this place during the war. Come on, be nice to an old friend of your family. Look what I have for you," he said as he reached into his vest pocket.

"Thank you for all you've done for them, sir, but I think it's better I remain here. A girl has to think of her reputation."

"Reputation? What does that have to do with it? If anyone were to see you with me they would say that you had made a good choice. There isn't another man in Augusta with my money or my good name. Think on that. From what I hear, your uncle is in a heap of trouble. He's about to lose his farm. I was thinking about being neighborly, doing the right thing by him since I've taken such a shine to you. I was thinking about it, but I could change my mind. Come on over here and let me see how this looks on you," he dangled a pendant on a slender gold chain from his pudgy fingers.

Alice stared at the gift as the awful words he'd said sank in for a moment. She didn't want to accept his gift; she would be obliged to him if she did. She was repulsed to think what favor he might request as he waved the necklace, the bright gold shining in the afternoon light. With the creaking of the hinges on the front door, her aunt came bustling out of the house holding a tray of drinks. She did not meet Alice's eye, but Alice had the terrible suspicion that her aunt would do little to save her from the affections of this terribly domineering man.

"Mrs. Cleary, you've done a fine job raising Miss Alice here to be a God-fearing woman, but tell her there's nothing wrong with treating your guest hospitably. I'm offering her a fine present and she won't accept it. I'm feeling mighty insulted," he said.

Her aunt did not look at her, but spoke to the colonel. "Has she been rude to you? You must forgive her. She is quite young, just nineteen."

"Nineteen. What does that have to do with it? My first wife was seventeen when I married her. My second one was not much older. I wish for her to sit with me on the swing, so we can have a proper visit, and she insists on treating me like a stranger."

"Alice, tell the colonel thank you for his lovely gift. Now go on, and have a seat beside him. You mustn't let him think you don't mean to be polite."

Alice was frozen in her seat. She had no desire to get anywhere near the colonel, but she didn't know what to do. Her brother, Will, had warned her that her uncle was in trouble because of the Yankees. The war was over, it had been for ten years, but still the northerners came to the South to punish every southerner for rebelling in the first place. These Yankees stayed on, making their homes in the finest houses, taking the farms and businesses of southerners when they could. These days, the Yankees (and anyone greedy enough to side with them) ran everything, making the business of rebuilding nearly impossible for any family who had fought on the side of the confederacy. Ten years should have been enough time for the North to extract its revenge, but it seemed that their thirst to punish every man, woman, and child was never going to be quenched. The Yankees who ran the tax office at the county had raised the property taxes on every farm and plantation, all but one – and that one belonged to the colonel.

There were few who could afford to pay the taxes. Everyone else was in the same terrible state as the Clearys, scrambling for money, unsure what to do or what the future held for them. Alice knew what was at stake. She was being leveraged like property, used to court the good favor of the one man in Augusta who could convince the Yankees to forgive the debt on the Cleary farm. With a chill, she realized she might have to do more than sit beside the man she loathed. Would she have to marry him so that her uncle and aunt wouldn't lose their farm? As she forced herself to stand, to make her feet carry her closer to the swing, she watched her aunt's shoulders tense with some unknown emotion. Maybe she could manage sitting beside the colonel for a few minutes.

She carefully wedged herself into the space beside him and tried to think of nice places she would rather be as he slid the necklace around her neck. His fingers brushed against her skin in a way that felt improper. She wanted to vomit as his rough fingers fumbled to clasp the necklace. At last, it was on and

Alice tried to smile, but found all she could manage was a weak, "thank you."

Her aunt left the tray of drinks on the table and made an excuse that she had something on the stove. Alice felt very alone as her aunt rushed inside the house, her head down, her face twisted into a frown. With the slamming of the door behind her aunt, Alice wanted to run away. Anger began to burn in her chest. She would have loved to strike the colonel in his fat round face and run down the lane as fast as she could, but she knew she couldn't do that.

He reached for an errant dark curl that fell on her shoulder, fingering her hair. "You don't favor the rest of your kin, not the way I see it. Your hair is dark as night. You got those deep colored eyes like a gypsy, but your skin is fair as milk. I bet you got a secret, don't you?"

"A secret?" she asked as she tried to forget that he was still rubbing her hair between his fingers.

"You can tell me. I don't mind a little secret; lots of people got them. Your aunt and uncle, they have a secret, but I didn't come here to talk about them. They have done good by you, raising you like you were one of their own youngins, but we know the truth, you and I."

"What truth is that, that I'm their niece? That's hardly a secret," she tried to laugh, but she knew that wasn't what he meant.

"I think they're not telling you all of it, but I don't mind. You got the features of someone who isn't all white. I was never opposed to a little mixing of the races, if you know what I mean. When I had a plantation full of slaves, I wouldn't turn down any pretty women who wanted to show me their gratitude. You can tell me your secret. Maybe I won't tell no one, if you're nice to me."

She stared at him, appalled. "What do you mean, nice? What are you implying?"

"Come now, you know what I'm implying. Your brother looks like the rest of the Clearys, but not you. You with your fair skin and dark hair. You have the dark eyes of what, you're not a gypsy, maybe you're an Indian. Look at your face. If you were dark-skinned, I bet you would look like one of those heathen savages. You could almost pass for an Indian. Is that your secret? Or is it something else?"

Alice had heard vague stories from her family when she was growing up, that they had a grandmother who was a healer, that her grandmother may have been an Indian woman. She didn't know if any of it was true. She was far too young when she heard it and there was no one who talked about it anymore. She knew that her hair was darker than any other Cleary's and her features were markedly different, but she never put much stock in any of the old stories, until now. What the colonel was proposing was dangerous. If he thought she was Indian somehow, he could make trouble for her and her family.

"That's not true. I'm a Cleary, same as my brother," she said, but she knew whether she had Indian blood or not didn't matter. What the colonel said would matter.

With the Indians in the area still clashing with the settlers, word that the Clearys were their kin was not going to make things easy in town. They'd be shunned, and they could not afford that. If Colonel Chandler was insistent, he could make a case against her – and he was wicked and vile enough to do so. He was not content to use the threat to her aunt and uncle's farm against her, he was doing everything in his power to make sure she didn't have any way to resist him.

"Come on over and give me a kiss. You and I can be friends. If you're nice to me, maybe we can be more than that. I brought you a pretty necklace. Doesn't that make us friends? I don't mind what you are, I'll still take you for my wife."

He reached for her, and she froze on the spot. Her first instinct was to scream, but she clamped her mouth shut. As he slid his plump, sweaty hands around her waist, she closed her eyes, dreading what was to come. She felt her own hands ball into fists; she was going to hit the man, and she knew it. He deserved to be hit, again and again, for his villainy. Closing her eyes tight, she waited for the right moment. Just as she could feel his hot breath on her face getting warmer, she heard a voice that she swore belonged to a guardian angel.

"Colonel Chandler, what are your intentions to my sister?" the voice said. Alice opened her eyes to see Will standing on the bottom step of the porch.

Will was two years younger than Alice, but he was taller by a foot, and he looked like a grown man. With his wiry figure and wispy blond hair, he resembled every other Cleary. His fair skin was splotched red as he glared at the colonel.

"Will, my boy. I don't know what you're suggesting. We were just sitting a spell on the porch together, weren't we?" The colonel said as Alice made her getaway.

Standing up, she dusted off her dress. She briskly brushed where his hands hand been, as though he had dirtied the material with his touch. "No, Colonel, that's not what was happening. You were threatening me, and I was about to hit you."

"Colonel, I'm not a boy. I expect you to apologize to my sister for insulting her," Will stated as he reached for Alice's hand.

Alice held his hand as he pulled her to his side, whispering, "Are you hurt?"

She shook her head no. She didn't know what the ramifications of her actions, or Will's, were going to be, but she knew that she couldn't allow the colonel to touch her or kiss her, not for any reason.

"Apologize for what? I wasn't doing a thing wrong. You should be proud I chose your sister to court, your uncle and your aunt sure are. If she wasn't putting on airs she would be proud that I want to spend time with her."

"My sister does not *put on airs,* nor does she wish to be courted by a man like you," Will said as he glared at the older man.

"We'll see about that. Let's see how high and mighty you both are when your uncle turns you out on your ear and he loses everything. A fine lot you two are, Will with your proud ways and your sister – if you can call her that – bewitching me like one of my servant girls. You two are going to get a comeuppance, just like the rest of your family. Miss Alice, I'll have what I want from you or your uncle will find himself without a farm. Don't forget I can have the sheriff down here arrest you any time I like!"

"I don't care what you have to say; my uncle won't stand for it. The old days are dead. You can't order me around and you can't have my sister!" Will declared.

"We'll see about that," the colonel said as he pushed past Will and Alice, nearly knocking her from the steps. Together they watched him go.

"Oh Will, what am I going to do? He threatened me, he threatened Uncle Henry."

"Don't let it worry you, I'll think of something. No one is going to make you marry that man, not if you don't want to," he said as he held her close to him.

"What am I going to do without you? You'll be out west with Louisa and I'll be here, all alone."

"You won't be alone, Alice. I promise," he said as she wept in his arms.

*****

Dinner at the Clearys' was never a boisterous affair. Her uncle and aunt were quiet, their five children (ranging in age from twenty to twelve) sat on either side of the table, keeping to themselves or talking in whispers. Will and Alice sat together at the far end, a subtle reminder that they were not *quite* welcomed as part of the family. This reminder was unnecessary, as Alice was aware of it every day. Will never complained, but he confided that he felt like a hired hand, and not a cousin.

From their hand-me-down clothes to the way the other Clearys treated them, Alice and Will stood apart, but clung together. They were not only brother and sister, they were close friends. Alice often wondered if it was necessity, or the tragedy they'd experienced when they were children that drove them to become so inseparable. Together they were taken in by their Uncle Henry, while their other brothers and sisters were scattered across Georgia, living with relatives after the heartbreak during the war when the Yankees had come through the state, burning everything in their path. Alice and her siblings had lost their parents; the farmhouse was destroyed, and their land taken. Their oldest sister, Louisa, had left Georgia ten years ago, seeking a new life out west. Her letters were a constant source of hope for Alice and Will, as their lives in Georgia were difficult.

On this evening, there was a terribly dark mood at the table. It had been building over the few days since the colonel had threatened Alice using every means at his disposal. Uncle Henry, a steadfast man who rarely said much except at prayer or to order his wife and children about, was silently fuming at Alice. She could feel the intensity of his glare as she picked at the ham and beans in her bowl.

These days, there were not many suppers of fancy roast chicken and all the trimmings. Beans, potatoes, and bread were staples, supplemented by any wild game Will or one of the other Clearys could shoot. The scraps from one meal became a watery soup the following night, served with bread. There wasn't much money to go around for food, or much else. The family was in trouble, and their livelihood depended on her. The guilt she felt was almost equal to her revulsion at the thought of marrying the colonel.

Alice knew the colonel was right; she did owe this family everything. Without their generosity, she and Will would have starved, or even worse, been left at an orphanage. Her uncle's glare wasn't the only one she saw as she glanced at the other faces around the table. From her cousin Nell, the small, pretty girl whose dress and shoes she sometimes wore, to her cousin Jeb, all faces were sour. She knew what they were thinking. Will met her gaze. With a quick squeeze of her hand, he reassured her in his silent way that all would be well. He always knew what was troubling her.

"Don't you care for your nourishing dinner, Alice? It's a pity; soon you won't be eating this fine anymore – and neither will we! What's wrong with you? You could have nice clothes and food every day if you weren't so uppity! But beans is too poor for you? You'll soon be starving when you could have been feasting!" Nell said as she threw down her napkin.

Nell was a beauty, a tiny woman who was twenty years old and still threw temper tantrums to ensure that her mother and father gave whatever she wanted. For a decade Alice had shared Nell's room, sleeping in a trundle bed beside Nell's great canopied four-poster bed. When she was a child, crying to herself at the loss of her mother and her sisters, Nell would laugh at her and call her mean names.

When she needed to, she would leave Nell's bedroom and find her way down the long hall to the room Will shared with two of his younger cousins. She couldn't help but feel responsible for him. She would lay her hand on his head, kiss his forehead and watch him sleep, swearing that she would never let anything harm him. By caring for him, she was able to forget about all that they had lost. Some nights, Will had terrible nightmares, and he would come find her. She would comfort him in the dark, forgetting that she was small and alone in the world.

But now she was nineteen, and Alice knew she couldn't stay at the farm much longer. Whether the family lost it or not, she was no longer a child and could not count on anyone to take care of her anymore. How she wished she could journey out west with her brother to find a new life. She often thought she would like to be a teacher, but there was no money for her to learn how to become one. Her only hope was marriage – and her only prospect was Colonel Chandler.

"Nell, if you think so much of fancy clothes and food, why don't you marry the colonel? Leave Alice alone; she doesn't feel well. Have you no heart?" Will spoke up for his sister.

"I have a heart, but does she? What do you care what becomes of us? You're as unappreciative as Alice, if you ask me. After all we've done for you, your sister Louisa sends for you to come out west, and you go. You're all set to leave, having no care for us, no care to look after the farm and your uncle, who took you in!" Nell said with venom in her voice.

"Nell, hush up! It's not Christian to say such things," a young woman hissed at her sister. Ernestine was Nell's younger, plainer sister. She was often sympathetic to Alice, as she too suffered from Nell's mistreatment.

"Ernestine, you hush," Aunt Cleary scolded her daughter.

Ernestine shot a sad look in Alice's direction as she recoiled, slumping into her chair.

Will replied, "Nell, is that how you feel about me and my sister? That we're no better than your servants? That we owe you for the rest of our lives? I've paid my debt to this family. Every day I've spent hours in the fields, working, bent over the rows, weeding and plowing. Don't you tell me about work and paying my dues, when you sit up here in this house while Alice works and scrubs like a maidservant!"

Alice shook her head and whispered, "No Will, don't say anything. She won't understand. None of them do."

Alice's uncle Henry was a thin man who physically resembled her father but whose stern demeanor was opposite to the warmth and love she had received from her dear departed Papa. "What don't we understand? We have given you everything you have now, the roof over your head in the winter, the food on the table, a Christian education. You're nineteen, and what have you done? You don't do a thing that a hired girl couldn't do. Our lives depend on you and you won't hear of helping us. By God, you will help us. You'll marry Colonel Chandler if he asks for your hand, or you'll find yourself on the street!"

Alice understood why she was being glared at. This family was convinced that she owed them her life, her virtue, and her future. Her choices were down to two: she could accept the colonel, a proposal which made her nauseous, or she could leave. Without any skills or a trade, what would become of her? She stared at her uncle. His intense glare felt like a weight on her chest; she could barely breathe.

Throwing her napkin onto the table, she sprang up from the dinner table and bolted from the room with Will on her heels. She could hear her uncle bellowing as she ran. Not waiting to hear his words, she raced through the dimly lit farmhouse, down the back steps past the kitchen and into the night. She didn't know where she was going, but she seemed to be heading towards the barn. Will soon caught up to her.

"Whoa, where do you think you're going? If you're not careful, you'll get your shoes mucky. It's been raining the past two days," he said as she spun her around.

"Will, they hate me! They always have. Did you see the looks on their faces? Did you hear the anger in their voices? They expect me to marry that fat, disgusting old man because ten years ago they did what was Christian by giving me a home. They act like they own me. Do they?"

High overhead, thunder rumbled and the first few drops of rain fell, but Will's voice was calm. "Don't say that; they're all just scared. They survived the war, they kept their farm, while we lost everything. They haven't had to face the same hardship that happened to us, or to the Burkes who took in Louisa. It doesn't make them right, but they don't know what to do. You can see it in their eyes."

Alice felt betrayed. "Do you agree with them? Should I marry the colonel?"

"No, I don't agree with them. I would wish you sick and dead before I let that bloated old man touch you."

"That's not very Christian," she whispered as they ducked inside the barn. The rain fell much stronger now, the droplets turning to a torrent.

"I know. I'm sorry. If you loved him it would be different. I can't watch you sacrifice your life. Why should you? So this family may keep their farm, so that Nell may live a life of ease and contentment? If she wants her father's farm to be safe, let *her* marry him. I don't see her doing that, do you?"

Alice snorted. "Still, I can't be the cause of their misery, no matter how terrible they've treated me. They took us in, they fed us, and gave us a place to live. I don't know what to do, but I know I would feel terrible if they lost the farm because of me."

With the coming of the rain, the temperature dropped. A chill in the air made Alice shiver. She was glad there was no light in the barn; she didn't want Will to see the tears streaming down her face. She wished that the colonel had never laid eyes on her. She wasn't beautiful; there were far prettier girls in Augusta than her. Why did he choose her? Why didn't he choose someone like Nell?

She didn't have an answer to that question. Every time she thought of his thick lips on hers, his breath reeking of liquor, she wanted to vomit. But then when she thought of her family destitute on the street, she was torn in a way she had never been before. If she could only find a way to make herself marry him, the Cleary farm would be safe, and she would never want for anything ever again.

"If I married him, I would have new clothes and a carriage. The colonel is rich," she said to Will in the darkness.

"Rich he may be, but never forget, he's cruel. You would have no peace, you would find no happiness in your wealth. He would demand more than you want to give."

"I can't be the reason our family loses their house and their farm. Why does it have to fall to me? Why does it have to come to this?"

"You aren't the reason, so don't blame yourself. You didn't choose to raise the taxes on the farm and you didn't choose to be courted by the colonel. Tell me the truth, if the farm wasn't in danger, if you weren't threatened by the colonel, would you marry him? Would you ever think to stoop to such a terrible fate?"

"No, I would never marry him. Will, he stinks of drink and he's mean."

"There's your answer. You can't marry him," Will said with a tone of finality in his voice.

"What am I to do? You heard Uncle Henry. If I don't marry the colonel, if that's even what he wants now, what shall I do? I have nowhere to go and no money. You're leaving me. You're my only real family."

Will grasped her hands. "I never meant to leave you for very long. I was going to go west and send for you as soon as I had enough money saved for a ticket. You know that's what I wanted to do. I didn't intend to leave you to the mercy of Colonel Chandler." He fell silent for a moment, and then continued. "I tell you what, I won't go. I'll stay right here with you. We'll both leave, we'll go to Atlanta. I can find some kind of work, and maybe you can, too."

"No Will, I won't have you giving up your chance to leave Georgia for me. I would never forgive myself for making you stay. You know there isn't much more in Atlanta than there is here. Not for us. You might find work in some drudgery of a job. All I wanted was to become a teacher. What can I do? Wash dishes, cook and clean?"

"Well, I can't leave you, not like this. If you had to marry that man, or if you were thrown out and I did nothing, I would never forgive myself."

"Will, I'm supposed to be the one who's responsible, remember? I'm older than you."

"It doesn't matter, not anymore. I wish there was some way for you to go with me. If we leave together, we could leave the colonel and our family behind. Let them sort it out. It was wrong of Uncle to put this burden in your hands."

"Do you mean that? What if I could go with you? What would Louisa say?"

"I don't know what she'd say. She sent enough money for me to purchase a ticket. Just one ticket, Alice. Aside from that money, I don't have more than two dollars to my name, how much do you have?"

"A dollar and a few pennies," she said.

"We're going to need more than that if you're going to buy a ticket."

"I could sell my hair, my clothes, whatever I have."

"Don't sell your hair; not yet anyway. We'll find a way, we have some time."

"Not much time. Oh, Will, I really want to go to Kansas. I could start a new life there with you and Louisa. Remember her? I can, but only barely. She used to tell me stories when I was sick, she would stay beside me. I miss her, I miss all our brothers and sisters. I miss our parents."

"So do I, Alice. Don't despair. We'll find a way. I promise," he said. His voice was reassuring in the darkness of the barn while the rain pounded on the roof.

Alice's mind was troubled. How would they ever find the money to buy a train ticket for her? They had three dollars and a few pennies. That wouldn't get her to Memphis. She needed a miracle. As she leaned her head against her brother's narrow shoulder she made a decision. In the morning she was going to walk into town, to the place that beckoned to her in times of trouble. There was somewhere she could go where she felt safe and secure, where she could think and pray. Tomorrow morning, she was going to Augusta and she wasn't going to let anyone stop her.

Chapter Two

April 11, 1876
Augusta, Georgia

Alice woke early, as she always did. She dressed quietly, making sure not to wake Nell, who snored in her bed. It was still dark outside as she crept down the stairs and out the front door. The rain had ended, and there was a chill in the pre-dawn air. In the sky-high overhead, the stars were twinkling as the moon dipped towards the horizon. It would be light soon, and she didn't want to waste precious time. Someone might wake up and ask her where she was going.

As she walked towards the lane, she heard the sound of footsteps behind her. Someone was awake, and the only person it could be was her uncle. He didn't sleep much these days – often, she would find him awake when she came downstairs to make breakfast. She sighed, he must have heard her leave the house. Turning around, she was expecting a scolding for leaving, but instead she saw the tall, lanky form of her brother.

"Will!" she hissed, her voice sounding loud in the dark. "You scared me half to death."

"I didn't mean to scare you. You talked about going to Augusta first thing. I don't know where you're heading but I don't think it's safe for you to be walking alone. Not with the colonel and who knows what ruffians about these days."

Sighing in relief, she said, "You're going to town with me? That would be lovely, I could sure use the company."

"Then it's settled, I'm coming with you. Now, where are we going?" he asked as they walked down the narrow dirt lane.

"St. Theresa's," she answered.

"We're going to church? It's not Sunday."

"I know, but I need to pray. Can you think of a better place to pray?"

"No, I can't. What shall we do afterwards?"

"I don't know. I haven't spoken to anyone but you since dinner last night. I don't know what happens afterwards."

"Mind your skirt, it's muddy here on the road," he cautioned as he sidestepped an enormous puddle.

"I don't care about what I'm wearing. Today I have on old boots that fit me, and a dress that has seen better days. I refuse to dress up for anyone ever again."

"Don't say that. When we get to Kansas, maybe you'll meet someone who makes you forget all about the colonel."

"It will be a long time before I can do that. What if all men are like that, or like Uncle Henry? I can't be demure; I can't be silent and dutiful. Maybe I will never be married."

Will laughed. It was a cheerful sound that made her feel better right away. "I'll remind you that you said that one day. Maybe on your wedding day, when you're getting ready to marry some cowboy."

"A cowboy? Well, anyone would be better than the colonel," she laughed, feeling better than she had in days.

They walked to Augusta as dawn lit up the sky above the fields and pine trees of Georgia. Alice wondered what the west looked like. Were there trees, or was it as she imagined, nothing but emptiness, a barren landscape for miles?

Her imaginings of the desert were not all that filled her mind as she walked towards Augusta. She had never considered leaving home, and the town of Augusta was her home. She knew the streets of downtown as she did the dirt wagon paths of the Cleary farm. She knew the mighty Savannah River, and had eaten many fish Will and her uncle had caught from its banks. She couldn't imagine leaving, but she couldn't stay if there was no one here who loved her. There had to be a way for her and Will to leave together.

They approached downtown to the sound of dogs barking in the yards and carriages clattering along the street, the horses' hooves echoing in the quiet of the morning. In the soft light of the early hours, Augusta was at her most beautiful. The trees were bright green with new leaves, flowers bloomed in window boxes, and everywhere Alice looked was pink with azaleas and lilac and blue of hydrangeas. She would miss the colors of her world, but she didn't want to stay if it meant being forced to marry the colonel.

Soon they were on the steps of St. Theresa's, and all her terrible thoughts were quickly supplanted by a peace. This peace was as familiar to her as her own face was in a reflection. She felt it every time she walked up the gray stone steps leading to the red brick church surrounded by its high brick wall. Under the sheltering willows and the tall pecan trees that lined the garden of the church she could believe in the love of God, even after the horrors of the war.

The parish of St Theresa's had welcomed her as a child, when her world was destroyed. Her aunt and uncle were Catholic, like so many other people who had come to Georgia from Ireland many years ago. The broad oak doors had stood open to her when she was young, and they did now.

Walking inside, Alice breathed in the familiar scent of incense and candle wax. As the light streamed in through the stained-glass windows, she felt serene – as though nothing bad could ever happen to her. She looked at her brother, and found his face was like hers, peaceful. His brow was no longer troubled as they kneeled down in front of the altar for a quiet moment of prayer, before finding their way to a wooden pew.

Alice made the sign of the cross and closed her eyes. Folding her hands in prayer, she began to pray, silently pouring out the troubles in her heart. When she was done she expressed her gratitude for her life, her brother, and this day. Then, spent and cleansed for the moment, she simply sat silently.

She was not aware of time passing until the aching of her knees and her back reminded her that she was still kneeling. Opening her eyes, she slid onto the pew beside her brother.

Will looked peaceful, as though he had found guidance, if that was what he sought. She hadn't received an answer, but she was reminded to have faith. It was faith that brought her to St Theresa's so early in the morning. It would be faith that would see her through this trial. Feeling better, she breathed contentedly. She whispered to Will that she was going to walk outside in the garden. He nodded, and she quietly left the pew.

As she walked down the aisle, Alice saw that other people had come into the church while she was praying. Respectfully, she tried not to stare, but she was touched by the men and women she saw in the pews. Their heads were often bent, some held rosaries in their hands. These days, there was much to pray about in Augusta. Her dilemma was difficult, but she had faith that she would find a way to join William in Kansas.

She had prayed about it, and she had prayed for the Clearys. No matter how badly they treated her, she didn't wish for them to lose their farm. Being homeless was a pain she knew too well.

Leaving the sanctuary, she walked out a tall, narrow door into the garden. The cool mist of the spring dawn was gone, replaced by the warm breeze and sunshine of a beautiful day. Sunlight filtered through the trees, bathing the green grass of the garden in a soft hue. Looking down at her boots, she longed to unlace them, to leave them behind as she ran barefoot through the garden. With so much else to trouble her, it was a rare moment of joy. It was foolish, she knew that, but she felt exuberant in the face of her problems. For a moment, the weight of her troubles lifted, and she reveled in the feeling. Soon she would have to choose to marry the Colonel, leave the Clearys' home, or go with Will. The third choice seemed out of reach, but she prayed that somehow, if it was God's will, He would show her the way.

Leaning down, she reached for the lace on her right boot. She did not expect anyone would be in the garden with her.

"Miss Cleary, what brings you to the garden on this fine morning?" a woman called out from behind a large azalea bush.

"Sister Agatha! I didn't see you there," Alice said as she bolted upright.

Sister Agatha was a cheerful older woman with a kind face and a compassionate disposition. She wore the traditional habit of her order even as she hunched over the flowers with a spade in her hand. Alice had long marveled at the woman, the Abbess of St. Theresa's in Augusta could be so kind.

"My dear child, I hope I haven't given you a start."

"No, Sister, I was about to forget myself entirely. I am thankful you have returned me to my senses," Alice replied as she walked across the green patch of lawn to join the sister. "Hand me a trowel, and I shall be happy to help you." Alice sat on the grass beside the small plot of flowers. It was still damp with dew, but she didn't mind getting her dress soiled if she could have a few minutes with Sister Agatha.

"I couldn't ask you to do that; you're getting dirty enough already. Sit a spell and talk to me. Keep me company, that is all the help I need."

"I do have a question you may be able to help me answer."

The older lady glanced at Alice and sat back. "You look troubled, what is bothering you?"

"I don't want to burden you, Sister. You have been so good to me, since I was a child. It's a comfort to me just to sit here in the garden with you."

It was true. Sister Agatha had a way of reassuring her even if she didn't say a word. To Alice, this kindly Abbess was the grandmother she never knew or maybe she reminded her of her own mother, a woman she distantly recalled.

"It's no burden to me; you can tell me anything. It does my heart good to see you and your brother when you pay us a visit here. I know how much trouble you have both seen in your young lives."

Sighing, Alice spoke haltingly at first, but then her words came pouring from her lips, one after another in a torrent to rival the rain of the previous night. By the end of her lengthy recounting of her worries, she was weeping silently. Her guilt and her despair were equal in their torment.

The abbess simply sat, her spade forgotten as she listened to Alice's troubles. She didn't offer any advice or suggest a way out but she was attentive, nodding as Alice told her about all that was looming like a terrible fate in front of her.

"So now you know why I seem troubled. I have faith that God will show me the way. I do not despair, but I wish I knew what that way was. I would sleep better at night if I knew whether I was about to be thrown out in the street or married to a cruel drunkard. How I wish I could go to Kansas, and start over in a new place. If I could go to Kansas with Will, I know I could find some way to become a teacher. I've always wanted to be a teacher. Ever since I was a little girl, I wanted to teach in a small school. What am I to do?"

The older woman looked at Alice. She didn't speak, but her silence was not evidence of her lack of concern. Alice knew the abbess well enough to know that she was a woman who was cheerful, but moderate in her speech. Her words were well chosen, as were her actions. If she was silent, Alice decided to let her remain so. Any advice she may give would be worth any amount of waiting.

"Why do you want to be a teacher?" Sister Agatha asked as she smiled at Alice, patting her hand.

"I don't know; it's what I always wanted to do. When I was a little girl, back before the tragedy happened to my family, I can remember lining up my doll and my sister's dolls like children in a school room. Its one of my fondest memories. When I went to school, I wanted to learn everything there was to learn so I could one day teach. When I see myself in the future I don't see myself falling in love, I see myself happily spending my days teaching."

"You have no wish to marry the colonel?"

"No, Sister. I know it's not Christian to speak ill of another person, but he's cruel, he's threatened me, and he drinks. I don't mind that's he's old or fat, but I do mind that's he's mean."

"Tell me, Miss Cleary, have you given any thought to working in a mission, somewhere farther west than Kansas?"

"A mission, what would I do there? I don't think I would make a very good missionary."

Sister Agatha laughed, her voice as melodious as a singing bird. "My goodness, no. Dear me, that sounds dreary; I should know. I meant as a teacher. In my order, we have several missions in New Mexico. One of my dearest friends, Sister Cecilia, writes to me of the need they have in her mission outside of Santa Fe. They are desperate for teachers, for nurses, for anyone of the faith who can lend a hand. There are not enough sisters to do the work."

"New Mexico? I would be lying if I said I have ever thought of myself in New Mexico, but now that you've mentioned it, I would be pleased to teach in a mission. I would gladly go where the Lord calls me, but I have no money for a train ticket, and I don't have the education."

"God will find a way, if we pray. You told me that you and your brother have a modest amount of money. I can give a small gift from the mission fund, but you must find the rest. About your education as a teacher, that can be completed at the mission. Sister Cecilia needs help, so I know she will not turn you away. She will find a way to help you become a teacher."

"If I stay to teach in a mission, is that it?"

"Yes, Miss Cleary. I say, this is providential. Do you not agree? You wish to become a teacher, and my dear friend is desperate for teachers at her mission. How magnificent is the Lord in his bounty?"

"In New Mexico."

"Yes, in New Mexico, The journey will be arduous, but if you wish to help Sister Cecilia, if you do this in good faith, the Lord will see that you arrive safely."

"Tell me, Sister, does a train go to Santa Fe?"

"I'm told that it will one day," Sister Agatha smiled as Alice laughed.

"New Mexico! I never would have dreamed I would be led there. I did pray to go west. Perhaps I prayed too hard," giggled Alice.

"I would say that God must have heard you! Alice, do not let me convince you, do you wish this?"

Alice beamed as she watched her brother walking towards her. In New Mexico she wouldn't be on the farm with him, but she would be closer to him than if she remained in Georgia. Smiling, she waved at him as she answered, "Yes, Sister, I do. I did not expect to find an answer to my problems in the garden, nor did I expect that my future awaited me in New Mexico. Please write to Sister Cecilia. I shall be honored to come to her mission. I'm grateful for your faith in me."

"It's not my faith in you, Miss Cleary, it's my faith in God. See how he has answered your prayers and the prayers of Sister Cecilia?"

Will held out his hand, helping Alice to rise from the ground. As she leaned over, brushing the dirt of her skirt, the sunlight glinted on the metal of a necklace she had forgotten she was wearing.

"My, what a beautiful necklace you have," Sister Agatha remarked.

Impulsively, Alice's hand went to her throat. The cold weight of the necklace reminded her of the man who had slid it around her neck. She couldn't imagine how she hadn't noticed it was still there.

"I've been wearing this for days; how did I forget it was there? Had I remembered it, I would have thrown it at the colonel's face. Sorry, sister." She reached up to unclasp it from her slender neck.

"You might be glad of that," said Will.

Sister Agatha smiled. "Perhaps you choosing not to use this gift as a weapon is a sign that there is another reason for this gift, one that was not intended by the giver."

"I do need to raise the last of the money for the ticket," Alice replied as she fingered the gold chain and the pendant sparkling with jewels. "Sister Agatha, I think you're right – even the colonel's gift is providential. God does want me to go to New Mexico."

"New Mexico?" Will asked, his brow furrowed in confusion.

"Yes, Will. I'm going to be a teacher!" Alice exclaimed, her sorrow lifted from her heart. It seemed that she would have the money to leave the colonel, the Clearys, and Georgia behind, after all.

Her smile faded when it occurred to her that she would also be leaving Sister Agatha. Wiping away the tears, she promised to write to the Abbess. Sister Agatha gave her a blessing and a small sum of money – a gift, she said. Alice was speechless. She knew that other people in town needed this money, the missionaries needed it, but Sister Agatha was so happy to help her, and she was so desperately in need, that she could not turn it down. Not if it was God's will.

*****

April 17, 1876
Augusta, Georgia

    Alice packed what few belongings she had in a threadbare bag, and the remainder in the trunk she shared with Will. There wasn't much. A few changes of clothes, a jacket, a coat, and a pair of shoes for each of them. Packing didn't take long at all, especially since Nell took back anything she had given to Alice that was still in good repair.

    "You won't be needing my old blue dress, will you? Not where you're going, anyhow. It never looked good on you anyway!" Nell declared as she pulled the dress from Alice's bag.

    "You won't be needing the shoes that I gave you, or the bonnet!" Nell continued to take things as Ernestine stood in the doorway, looking even more sad and forlorn than usual.

    Ernestine cried, "Alice, I don't want you to go! Take me with you!"

    Alice stopped to comfort the young girl, a lump welling up inside her throat. "Ernestine, I can't take you with me. Your mother needs you here to help in the kitchen and with the mending. No one sews as well as you. You have to stay."

    Nell threw the clothes down on her bed and turned her malicious attention to her younger sister. "Stop crying, Ernestine! Stop crying this instant! Why would you want to go west? There's Indians out there! They eat people and drink their blood; they burn down houses and kill children just like you!"

"Stop it, Nell! You're going to give her nightmares!" Alice yelled as Ernestine ran to her arms.

"I don't care if I do. She deserves nightmares, the weak sniveling little baby!" Nell replied as she pinched her sister.

Ernestine howled as Nell continued her attack on Alice. "What I want to know is how did you find the money for a ticket to Kansas? What did you have to do? I wonder that you have any claim to virtue left. Don't think I didn't see that necklace the colonel gave you. What did you have to do to earn that, hmm?"

Alice felt her face turned hot. She had prayed that the man she'd sold the necklace to wouldn't recognize it as being a piece of jewelry bought by the colonel. She prayed that the colonel had bought it somewhere else, like Atlanta or Savannah. She wondered if anyone besides Will and Sister Agatha knew anything about it. With a sinking feeling, she thought about her aunt. Her aunt knew about the necklace, and so did Nell.

Would the colonel come and ask for it back?

"I can see you're blushing, Alice. My, my, I wonder what you did. Is it too terrible? Should I be even more ashamed to be seen with you than I already am? Are you a fallen woman?"

Alice's first instinct was to defend herself, but she knew it was quite impossible against a woman as vile as Nell. Holding a sobbing Ernestine close to her, Alice glared at her cousin. "You can think whatever you want. You can say whatever evil and wretched things are in your heart, but I'm leaving to go somewhere you and Colonel Chandler can't find me."

Nell hissed, "You're going out west to live with the rest of the savages and the poor people, and that is just what you deserve. I bet you'll be dead in a year. I hope a rattlesnake bites you, or an Indian scalps you!"

Feeling emboldened, Alice answered, "I would rather face a rattlesnake any day than stay here in Georgia with you. If you're lucky, maybe your father will trade you to the colonel, the same way he did me. What do you think of that? You like silks and satins so much, maybe you can marry that fat, bloated old fool and get as many dresses as you want. I think you would make a fine wife to him. I wonder which of us would outlive the other? Be careful, he may tire of you – and you know what he did to his first two wives!"

"I wouldn't marry him for all the money in Augusta!" Nell screamed as she ran out of the bedroom.

"Is she gone?" Ernestine asked, her face still pressed against Alice's shoulder.

"She'll be back, Ernestine. You have to be brave and strong for me, can you do that?"

"Don't go, please Alice."

"I have to; your father won't let me stay here anymore. Pray that your sister gets married soon, so she won't hurt you anymore."

"I'll pray she marries that colonel fellow."

Alice laughed as Ernestine went out of the room, leaving her to her thoughts and to her packing. There wasn't much left to pack. Her traveling clothes were laid on the chair with her one pair of boots. An old bonnet sat on the writing desk. She picked up the bonnet and held it her hands. There was a new ribbon sewed to it, a gift from her friend Daisy as a going away present, that and a tin of biscuits for the train. She was going to miss Daisy, and Ernestine, and Sister Agatha, but she could not stay. Her uncle had been furious when he discovered she was leaving with Will. He hadn't spoken to her since, and neither had her aunt. It was just as well, she didn't have very much to say to them.

A terrible thought passed through her mind, that Nell would try to steal the money for her train ticket. She was spiteful enough to do just that. With a sigh of relief, Alice remembered that Will had her money in his safekeeping.

It was strange how differently her family treated him. They were disappointed that he was leaving, but they were going to see him to the station. Her aunt was even packing him a hamper filled with food. But when she announced that she, too, was heading west, their reaction was just the opposite. Her uncle forbade it, then realizing that he had no ability to make her marry the colonel, he wished her misfortune in her future.

His anger made leaving easier for her, confirming that it was a good thing that she hadn't sacrificed herself for a family who would never have appreciated it. For a moment she saw a vision of herself, miserable and desperate, while her uncle and his family never gave her despair a second thought. She thought of Nell, of her years of mistreatment, and her aunt who had insisted she be polite to the colonel when it was clear that his intentions were far from honorable.

There was no life for her here in Georgia. There was nothing to hold her to this town or the state anymore. Even her own brothers and sisters were like strangers to her. She received a letter once and again, but they were all so distant from each other that they seemed like people she'd once known, and not like her family. Will was her family now. Heading west with him was the best decision she could have made. She was thankful that Sister Agatha and the colonel's necklace had made it possible.

That night she slept fitfully. She was scared and her dreams were dark. She dreamed that the colonel snatched her from the train station. She had visions of her uncle forcing her to marry Colonel Chandler. She saw Nell setting fire to her money, and locking her in the bedroom so Will left without her. Finally, haunted by dread, she gave up on sleep and went to the window.

God was being so good to her; why did she feel like she didn't deserve his grace? Perhaps the sale of the necklace was weighing on her mind. When she looked inside herself, she saw her own guilt at selling it. May God forgive her for her sin, she prayed silently as she waited for the night to end.

When the sun rose she was fully dressed. The trunk sat in the hallway downstairs. Will would be up soon, and so would her uncle and her aunt. Alice's stomach growled. She crept downstairs to the kitchen as quietly as she could.

Will had a hamper filled with what food Aunt Helen had packed for him, and Alice had a small tin of biscuits. It would have to be enough to get to them to Kansas, as there was no money left to spend on food along the way.

She didn't know how much a stagecoach ticket may cost beyond that, or what else she would need before she reached Santa Fe. The sale for the necklace had yielded enough to get her to Kansas with a precious few dollars left over, but that was all.

Perhaps, she mused, there was crust of bread and slice of cheese in the pantry. A paltry breakfast would be better than nothing.

The floorboards creaked under her weight as she moved as silently through the house as she could. Her uncle had a habit of waking early – or never going to bed, she could not decide which. She had no wish to see his scowling face when she was hours away from never seeing it again. In the kitchen, all was dark and quiet. Dawn would soon be breaking; her aunt would be coming down the stairs any minute. She needed to hurry. There was no time to waste if she was going to have any food in her belly at all.

Finding a half of a loaf of dry bread, she pulled off a piece, which she nibbled as she looked in the pie safe. These days there wasn't much to be found inside the pie safe, but there was a small portion of cheese, and part of a meat pie. The meat pie contained what

42

was left of the chickens that had once paraded around the backyard. Sliding the pie out of the safe, she decided to eat a small piece. That and the bread would have to be enough.

"Alice?"

Alice almost screamed as she was startled by her aunt, who was standing in the kitchen, a pitcher of water in her hand. She wasn't sure how long her aunt had been standing there, but Alice self-consciously slid the crust of bread behind her, and pushed the pie tin back into the cupboard.

"Alice, what are you doing?" her aunt asked as she set the water down on the table.

"I…I was just getting something to eat."

"You were stealing, weren't you? You no longer live here. You don't deserve any of our food since you've sent us into ruin."

"*I've* sent you into ruin? How? Because I don't want to marry the colonel?" Alice asked as she dropped the crust of bread onto the table.

"You ungrateful child, after all we've done for you. Where are you ever going to find a husband as wealthy as the colonel? Not out west."

"Is that all any of you think about, money?"

"How could we think of anything else? We *need* money, don't you understand? We need money or else we lose the farm. It's all your fault! You could have married the colonel just like we promised him you would, and none of this would be happening."

43

What guilt Alice felt was soon replaced by curiosity. "You promised him I would marry him? How could you promise him that, when you never asked me what I wanted?"

"What does it matter what you wanted? You're a stupid girl, an orphan. You don't have the privilege of deciding what you want!" her aunt spat, looking less demure and more like her daughter, Nell.

"When did you promise him he could marry me?"

"I didn't promise him anything, your uncle did. The colonel was going to lend us the money to pay the taxes, and now we won't have it because of you!"

"No, Aunt, it's because of *you*. If you wanted to save this farm, you could have promised him Nell!"

"Not my daughter. How dare you suggest that!"

Alice grabbed the crust of the bread from the table. "You don't own me; you never did. I am grateful that you took me in, that you gave me and my brother a place to stay. Thank you for that. I will not let your anger take away my gratitude. I forgive you for what you were willing to do to me, to barter me off to the colonel. I will pray for you."

"Your prayers are useless. Who would listen to a dark-haired outcast like you? You're no better than an urchin on the street. I told my husband that we should take Will and leave you. He was a boy. We could use his help on the farm, but what good have you ever been? You've had everything we could give you, benefited from our kindness, and this is how you show your gratitude?"

"I will pray that God lightens your loads and that you will come to understand the wickedness of your ways," Alice said. As she passed her aunt on the way out of the room, she deliberately took a bite of the bread. Will was waiting in the hallway.

"Are you ready to go?" he asked, glancing in the direction of the kitchen.

"How much did you hear?"

"Enough to know that it's time to go. We've overstayed out welcome here."

"Yes, we have. I'm ready when you are."

Will smiled. "I've been dreaming of this moment ever since Louisa left for Kansas. Let's go, Alice. We can't keep our sister waiting."

Alice didn't look back as she climbed into the wagon beside Will. Her aunt declined to come to the station, and so did the rest of the family. Her uncle wordlessly drove the wagon down the wood-lined lane into Augusta. Soon Alice saw the steeple of St. Theresa's rising high above the trees. She thought of Sister Agatha's generosity, and wished that one day she might see her again. But right now she would go to Kansas, and then on into New Mexico. She would seek out Sister Cecilia and endeavor to become a teacher, just like she promised. Wiping away a tear, she reached for Will's hand. Soon they would board the train and say goodbye to Augusta.

She knew in her heart that she was leaving for good.

Chapter Three

April 26, 1876
Fort Monroe, Kansas

Louisa Cleary Burke held the little girl's hand tight in her grasp. The child, a precocious two-year-old, stared at the sights all around her as she gripped her mother's hand with all her might. Louisa knew that her youngest child was frightened by the noise of the approaching steam engine, but she was also excited at the same time. Louisa knew that if she were to let Miriam's hand loose for a moment Miriam would cry, but then run as fast as her little legs could carry her towards whatever caught her eye. In this case, Louisa knew it would be the train.

In a way, Louisa understood the marvel that her eyes beheld, though it had been a decade since she'd ridden on a locomotive. In her eyes, the mighty trains

47

that had come west were beautiful and wholly unreal. How had man created such a wondrous thing, she wondered as she watched her daughter gazing at the enormous machine that spouted steam from its stacks. The train was part of how she came to Kansas, and how she escaped the terrible aftermath of the war.

The war seemed such a long, long time ago, and yet it had only been ten years since Louisa's parents had died, and her family farm was burned and taken by the Yankees. She'd been a young woman when her brothers and sisters were sent to live with relatives. A tear came to her eye when she thought of how many years it had been since she had seen the tall green trees and red clay of home. It wasn't nostalgia. It was the persistent guilt she felt for leaving, for coming west and leaving her brothers and sisters behind, at the mercy of relatives.

It couldn't be helped, this splitting up of her family. How many times had she heard those words from her dear husband James, or her closest friend, Sarah? Louisa was just a young woman with no money and no prospects when she traveled to Kansas with the Burke family. She had no way to support herself or her siblings. James had told her time and again that she hadn't abandoned her sisters or her brothers; they were well looked after in the care of their aunts, and uncles, and cousins. His words were kind, but she never quite got over the feeling that she had just walked away.

But the years since she'd left Georgia had been filled with happiness and hard work. There was sorrow and hardship too, sometimes so much so that she'd thought they would be forced to leave Kansas, or they

48

would starve. James's father Samuel had grown old in recent years, and his eyesight was beginning to fail. He could no longer pull his weight on the farm, and that left all the work to James. Louisa helped when she could, but with three children and one as young as Miriam, she was not much help in the fields.

Her son, Thomas, was seven, and her daughter, Victoria, was five, and in them she could still see the traces of the hard winter. They were so thin, tiny in her eyes. They needed to eat more but the winter had been terrible, taking its toll on all of them. With the promise of the spring came the hope that this year would be better.

It wasn't just the promise of spring that gave her reason to hope. She was standing at the train station waiting for the arrival of someone she knew could help James. If James had another pair of strong hands, Louisa was sure that the farm could do better.

She thought of the money James had scraped together in the fall, money that could have been used during the winter. She consoled herself knowing that money was well spent, even if it had been a dearly felt expense. That money had been sent to William Cleary, one of Louisa's younger brothers. He had written to her of the longing he felt for a new life, a chance to make a start for himself somewhere far away from a land that bore the scars of war. She understood that desire, and she prayed he would find the new life he wanted in Kansas. There was so much more she wished she could do, but all she could offer to him was hard work and a chance to leave Georgia. Like her, he happily accepted the opportunity to come west.

She thought about William as she looked at her own son. Thomas was seven, the same age William had been the last time she saw him. William had the same wispy blond hair and light blue eyes that she had, and she remembered him as a sensitive boy who had cried pitifully when he was sent to live with his aunt and uncle in Augusta. It broke Louisa's heart, but she knew at the time that he would find food and shelter with his relatives, when she could offer him nothing. And he would not be alone – Alice, dark and capable even at nine, would be with him.

Now, ten years later, William was coming to Kansas, to help James on the farm and to start a new life of his own. The guilt she felt for leaving him in Georgia was assuaged, but only a little. It was not going to be an easy life for him.

"Do you know what he looks like? Can you remember him?" James asked as the train slowly came to a stop.

"The last time I saw him he looked like me, only younger and thinner," she said, anxiety rising within her chest.

Was it anxiety or guilt that made her nervous? Maybe it was the ten years and half a country of distance that separated her from her family in Georgia. Aside from the letters they'd exchanged, she didn't know Will. Was he tall, like her father had been? Was he still sensitive, or had the years of hard living in a place devastated by war taken that away?

Miriam pointed at the train and jumped up and down in excitement. Thomas was awed, and Victoria looked interested but cautious as she held her brother's hand tightly. Louisa prayed that William was on the train, that he was safely delivered to them. Peering at the passengers as they disembarked, she wondered if her brother would recognize her. Did she look like the same girl who came west, first on a locomotive, and then on a wagon train? Had the years been kind to her, or did she look as haggard as she feared?

The passengers gathered on the platform. Some were met with the cheerful embraces of family or friends, while others stood alone or in small groups with no one to meet them. The look of fatigue and fear in their eyes told her a story she knew so well. These were the new arrivals to the west. Some would continue on to Colorado or destinations even farther away. Some, as she had, would board wagons and head to places the train had yet to reach. From their clothing and speech, she knew that many of the new arrivals were from distant countries. They were hungry and poor, but here they were, looking for a new life.

Her eyes rested on a family who reminded her of the Burkes and herself when they arrived in Independence, Missouri. An older man and woman, who she assumed to be a father and mother, stood with wary eyes as their older children milled around them. Was that what she had looked like, with Sarah, James, and Matthew so many years ago? Was she ever that young, she pondered as her gaze fell on a gaunt young woman who was wearing a dress too short for her, and a tattered bonnet.

"I don't see any men standing by themselves. Are you certain he was arriving today?"

"Yes. I don't see him either; do you suppose something happened to him?" Louisa felt the stirrings of fear.

She thought her worry was justified. Will was seventeen, still young by her reckoning, but nearly a man by everyone else's. So many things could have happened. He could have missed the train, or he could have taken ill, or been robbed. He could have died. She tried not to let her fears get the better of her as she asked James to see to Miriam.

James scooped the child into his arms, and Louisa left her family in search of Will. She scanned the crowd, looking for a young man with blond hair. Walking past the family that reminded her of the Burkes, she tried not to dwell on past ten years. There was time to think about the past later. The past could wait, she needed to find her brother.

She walked past the new arrivals to Fort Monroe without discovering a single man who looked as lost as she felt at the moment. She decided that there was still time yet, perhaps not all the passengers had left the train. Consoling herself that he may still be on board, she waited and looked, walking among the crowd of people on the platform. From the corner of her eye, she saw a tall wiry man and a dark-haired woman standing side by side in front of a train car.

His hair was the right color, but he wasn't alone, so her eyes moved past him and continued to search. But the color – that pale blond – was uncommon in Kansas. She approached, hindered by a crowd of people who passed between them. Was it Will? Had he met someone on the train?

Drawing closer, she glanced at the young woman. The young lady's dark hair was tucked into a bonnet, but wisps of coffee-colored curls peeked out from under the ribbon. She was petite, like Louisa. When she turned her head toward Louisa, Louisa gasped. The young woman looked like her own grandmother. She had the same aquiline nose, and the same high cheekbones that appeared every so often in her family.

It was Alice. And Will. Of course, it was.

"Alice. Will." Louisa whispered. Her feet took her across the platform, where she gathered the two strangers into her arms.

"Oh Louisa! You look the same as always. How I've missed you!" the young woman said in her fluid southern accent.

"Alice, and Will! You're both here! I am so happy to see you safely arrived!"

As they embraced on the platform, the guilt Louisa felt for leaving them behind so many years ago melted away in tears of joy. Will and Alice were standing with her, they were alive and in Kansas. What a blessing, she thought to herself as she hugged them tightly, never wanting to let them go. Her family, or some of it, were together at last.

*****

April 30, 1876
The Burke Farm, Kansas

The Burke farm was three miles from the tiny hamlet of Tucker Springs. The small village was new, built over the last few years, with some buildings springing up seemingly overnight. Louisa had explained that the tiny village was an outpost, arising naturally from the needs of families who had arrived lately from the east – in particular of a large group of Tuckers who hailed from Ohio. The growing village would one day become a town, said Louisa. To Alice, who was accustomed to the stately homes and brick churches of Augusta, the plain roughhewn buildings of the small hamlet, situated on the banks of a wide rushing creek, didn't look very impressive. To Louisa, having the church, the post office, the blacksmith, and the brand new general mercantile within an hour's walk of her farm was a wonderful blessing.

Tucker Springs may have been rather primitive to Alice's eye, but she was impressed by the ingenuity and spirit which created this little town in the middle of the prairie. There was something optimistic in the people who came west, who built this little town from nothing in the middle of nowhere. The small, clapboard houses with their trim little gardens were a welcome sight to her. They were evidence of the promise of the West: that with hard work, anyone could change their lives and build something new.

The hamlet had been a stop along the way from Fort Monroe back to the farm, and it was where Louisa and James attended church with their children. The church was Methodist and not Catholic, but Alice didn't mind. The people treated her with kindness and no one stared at her for wearing a shabby dress. That Sunday, she was welcomed into the congregation as if she had been born Protestant. She didn't say a word about her own beliefs as they sat in the plain wooden pews and listened to the sermon given by a young man from behind his makeshift podium.

After church, all the Burkes assembled with their spouses and children at the Burke family farm. A large garden grew green in the warm Kansas sunshine beside a modest wooden frame house. The sod house that had sheltered them for that first long, terrible winter stood beside the smokehouse and the small barn. It was now used by Samuel Burke, who preferred the solitude of the simple structure, with so many Burkes living in the main house. Samuel was quiet and stern, and Alice could see he was the kind of man who liked to keep to himself. In the few days since she had arrived in Kansas she had heard him speak very little, except to say the blessing at dinner.

The other members of the Burke family, who lived on a nearby farm, came to eat Sunday dinner. There was Matthew and his frail, beautiful wife, Margaret. Sarah was Louisa's best friend, and she came with her husband Stephen Pate and their children, Katie and Freddy. The whole group together made a lively bunch, assembled under the shade of the young apple trees. James and Will spread quilts on the ground, creating a delightful place for the children to play and the Burkes and the Clearys to talk about old times and exchange stories.

Everyone was cheerful, despite the meager offerings of a thin, small chicken roasted with root vegetables, a brace of young rabbits stewed in broth, bread, and a pie made by Margie from the last of the blackberry preserves. Alice could see by the way the Burke children gobbled their share and asked for more that this was more food than anyone in their house had eaten in a long time. She wondered if adding two more people to the household would cause a hardship to Louisa and her husband, but that worry was soon lost in the laughter and small talk of the afternoon.

The sky overhead was a deep, bright blue with white, wispy clouds that floated by. Butterflies flitted among the wildflowers that grew on the edge of the field. The soft grass under the quilt tempted Alice to remove her shoes and stockings and run barefoot and carefree, as the children did. Beside her on the quilt, Will lay back in contentment, a peaceful expression on his face.

"It's hard to believe that just ten years ago, this house, the barn, and none of the fields were clear. We've done a heap of work since we arrived, haven't we, Pa?" James said to Samuel, who was leaning against the trunk of a young apple tree.

"It's been a lot of work, son, but with God's help we've tamed the land," Samuel said with an uncharacteristic faint smile.

Matthew reminisced, "Remember, Louisa, the Indians that camped not far from here that first winter? They were just over there, near where Tucker Springs is now."

"Indians?" Alice asked, remembering with dread what Nell had said about them.

"We don't see them anymore, not around here. They're still to be found in the world, places that are not settled. In Wyoming and up in the Dakotas," James replied.

"New Mexico, and Arizona, too. Some say there's more Indians in New Mexico than there are white men," added Matthew.

"I heard that all they speak is Spanish out there, because all those Spanish conquistadors settled in among the Indians. Lawless. Cattle barons, outlaws, and the like," said Sarah with a glance at the children.

Matthew said, "There ain't much left of that, not unless you want to go see one of those wild west theater shows. Guns blazing, Indians whooping around, it's all for show these days. I saw Buffalo Bill and Texas Jack at Fort Monroe last year, what a ruckus. All that shooting and smoke inside the Gold Mine saloon. You should have heard it, it sounded like a real commotion in there!"

"So there isn't anything like that anymore? No more shootouts on the streets, no more cowboys and Indians, as you call it?" Alice asked as she glanced nervously at her brother.

"Not here, not anymore. Maybe out in Arizona, and New Mexico. There's parts of the West that aren't tamed yet. I don't know if they ever will be; the train can't get to all of that land out there. We don't have to worry about Indian attacks or being robbed of our livestock by cattle rustlers. Not in Kansas, not anymore."

Alice didn't feel much better, but she decided that there wasn't much to be done about it now. She had given her word to Sister Agatha, and outlaws or no outlaws, she was going to New Mexico. But first, she wanted to enjoy being in a place that felt like home to her, being around people who bore her no ill will, and did not belittle her for being an orphan.

"Louisa, tell her about the time James was caught out on the wagon road from Tucker Springs. It was the blizzard of seventy-three; he was caught two miles from the house on the open prairie. James, you should tell your part first," Sarah suggested as she kept a watch on the children who were chasing each other around the yard. "It's one of my favorite stories!"

"After that, tell Alice and Will about the wagon train from Independence. We saw a twister so big that I thought I was dreaming!" Matthew said as he gently nudged Stephen. "Remember, your horses got spooked?"

Stephen answered, "You know there's a lot of things I can't recall. I guess taking a kick in the head will do that to you."

Will was sitting up now, his face turned to the Burkes and the Pates in apt interest. "All this really happened, a twister, Indians, blizzards? How exciting! All me and Alice did was survive the war and the carpetbaggers, and our aunt and uncle. The most exciting thing to happen to us was the train journey to Kansas."

"That's exciting. How I miss the train. I wish I could ride it again one day," Louisa said as she smiled at James. "Don't you miss it, James? Even a short trip to Colorado to see the Rockies would be nice, one day when the children are older."

Alice sat under the shade of the trees, the sun shining through the thin branches and the green leaves. She listened attentively to the Burkes and the Pates tell a decade's worth of tales of survival out here on the prairie. It was so hard to imagine the way the land must have looked when they arrived, when what she saw now was this neat and tidy farmstead. Ten years ago, it was nothing but open untamed grassland; there was nothing else as far as the eye could see. No sod house, no barn, no farmhouse. The garden was not here; they had built everything themselves from nothing.

The stories they told were of resilience and determination. As she listened to them recount their adventures, she wondered privately if she was brave like they were, to come out here to begin a new life for herself.

Will had arrived at his new life, and now he would find his way through hardship in this newborn land. Alice was facing a different destiny. She would head farther west and south, to a place the train had not reached. Where she was going to lay a world that was beautiful and only half settled with cattle ranches and towns built by the Spanish. It was a wild land, a free land, and she was going to see it for herself.

With a mixture of curiosity and trepidation, she silently thought about the fate that awaited her in a place that was as remote to her as a distant country. She didn't speak Spanish; she didn't know anything about the Indians and the people of the West except what she had read about in the sensational stories of the newspapers back home in Augusta. She had never given those stories very much thought, as the West seemed to be a place that existed only in those stories. How could she have ever known that she would one day be here in Kansas, headed even farther, to New Mexico? Who could have foretold that a poor girl from Augusta, Georgia, an orphan, would be so far away from home on an adventure that most grown men would hesitate to undertake? Listening to the stories on that sunny afternoon, her mind drifted to the future. She wondered what she would find at the end of her journey. Would she find happiness, or only danger?

*****

The days since Alice arrived at the Burke farm had been filled with so many tears, smiles, and stories that Alice didn't know if she would ever be able to remember them all, but she tried to tuck them away so she could think about them when she was in New Mexico.

60

Alice remembered the Burkes from before the war changed everything. In her memory, they were older than herself, but had always been kind to her when she was a child. She recalled with perfect clarity the day all the young men left Hartford County on their way to war. She also remembered that one of the older Burke brothers didn't come home. She had been so young when the war happened that her memories of it were a strange mixture of the excitement she felt among the adults in her life, then fear and sorrow. Eclipsing most of it was the death of her own parents.

Seeing Matthew and James again, looking older and wearier but very much the same as she recalled them, brought it all back to her. As she stood outside the modest Burke farmhouse on that night in April, she was astonished that she could remember so many things about that time that she had never thought of since. Those were happier times, when she still had a family of her own, when her parents were alive. She was filled with the sadness of it, which she thought had faded away many years ago.

"I thought I might find you out here," Will said as he joined her on the porch.

"It's a beautiful night. Look at all those stars." Alice wiped the tears from her face with the sleeve of her dress.

"I don't remember seeing so many stars back home in Augusta. There must be something about living out on the prairie that makes it possible. What do you think?" Will said as he leaned out from under the porch roof, gazing towards the heavens.

61

"Oh Will, you were so young back then, you don't remember much about the war, do you? Seeing Sarah again, and James and Matthew – even old Mr. Burke – brought back memories."

"No, I don't remember much about it. Only that you took care of me."

"That was a long time ago; now look at us. I would never have been able to come all this way if it wasn't for you," she said, turning to look at her brother.

He stood beside her on the long narrow porch of the farmhouse. When had he grown so tall? He was becoming a man in front of her and she hadn't seen it before tonight. In the moonlight, he could pass for much older than seventeen. Alice smiled as she thought of how he acted like a grown man, the way he was the one who was trying to protect her these days. When did that happen?

"It wasn't that long ago, it just feels that way. Out here, it would be easy to forget we ever lived anywhere else or any other way, wouldn't it?"

Her tears forgotten, Alice suggested, "Maybe that's the point of it all. Out here, no one cares that we're a couple of orphans trying to make our way in this world."

"You're not orphans anymore," Louisa replied as she closed the door behind her. "You have a home now, here with me."

"Louisa, I know I've already told you how grateful I am that you took me in. I intend to work as hard as I can for my keep," replied Will.

"I haven't taken you in, Will. You're here because you were like me, you wanted something more than what you had in Georgia. You don't have to feel like you're beholden to me. After a few weeks working on the farm with James you might regret leaving Augusta," Louisa said as she stood beside Alice. "What about you, Alice? You still haven't told me what brought you across the country. Why did you brave the train to come so far away from home?"

Alice thought about telling her sister what had happened back home, but she wasn't sure if she wanted to talk about Colonel Chandler. The old drunk made her feel dirty even though she hadn't done anything to feel that way. Was it the guilt she felt at accepting his necklace, the same necklace she sold to purchase her ticket to Kansas? Was it the guilt from having enough money to afford to go to New Mexico?

"I'm like Will; I wanted a new life. There wasn't anything for me in Augusta," Alice answered, hoping that her brother wouldn't mention the colonel. The colonel was like so many things in Georgia she wanted to forget, like Nell, her aunt and her uncle, and the terrible tragedy that tore her family apart. In the big, wide prairie, she was hoping that she would never have to spend another day looking back, even if that meant she had to say goodbye to Daisy, Ernestine, and Sister Agatha forever.

Louisa patted her sister's arm. "I wasn't expecting you, but I'm sure glad to see you both. Alice, my dear, with my children so young and all the work around the farm to be done, I could use the extra help."

For the space of a heartbeat, Alice tried to form the words to tell Louisa that she wasn't staying, but they wouldn't leave her mouth. She didn't want to talk about that, not yet. "I'm glad you didn't leave me at the station at Fort Monroe. I promise I didn't come here to be lazy. I intend to earn my keep as long as I'm here," Alice replied.

"I hope you're going to be with us for a long time. It's been years since I had my family with me. Seeing you two reminded me how much I missed having brothers and sisters around. Don't get me wrong – I love the Burkes, they have been as kind to me as if they were my own kin, but you two are my blood. You remember Ma and Pa, and what our lives were like so long ago. It will be good having you both around," Louisa said warmly. "Don't stay out here too long. Tomorrow is going to be a long day; we have plenty of work to do."

Alice and Will stood motionless as a cricket chirped in the bushes not far from the porch. In the distance towards the creek, frogs sang their nightly song.

Alice waited until she was certain they were alone. Quietly, she asked, "What do you think? Do you think she's as happy to see me as she says she is? Did you see her and James, and the children? They're all as thin as scarecrows. It looks to me like times have been rough."

"James said they had a tough winter, but he's certain this year's crop will be better, since I'm here to help. Alice, why didn't you tell Louisa about your plans to go to New Mexico, or about the colonel?"

Alice sighed and ran a finger along the rough wood of the railing. "I don't want to think about the colonel ever again. He's a part of my past that I want to leave dead and buried in Augusta."

"What about the teaching job?"

"I know I should have said something, but I just couldn't. Louisa seems genuinely happy to see us, to have us here with her. I don't know if she means what she said, but if she does, I don't want to upset her just yet, not when it's only been a few days. Maybe in a week, I'll tell her."

"You're going to have to tell her soon. You promised Sister Agatha you'd be in New Mexico by the summer. It's already May first tomorrow."

"I know, Will. I'm just not ready to leave yet. It's so nice to be together. It kind of makes me sad that we don't have the rest of our brothers and sisters together, the way it used to be when we were growing up. Besides, did you see how tired she looks? She looks worn out. If I can help her for a little while, what's the harm? I have plenty of time to get to New Mexico."

"If you say so, but I wouldn't wait. I'm going to miss you, and it's going to be hard to see you go."

Alice knew that she should have spoken to Louisa about her journey to New Mexico. In the company of her sister and the Burkes, she felt like she had come home. She didn't feel like she was an orphan anymore, or a poor relation. She felt something she could barely recall. In the snug little farmhouse she felt like she was loved, like she was among people who were genuinely happy to see her, to talk to her. It didn't matter that her clothes were old, or that her shoes needed repair. No one cared about anything like that. All they seemed to care about was each other, and how she and Will managed to come west.

There was a word for what she was feeling, something she hadn't felt since she was a little girl, a long time ago before the Yankees came and destroyed her world. The word she knew meant something in Kansas that it never meant in Georgia. That word was *family*, and out here in the middle of the prairie, she had found her family again. Only it wasn't just Louisa and Will, it was James and Sarah and the children who ran around, happily oblivious to any hardships. It was the feeling that she belonged here. How could she ever leave Kansas?

As she thought about the feeling of contentment that being part of big, extended family meant, she immediately felt terribly guilty. In New Mexico, a woman she did not know was waiting for her, needing her help. Alice knew she could not forget her promise to Sister Agatha, but she decided Sister Cecilia could wait for a few days, until she was ready to say goodbye to her sister and the Burkes, the family she wished she'd had every day since they left Georgia ten years ago. Now that she had them back in her life, how would she ever be able to tear herself away?

Feeling torn and guilty, she thought about her lifelong dream to become a teacher. She was going to need help to make that dream a reality. The help she sought was in New Mexico. If she didn't leave soon, like Will suggested, she wouldn't have the heart to ever leave. What a choice she had to make: to stay in Kansas, or fulfill her promise and her dream. As she followed Will into the house, she prayed that God would give her a few days to be Alice once more, little Alice who was part of a great big family, who was safe and content in the world. If she could feel that for just a few more days, she swore she would happily climb aboard the train and head as far west into New Mexico as it would take her. From there she would buy a ticket on a stagecoach, and if need be she would walk to the mission to see Sister Cecilia. Sister Agatha trusted her, and she did not intend to betray that trust, even if it meant saying goodbye to Will and Louisa for a long, long time.

Chapter Four

Tucker Springs, Kansas

"You're new to Tucker Springs, aren't you? I can't remember seeing you before last Sunday. Your sister told me you were a Cleary. What's your name?" The handsome minister stood on the front porch, holding his hat in his hands.

He was trying to be polite, so Alice stifled a smile. In a church that was one single room, how could he be in any doubt that he had never seen her before last Sunday? With her inexperience in the ways of romance, she did not realize that he was, in his own innocent manner, just trying to engage her in conversation.

"Yes sir, and you're Pastor Newland, or was it Newkirk?" Alice asked the young man as she wiped her hands on her apron. "Come on in the house and sit a spell. I can make some coffee if you like."

"Is that Pastor Newland?" Louisa called out from the kitchen.

"It is," Alice answered as she showed the young man into the parlor.

"I didn't come to be any trouble. If you have a pot of coffee made, a cup would be nice. If not, I will be just as happy with a glass of your finest cool water. It's already hot this morning and I don't suspect it will get any cooler until October," he said with a smile.

The pastor was a few years older than Alice, soft spoken, and he seemed very kind. He was not nearly as tall as Will, but he still stood several inches over Alice. His eyes were light brown, nearly golden, and they sparkled when he spoke to her. His hair was wavy, in a shade of dark blond. He was a handsome man, and as Alice soon discovered her perception that he was kind was not incorrect.

"Pastor, I wasn't expecting you today. What brings you out to the farm?" Louisa asked as she settled Miriam on her lap.

"I came out to see how your family was doing. I know it's been a hard winter for all of us; I thought James might need my help. I'm not the farmer he is, but I have my share of skills that I could put to good use. Hand me a hammer and I can fix a roof, or give me a plow and I can turn up a straight row ready for planting."

"That is very generous of you," Louisa replied.

Alice went to fetch a pitcher of water and a tray of glasses.

"Did you walk all the way from Tucker Springs?" Alice asked as the pastor drank thirstily.

"I rode my horse, Horatio. He needed a gallop; he's full of energy. If I don't ride him three or four times a week he gets restless," explained the young man, who looked longingly at the pitcher.

"Does he need tending?" Alice asked as she jumped up to go to the window.

Outside, she saw the white and brown horse drinking from the trough in front of the barn, Thomas holding the rein.

"What a fine horse you have; did you say his name is Horatio?" Alice asked as she returned to her seat.

"His name is Horatio, and he is a gentleman. I find he is more welcome at some farms than I am," laughed the pastor.

"The children adore him, there is no doubt about that, but I could not say that your horse is more welcome than you," Louisa replied.

"I'm afraid it's a burden I must bear. I am a man of God. Sometimes people don't see me as a man at all," Pastor Newland said with a glance in Alice's direction. "I have no interest in judging anyone, just doing what I can to help where I'm needed."

"Any help at all is appreciated on this farm, I can tell you. James and my brother Will are out in the south field, if you want to lend a hand. I'm sure James will be glad for it," Louisa said, bouncing Miriam gently.

"I'm confident Horatio is in good hands here at the house. I'll just be off to the field to see what James may need. Good day to you, ladies."

Alice stood as the pastor left the parlor. From the window she watched as he put his hat back on his head and waved to the young Burkes, who were feeding hay to Horatio. She wasn't sure if she imagined his lingering glances or the way his eyes sparkled when he looked at her. He was handsome – there could be no denying that, but was he just being neighborly? She stood still, her thoughts racing as her sister set Miriam down on her own small little legs.

Louisa, in true big sister form, immediately began teasing. "My dear Alice, you have been in Kansas less than two weeks and you already have a gentleman caller. You must have been a catch back in Augusta. I'm surprised you're not married."

Alice's face burned as she recalled the one offer of marriage she'd received. She deflected the implied question. "A gentleman caller? He wasn't here to see me, was he? He was here to see if James needed any help."

"That's what he said, and I believe him, but I don't think that was his only reason for paying a call to us this morning. I've never seen him pay the slightest attention to any of the girls in town before. He couldn't help himself, I don't think. He looked positively besotted."

"Besotted? What? With me?" Alice removed the pitcher and the glasses from the table and took them to the kitchen. She tried to change the subject. "These glasses are as pretty as anything I've ever laid eyes on. How did they not get broken on the wagon train?"

Louisa's eyes twinkled. "I don't think you care about the glasses or how they got here from Georgia. Didn't you notice how Pastor Newland stared at you?"

Alice carefully set the tray down on the table in the middle of the tiny kitchen. Biting her lip, she leaned over to tidy the baby's hair.

"Miriam, don't bother your aunt. Well, Alice, what do you think? He would make a good catch."

"What do I think? I think you are seeing something that isn't there. Look at me, I'm not the beauty you are. I'm too thin, and my clothes are dreadfully worn. I quite doubt I could catch the eye of a man like your pastor. I'm not even Protestant."

"Not Protestant? Oh, I forget that you were raised by the Clearys. You're Catholic, aren't you?"

"Yes, I am. I doubt I would get much attention from your Pastor Newland if he suspected that I did not share his religious views."

"No matter. You'll find that the differences that divided us in the East don't mean anything in Kansas. Not everyone who goes to the church in Tucker Springs is Methodist; there's a fair few Baptists in the mix and a Lutheran or two. We make do with what we have in this part of the country. And if I know the pastor, he didn't see your hand-me-down dress or your shoes. He was looking at you, at the young woman who just arrived to start a new life for herself."

"About that," Alice found herself saying as the kitchen door opened with a bang.

Thomas and Victoria were standing in the kitchen doorway, their freckled faces in smiles. "Ma, look who's just got here!"

Sarah Pate came bustling into the kitchen after the Burke children. "Go to the wagon and fetch the hamper. Be careful; it's heavy," she said to Thomas.

Thomas, who was nearly old enough to start working in the fields with his father, was elated to be given a task to do that employed his strength. He was tired of working in the kitchen garden and eager to show his ma that he was ready to work like his father, like a man. Louisa watched him as he nodded eagerly and bolted out the door.

"I know it's been a hard winter for us all, and you don't like taking charity, but I just had to share our good fortune with you."

"Good fortune?" asked Louisa.

Sarah removed her bonnet. "Yes! Matthew went fishing this morning up at the wide part of the creek, and he came home with a mess of fish. We can't eat them all, so I thought you might like some."

"Fresh fish? That is kind of you, but you could sell it up at the store. I can't take this from you. You know how your brother can be. He's proud, just like Samuel."

"I don't want to sell it, not when y'all could have it. Take it on my account. We've got plenty. Besides, Matthew would be hurt if you didn't take it, and so would Margie. She sent over some cornbread she made just for you."

Thomas came into the kitchen carrying the hamper. With a triumphant look on his face, he set it down on the table. Louisa and Sarah didn't seem to notice, and Alice realized that the mood in the room had changed. Smiling at Thomas and Victoria, Alice said, "You did a good job, thank you Thomas. Why don't you take your sisters outside, see if your Aunt Sarah's horse needs any water and hay."

Thomas was out the door with his sisters right behind him, but much slower. Victoria held Miriam's hand as they climbed down the back steps. Louisa pulled out a chair and sat down with a sigh.

"Thank you, Sarah. Please let me know when I can return the favor."

"There is nothing to repay, you know that. We're family. If it wasn't for you and Matthew, Stephen and I wouldn't have a farm. Take the fish and the cornbread, it will do you some good. There will be plenty more now that the summer is nearly upon us. Just you wait, we'll have a good harvest this year and you will soon forget how terrible this past year has been," Sarah said.

Alice turned away from the table and made herself busy cleaning up.

"I wish I could share your optimism. With three growing children—" she fell silent, and Alice knew that Louisa had caught herself before she said too much. But it was too late; Alice understood perfectly.

Into the silence, Louisa said, "Alice, I didn't mean anything about you."

Alice turned to face the older women. "You did mean me. I understand, you weren't expecting me to be here. There isn't enough to go around."

Louisa reached out to her sister, "Alice, it's not you, not at all. I love having you to help with all the chores around the house."

"I'm sorry Louisa, I know it's been hard on you out here, I know that. You have a lot on you and I am an extra mouth to feed. But I was just about to tell you that I'm moving on. I'm going to New Mexico, to a mission there. I'm going to be a teacher!"

Her heart ached as she spoke, but she smiled because she didn't want Louisa to see her pain. Alice had known that the invitation to come west had been extended to Will, and not to her. It wasn't meanness, only simple economics. They couldn't afford to feed her, though they would never say so. Louisa would not turn her away.

But, oh, she didn't want to leave.

Louisa looked relieved, but at the same time her eyes shone with tears. "Alice! I remember you playing schoolhouse with our dolls. Is it really what you want?"

"It is. I should have told you sooner, but I was really enjoying being here with you—"

Louisa stood and snatched Alice into her arms. "And I am so glad you came. How brave you are!" Pulling back, she swiped at her tears, and then Alice's. "I hate to see you go, I truly do."

Alice nodded. With the lump in her throat, speech was out of the question.

"So," Louisa said, turning back to the fish. "We will have fish. Thank you, Sarah."

Sarah was surreptitiously wiping her own eyes, and gave a choked laugh. "Maybe you can come back one day, Alice, and teach here in Tucker Springs!"

A little later, Alice made her way outside, where the children were playing chase. She couldn't help but smile as she watched them, and remember how it had been when she and her brothers and sisters were little, before the Yankees came. She'd found some of that same happiness here in Kansas, but she could not stay.

She had made a promise to Sister Agatha, and she had never planned to go against her word. Perhaps she had been a burden in Augusta, and she would definitely be a burden here. Her decision was made. She must continue on to New Mexico, and she would go very soon. And whenever she could, she would send money back to the family she loved, here at the Burke farm.

*****

77

May 21, 1876
Western Texas

Alice was hungry. It had been several hours since she'd eaten anything, a piece of bread and a thin slice of cheese sold at the last whistle stop. That was in Kansas, and it seemed like days ago. She hoped that at the next station there would be something more to eat than bread, but she doubted it. She didn't have any food with her except for a piece of pie and an apple left in the hamper Pastor Newland had given to her at the train station, and she was saving that pie for when she arrived in New Mexico. From what she heard, the place was wild and virtually lawless. Food may be scarce, she reasoned, as she peeped inside the hamper, her mouth watering.

She thought about the pastor, her brother Will, and her sister Louisa standing at the station at Fort Monroe. Will had struggled not to cry, Louisa looked stricken, and Pastor Newland made Alice promise to write to him as soon as she arrived safely at the mission at Santa Maria. Unlike Will, Alice didn't try to appear stronger than she was. She had never spent a day away from her brother. All her other brothers and sisters had been scattered after the death of her parents – everyone except for Will. She had cared for him and protected him every day of their lives, and now for the first time, they would be apart.

As she stared out the window at the spartan terrain of brown dirt, low scrubby bushes, and dark brown hilltops on the horizon, she wondered if she would ever grow accustomed to a place that was so different to the lush green world of Augusta. The view from her window was desolate; there were no tall trees to offer shade, no buildings, no homesteads. The landscape itself was lonely, and she knew she was going to feel that way, too. Would Will be ok without her?

She realized she was being silly. Will had Louisa and James; he had his nephew and his small nieces who adored him. He had no reason to feel lonely. Alice, on the other hand, felt alone and scared. No one she had ever known had ventured this far from Augusta.

James had been livid when he discovered she would be traveling by herself, and Louisa was frightened for her. They said the trip would be dangerous for a young woman all alone, and they had even tried to change her mind, but she would not listen to their arguments. She knew that she was one more mouth to feed in a family that couldn't afford it. She wasn't the one they'd invited to come to Kansas, she wasn't wanted at their house any more than she was wanted in Augusta. Stubbornly, Alice refused to listen to them, and so she found herself on the train headed into New Mexico Territory, to a place where she knew no one and no one would be waiting for her at the station.

Sister Cecilia was expecting her, but she was not going to be waiting with a carriage. There was a station south of Santa Fe; from there, Alice would have to purchase a ticket for a stagecoach destined for Santa Fe, and then north to Santa Maria.

She was apprehensive to be traveling alone, to be so far away from anyone she knew. What if something happened? What if she was robbed? What if she arrived at Santa Maria and there was a mistake? She didn't have enough money to return to Kansas, and that thought was nearly as frightening as what waited for her in New Mexico. If Sister Cecilia didn't take her in, then what would she do out there all alone in a strange place?

"Miss, is this seat taken?"

Alice turned away from the window, her jumbled thoughts forgotten. Standing in the aisle of the train car was a tall man with wide shoulders and a disarming smile. His dark hair and deep-set dark eyes gave him a mysteriously handsome air. He was dressed in a black coat and deep blue brocade vest that must have cost more than all the clothes in her trunk.

He bowed. "Miss, did I startle you? It was not my intention; please forgive me."

Alice looked around the train car nervously. She was not accustomed to being addressed by men she didn't know, much less by men who were as handsome and well dressed as this one. But there were other passengers in the train car – more men than women, but their presence made her feel less anxious. No matter how charming he may be, she had an inherent distrust of strangers, especially when she was this far away from home.

"I don't believe I know you," she said politely, if a little coolly.

"No, you do not. Would you like to?"

Alice was taken aback. "Sir, that is not a question to pose to a lady, is it?"

He smiled. "No, it's not. I'm not used to speaking with ladies. Allow me to introduce myself, and perhaps we may begin again. I am Jonathan Keene, at your service."

Alice regarded him suspiciously, doubting the character of a man who would approach a lone woman and speak to her. "Mr. Keene, I am not at all certain I know what you wish to achieve by introducing yourself to me. There are countless other seats on this train."

She opened her book and looked at the page, ignoring the man. He took a seat across the aisle from her, and seemed to be ignoring her in return, except occasionally she had the feeling he was looking at her out of the corner of his eye.

She wasn't actually interested in reading, and his sideways attention was very distracting. She made a peevish sound in her throat, and thought she heard a small chuckle from his direction.

"If you told me your name, we could have a conversation," he said.

"Your behavior is inappropriate, sir."

With a nod, he replied, "You're quite right, whatever your name is; I'll give you that. You're perfectly right to be cautious. For all you know I could be a cheat, a scoundrel, or a thief."

"Are you, Mr. Keene? Are you any of those things?"

"No, Miss, I'm not. I do gamble from time to time, but there isn't a decent game to be had aboard this train. I pride myself on my skill and not having to rely on cheating or thievery for my living. Are you finally convinced I mean you no harm?"

Alice shook her head, and kept her eyes on the page. She had no idea what was written there. "Why should I be convinced? You could say anything at all, and then be off with my meager purse. At any rate, judging from your fine clothes, I would think your attention would be better spent elsewhere. I have no jewelry, no valuables of any kind."

"Are you suggesting I should choose a wealthier traveler on whom to exercise my charms?"

"Your charms, Mr. Keene. How you talk! I have never met a man as bold as you."

"Bold, Miss? I'm bold because that is the only way for a man to be. After all, I have to live by my wits and my skill at cards. Tell me something else, if you will not tell me your name. What part of the South are you from? Your accent sounds like Georgia, but I could nearly place you in the Carolinas."

"Your accent, sir, is unlike any I have ever heard – except by the Yankees."

"Ah, yes. Then you are a southern belle traveling alone; that will never do."

"It would do fine, sir, if you would leave me alone."

He turned toward her, his face even more handsome this close to hers. "See? My charms have you ensnared. You are enraptured."

Giggling despite herself, Alice replied, "You may be charming, sir, but you are arrogant *and* a Yankee. I have no interest in befriending a Yankee."

"I admit that I am from the North, but I am not a Yankee. You see, I am far too young to have fought in that war. Don't let my accent fool you, and I will not let yours fool me. Neither one of us belong to that world any more. If you were a southerner, a true, dyed-in-the-wool confederate, you wouldn't be on this train heading west, and you wouldn't be talking to me."

"What choice have you given me? You started talking to me; you sat down beside me."

"I can see how that would cause you distress. If you insist, then, I will leave you alone with your lovely view of the dirt." He rose to leave.

"It was good to meet you, Mr. Keene. I wish you a safe journey." Perhaps this bold, irritating manner is common among northerners, she mused.

"You as well, Miss. Since you are not going to ask me to stay or tell me your name I suppose I shall have to give you a name that suits you. What about Katherine, or fair Bonnie? Maybe you are a Colleen?"

Alice did not tell him her name. With a smile, she dismissed the handsome stranger. "Good day to you Mr. Keene; it has been interesting."

"So, it has, thank you for the diversion. I shall pester you no longer," he said.

Alice didn't know what to think of the handsome stranger, but when he was gone, she checked her purse, which resided with her hamper below her seat. Her money was still there.

*****

Alice didn't know exactly when the train traveled across the border from Texas into the New Mexico Territory. She had managed to fall asleep in her seat, after spending far too long musing about the intentions of the charming Mr. Keene. He was a welcome distraction from her uncertainty and trepidation about her journey to Santa Maria. The train was nearing the station south of Santa Fe, according to the conductor, as he made his way through the train. It would be arriving in the morning. As she yawned and dozed off again, she prayed that she would soon be at the mission in Santa Maria, and that a bed and a hot meal would be waiting.

The next morning she woke to the rhythmic jostling of the train car as the sun rose over the horizon in the distance. The terrain was coming alive as the light of the day was creeping up over the mountains. The view was breathtaking. Was this to be her new home? Did Santa Maria look like this? She reached for the letter penned by Sister Agatha. It contained simple instructions to reach Santa Maria, twenty miles north of Santa Fe, and Santa Fe was several miles north of the train station. Would the country be as beautiful that far north?

The anxiety she had fought to conceal came back as the train slowed to approach the station. From her vigil at the window, Alice did not see much to recommend the station, or the town that surrounded it. There was a small, adobe building by the platform, surrounded by other adobe buildings scattered haphazardly around it. Smoke rose from chimneys in the cool air of the morning as the train came to a stop. Alice stood, stretching her legs and her arms. It felt good to move around again, she mused as she shivered. The morning was cold, but she had heard from the other travelers on the train that by midday the temperature would be intolerably hot. Looking out the window, she realized there wasn't a bit of shade, not from a single grove of trees, not like in Georgia where on hot summer days, she could always find shelter under the oaks and pines.

With her hamper in one hand and her purse in the other, she stepped down from the train onto the platform. She felt better seeing several other travelers standing on the platform as they waited for their trunks to be unloaded. She recognized one of them. With a tip of his hat, Mr. Jonathan Keene walked towards her.

"Miss, is this your destination?" he asked, smiling.

"No sir, not quite. Is it yours?" she asked feeling bolder than yesterday.

"I'm heading for Santa Fe; what about you? Are you going to the same fair city?"

She hesitated, but feeling a strange mixture of courage and loneliness, she told him the truth. "I'm heading for the mission at Santa Maria."

"Ah, Santa Maria. A wonderful place."

"Thank you. It brings me comfort to know that it is nice there."

"The mission is lovely, and so is the church – but the town is no place for a southern lady traveling alone. Cattle rustlers and other men of poor reputation gather in saloons. Have you ever been to saloon? No, I would think not. You look too wholesome."

"Saloons? They have saloons in Santa Maria?"

"They do, and saloon girls, but I probably shouldn't be telling you about that. It's not considered proper conversation for a lady."

Alice could feel her face turning crimson. "Saloons and saloon girls? Are you having fun at my expense?"

"There's no reason to believe me, but I have been there, and I must confess that I did very well for myself. It's been a year or two since, but I doubt much has changed. Another thing, you may want to learn a few words of Spanish, that will help you with the people who live there. How do you feel about Indians? There's a pueblo outside of Santa Maria that rivals any of the buildings I've seen in St. Louis. Quite a place, that Santa Maria, if that is truly your destination."

"Indians in a…what did you call it, a pueblo? Spanish and saloons? You make Santa Maria sound like it should be in a wild west show."

He smiled. "Maybe it's not as bad as that, but I give you my word as a gentleman, you have never seen the like before in your life. And yes, the word is *pueblo*. It's a tall Indian city built of stone and adobe that rises from the desert. Quite impressive."

"A pueblo. Maybe I shall see it for myself one day."

"Maybe so. Here are the trunks." A porter unloaded the trunks onto the platform. "You'd better not tarry purchasing your ticket; there's only one stagecoach to Santa Fe. You don't want to ride up top in this heat."

"Thank you, Mr. Keene. Where should I purchase a ticket?"

"Come with me; I'll make sure you get a good seat."

Alice followed him into the cramped adobe station. Inside the waiting room were a few benches and a cast iron stove for heat and, she suspected, for coffee and tea for the stationmaster. The old man at the ticket window spoke with her companion at length about the seating on the stagecoach as he took her money and presented her with a ticket and a dire warning.

"Are you going to Santa Maria? I hope you aren't travelling alone, Miss."

"No, she's traveling with me. One for Santa Maria, please," Jonathan Keene said as he handed his money to the stationmaster.

"Wait, Mr. Keene. I thought you were heading to Santa Fe."

"I was, but I can't have an innocent young woman like yourself at the mercy of strangers on the road, now can I? That would not be the conduct of a gentleman."

Alice held her ticket in her hand and looked at it, thinking about this man who stood beside her, this Yankee who talked about saloons and playing cards as casually as if he were discussing the weather and farming. Looking up, she smiled at him. "Mr. Keene, I don't know why you have taken it upon yourself to be my protector, but I'm glad you have. I shouldn't trust you – I shouldn't even be talking to you – but there is something about you and your manner that I find honest, even if I suspect your profession isn't."

"So you trust me enough to sit beside me all the way to Santa Maria?" he asked as they left the station.

She gave him a stern look. "I may regret it, but I suspect my chances of arriving safely are better with you, than without you."

"You aren't going to become a sister, are you? You don't plan to take the vows; that would be a terrible waste."

"How you talk, Mr. Keene. No, I'm not going to become a sister. I am going to Santa Maria to become a teacher. Sister Cecilia needs teachers, and from what you said about Santa Maria, the town needs the mission."

"A teacher! I should have known that you would turn out to be as wholesome as I presumed," he teased.

"I am wholesome, if that's what you want to call it. and for that matter, I suspect there may be some good in you. Why else would you spend the money to take me to Santa Maria?"

"I have a weakness for wholesome teachers with southern accents," he replied.

She huffed, and hid her amusement rather well, she thought. "Say what you will, but I am grateful. Thank you, Mr. Keene."

"You are welcome, Miss…"

"Miss Alice Cleary, from Augusta."

*****

The road to Santa Fe had been well trodden by the hooves of horses for many years, but it wasn't smooth; the stagecoach was a bumpy way to travel. After the lulling rhythm of the train, the coach was jarring as it flew across the barren land. Inside the coach, Alice sat beside her traveling companion, Mr. Keene. Seated across from her was a wiry man, and a large man who smacked his lips as he ate beef jerky washed down with the contents of a flask. His companion was a woman who was dressed garishly in crimson and black, with rouge on her cheeks. Alice tried not to stare at the fat man or his colorful companion but she found she could not help herself; they were sitting right in front of her. She had never seen a woman who wore makeup, nor had she ever smelled the sickly-sweet scent of perfume in such close quarters. Fighting the urge to be sick from the tumultuous ride and the perfume, she held her handkerchief to her nose.

"What's wrong with your wife? She is your wife, isn't she? She's turning green." the large man said as he gestured with his flask.

Even with the handkerchief held to her nose, Alice could not escape the aroma of alcohol that rose from the open flask. She had never touched a sip of spirits but she knew her uncle kept a bottle for medical purposes. The smell made her even more nauseous, and she swallowed the saliva that pooled in her mouth.

"Aye, a lovely thing she is, my sweet Colleen. My dear, you've worn your worst dress for the trip. We should buy you a new one when we reach Santa Fe. What do you say, my pretty, would you like a dress and a bonnet to match?" Mr. Keene said in a thick foreign accent. He sounded vaguely like one of the sisters from Augusta, an Irish woman who hailed from Galway.

"Aye," she whispered with an attempt at a smile.

"There, there, the coach will be stopping soon for a change of horses. Some fresh air will be just the thing to cure what ails ye."

Alice nodded, wondering why he was speaking so strangely, and why he insisted she was his wife. As she concealed her distress as best she could, she decided that those questions would have to be relegated to another time. At the present, she was feeling far too queasy to concern herself with much else.

"Here, take one of these. They help me every time I feel sick to my stomach," The painted woman said as she dug into her purse and produced a tin of candy.

Alice didn't want to accept anything from a stranger. She glanced helplessly at Mr. Keene.

"Please excuse my wife, she's a might picky about her sweets. Thank you just the same, that was mighty generous of you," he said.

"Just trying to help," the woman said in a huff as she closed the tin with a sharp click.

"Now, Harriet, there's no need to be angry at the woman; she's green as green can be. She don't have no kind of appetite. She didn't mean no harm by it. Here, have a drink and don't let it worry your pretty head." The large man handed the flask to the woman in crimson.

"Don't mind if I do," she answered as she drank a swallow of the liquor.

"There's the outpost up ahead," Mr. Keene said as he gazed out the window.

The stagecoach came to a stop at a wood and adobe building sitting along the narrow, dry road. The passengers disembarked from the stagecoach to freshen up at the well and walk for a few minutes in the blistering hot air. While the horses were being changed for a team of fresh ones, Alice gestured to Mr. Keene to speak with her away for the other passengers. Standing on solid ground again, she was beginning to forget how sick she had been, but she hadn't forgotten his antics.

"Mr. Keene, I don't understand you! Why do you claim we're married? Why are you speaking like you're from Ireland? What are you doing?"

"I think my accent was spot on, don't you?"

"That it may be, but why were you speaking like an Irishman, and why have I suddenly become your wife?"

"Oh that. That was for your own good. The man who was seated in the stagecoach with us was one of the least reputable men you will ever meet in the territory."

"You mean the large man who was drinking?"

"No, he's harmless; he's a gambler like me. I'm referring to the other one, the thin one," he said as he glanced in the direction of the stagecoach.

The thin man was smoking a cigar, and he was watching Alice and Jonathan. There was something cold in his gaze, something that made Alice shudder despite the heat.

"For God's sake, don't stare at him."

"Sorry, I couldn't help myself. He's looking at us," Alice said as Mr. Keene gently held her arm and guided her in the opposite direction.

"He's been watching you ever since you got on the train in Kansas. You may not realize it, but he was seated a few rows back from you in the train car. I don't know if he buys my story that we're together, but at least he knows you aren't traveling alone. The accent was just to throw him off my trail – he owns two of the biggest saloons in Santa Fe. If I want to make any money this trip, I don't want him to recognize me when I sit down at his tables as myself."

"How do you know he was watching me?" she asked.

"I don't mean to alarm you, but I was also watching you. You have 'innocent naïve girl' written all over you. You have no business traveling alone in this part of the territories. If you have any family at all, I wonder that they allowed you to board the train."

"They tried to stop me," she admitted.

"You should have listened to them. A man like him preys upon young women like yourself. If I hadn't come along, he would have seen you safely to Santa Fe, and into one of his business that *aren't* saloons."

Alice looked blank for a moment, and then gasped. "I wouldn't have gone with him, not for anything."

"If he drugged you, you wouldn't have had much choice, now would you?"

"Drugged me?"

"Yes, with laudanum or some other devilish device of his. If I hadn't come along, I fear to think what would have happened to you."

Alice studied the man at her side. His smile was gone, and in its place was an expression of such earnestness, she regretted questioning his motives. Still, she asked, "You don't know me, Mr. Keene. Why have you taken such an interest in my safety?"

"I may be a sinner, Miss Cleary, but I'm no villain. Where I come from, I have seen too many young women fall prey to the evils of men. I couldn't stand aside and watch the same thing happen to you."

Alice nodded thoughtfully, and for a few moments they were silent, pacing slowly along the track. "The reason I came to New Mexico was that I, too, was nearly preyed upon by a terrible man."

"Miss Cleary, I'm sorry to hear you say that. He must have been terrible indeed to send you to the territories in search of refuge."

"My uncle tried to sell me in marriage to a wealthy but cruel drunkard." Hearing herself, she laughed self-consciously. "I must trust you after all;

you are the only person besides my brother Will who knows the truth."

"Will? Where is he, may I ask?"

"He's back in Kansas, in a little town called Tucker Springs. Oh, how I miss him," she said as she fought the urge to cry.

"It looks like we're boarding again; the journey to Santa Fe is nearly over. I shall give you the seat by the window. If you look out and watch the scenery go by, you won't feel as sick."

"That's very kind of you," she said as they walked back to the stagecoach.

"Anything I can do for my fair wife," he replied as he held the door one for her and gave her his hand to steady her.

Alice knew the thin man was watching her, studying her. She didn't know why she hadn't noticed him on the train. But Mr. Keene had watched over her, even when she didn't know it. She was suddenly embarrassed. Had he seen her check her purse after he left her on the train? What must he think of her? He had been so kind, and she mistook him for a common thief. As she settled into the seat by the window, he reached out and patted her hand. It was a kind gesture, forward and bold from a man she barely knew, but she didn't mind. She no longer felt he was a stranger.

*****

95

The stagecoach did not go to the mission in Santa Maria. It stopped at a hotel in the town, one situated across the street from a saloon and a general store. The hotel was like the other buildings in the town – not very large, but sturdily built, a combination of wood, stone, and adobe.

Santa Maria was just as Mr. Keene had described it. It seemed lawless, with its tough, frowning men walking along the street, and the saloons and other business that lined the roadway, but it also looked civilized. A big general mercantile store stood in the middle of the main street, beside a post office. A family of fair-haired children were leaving the post office with their mother, holding hands.

Along the main street there was a central square, a market, and church. Alice gazed at the church. "Is that the mission?" she asked.

"That's Our lady of Sorrows. The mission is outside the town," explained Mr. Keene as he stepped away to inquire about the hire of a wagon.

Alice was excited by the strangeness of the town, but also thrilled by the beauty of the church and some of the buildings. This was her destination, a place farther away from Augusta than she had ever imagined she could be.

When Mr. Keene joined her once more, she said, "This town, it's everything you said and much more. I've never seen anything like it!"

Mr. Keene took a long deep breath. "Ah, do you smell that? Spices, chili, and beef. It's been too long since I had any real food; how I've missed New Mexico."

"What is that smell? I've never smelled anything like it," she said as she realized that she was extremely hungry. The travel sickness was a distant memory as she inhaled the unfamiliar but pleasant scent.

"That, my dear, is a dish they make here, beans and chilies with a warm tortilla. It's just the thing to stave off hunger."

"Do we have time to eat? What about our trunks? What about your passage back to Santa Fe?"

"I can catch the stage tomorrow. The carriage will be along in a moment, in the meantime, you wait here. Guard our trunks and don't leave this spot, do you understand?"

Alice nodded as she watched him rush across the dirt street to a tiny store by the post office. Alice didn't know what the sign said (it was in Spanish), but from the smell of the food, she guessed it must be some kind of restaurant. She waited and watched the people of Santa Maria pass her on the street. She heard languages spoken she had never heard before, and she saw all manner of people, some of whom might be Indians, with their thick dark hair and golden skin. She tried not to stare, but she was curious. In Georgia, being Indian was dangerous. Here, she wasn't so sure that was true.

"Try this. I promised to bring back the plates when we're done," he said as he invited Alice to sit down on the trunk by the front of the hotel. He passed her a plate of beans and a round flat piece of something that resembled bread.

"Are we going to eat right here in the street? How am I supposed to eat this; where are the knife and fork?"

He laughed. "Forget about being proper; you don't need a knife and fork for this. Eat it like this, watch me," he said as he demonstrated how to fold the tortilla and scoop the beans. "Try it, but be careful. It's not what you're accustomed to eating."

Alice scooped up the beans after several tries and carefully bit into the flatbread and the beans at the same time, like he was doing. The *tortilla*, as he called it, reminded her vaguely of buttered cornbread, and the beans were flavored with something more than a ham hock. She liked the flavor immediately.

"That my dear, is what they eat in Mexico. A friend of mine told me they were eating food like this before the Spanish came. I'm glad you like it, because you will be getting a lot more of here in the territories."

"It's so good, but what is this flavor? It's making me cry."

"Chilies. Mama Rosa uses plenty of chilies in all her cooking."

"Mama Rosa?" Alice asked between bites, all thoughts of propriety dismissed as she ate the simple fare.

"The nice lady who runs the café across the street. Best food in Santa Maria, if you ask me."

"Tortillas, is that what this is called?" asked Alice.

"Yes ma'am. It's the equivalent of bread; you'll get used to it."

"I like it. It's a bit like cornbread, isn't it?"

"A bit. I'd better be taking these plates back or Mama Rosa won't serve me another mouthful, ever."

Alice's mouth was burning from the spices but she didn't say anything to Mr. Keene. He'd been kind to buy her lunch after the long ride from Santa Fe. He dashed across the street a minute later with a jar full of water, which he handed to her. "Drink this, and you'll feel better. I remember my first time eating this – I cried for an hour afterwards."

Alice drank the water, feeling the quenching coolness slide down her throat. She handed the remainder of the jar to her companion. "Thank you, this has been an adventure. In Augusta I never would have dreamed of eating outside on the street. I may be an orphan, but I'm not a field hand."

"In Santa Maria those old ways no longer mean anything. You aren't in Augusta anymore, you aren't even in a *state*. This place is different. It was Spanish, and before that it belonged to the Indians. No, my dear, you are far away from the laws that you lived by in Georgia. How does that feel?"

Alice frowned. "I don't know. I've never lived my life by any other laws and rules but what I was taught as a child. Do you mean that here I can do what I want to, and say what I please?"

"You can, if you like. There's no one to stop you. You can change your name and become a new person if you wish. Lots of people do it."

"Lots of people…like you? Is that why you can sound like an Irishman?"

"I have talent for mimicry. It comes in handy."

"What about your name? Are you really Jonathan Keene?"

He tipped his hat to her as an older man brought a wagon around to the front of the hotel. "Looks like that's our wagon. I'll just be a moment; I have to make arrangements for my room and board tonight and see to my own trunk, then we'll get you to your mission."

"You didn't answer my question, Mr. Keene."

"I know," he said with a smirk as he disappeared inside the hotel.

Alice suspected that he may never give her an answer other than a smirk and a tip of the hat. But if he saw her safely to the mission, she decided that maybe she didn't need to know who he was.

"The mission is two miles from town, near the pueblo," her traveling companion explained as the driver silently steered the horse along the street. Alice was nervous, not from fear this time, but because she was nearing the end of her journey and the end of her time with Mr. Keene. In the short time she had come to know him, she had become a little attached to the man. He acted like no one she had met before. He protected her, but he talked freely about saloons and saloon girls. He was a mystery, and one she wished she had more time to study – but she didn't come to New Mexico to meet men. She came here to teach.

"Look, see the bell tower? If you look carefully you can make it out. See how it stands high over the desert?" He pointed to a place on the horizon.

Alice peered carefully into the distance. Along the horizon was the gray outline of mountains, but here along the wagon trail there was dirt, rock, and the occasional low bush or pointy-looking plant.

"Do you see it?"

She squinted until she could see the bell tower clearly, far off. "I do, is that it? Is that the mission?"

"It is. When we get closer you can see the village that has grown around it and just there, past the mission, is the pueblo."

Alice wasn't sure which was more exciting to her, the mission or the pueblo. She had never known that Indians lived in cities or that they dwelled openly in the West. The Indians in Georgia had been sent away, or else they lived in fear. This was a place like no other she had ever known. She smiled as she realized that here she may have found the place she belonged, this place was to be her home.

Chapter Five

May 24, 1876
Santa Maria, New Mexico Territory

Alice woke up in a narrow bed in a tiny room. The chilly morning air made her snuggle deeply into her blankets as she looked at the ceiling above her. It was constructed of wooden beams that looked sturdy and old. The walls of the room were painted white, and a crucifix hung above the bed as the only decoration. Glancing around the room, she saw a candle on a round table at her bedside, and a bench at the foot of the bed, near a table. Her trunk sat beside the wall of the austere space.

Forcing herself out of bed, she pulled the blanket around her shoulders and walked across the colorful rag rug to the shutters. Pushing them back, she gasped at the serene view which greeted her. Before her lay the mission garden and the soft greenery of trees that shaded a small patch of green grass. Here, behind the walls of the mission lay a piece of earth that was not brown and dusty, but a lush, green paradise of flowers, blossoming trees, and a thriving garden. In the branches of the trees she heard birdsong, reminding her that she was far too late to join the sisters in morning prayers.

Turning away from the view, she washed her face and freshened up using the water in the pitcher and basin on a stand by the table. There was no mirror in her room, and she doubted there were any at the convent. Vanity was a worldly vice and one that had no place in the abbey.

Jonathan Keene was gone. He had not been permitted inside the abbey, though he'd insisted that he carry Alice's trunk. How gallant he was, right to the end. Alice laughed to herself. Gallant and terribly old fashioned, despite being a scoundrel and a gambler.

Of course there were no words of affection to pass between them. He made no promise to write, and neither did she. After all, what was he to her but a helpful stranger she'd met on a train? But she did wonder, as she reached for her hairbrush, if she would ever see him again. She didn't know where his home was, if he had one. She had no way to find him, even if she wanted to.

When she'd bid him farewell and thanked him again, he'd slipped a few coins into her hand and wished her good fortune, and then he was gone.

Alice finished brushing her hair, braiding it, and pinning it into place. From her trunk she selected the nicest of her dresses, gray with a wide, white collar. It was plain, and Nell had barely worn it when it was hers, but Alice loved it for its simple tailoring and the modesty of the collar. Satisfied that she was presentable, she left her room and went to look for the dining hall to see if she was too late for breakfast.

Sister Cecilia was nothing like what she had been expecting. She was a tall woman, young for an abbess, and as serene as her surroundings. She greeted Alice warmly, praising God that she was safe in Santa Maria after such a long trip. She had given Alice a bowl of stew for dinner, and showed her to her room, where Alice fell into a deep sleep until this morning.

Today, she would learn about her position at the mission, what Sister Cecilia expected of her, and how she would become a teacher. After a good night's sleep, Alice was ready to face her future, as soon as she found something to eat. She tried to recall where the dining room was and walked down a narrow corridor.

She came to an arched wooden door. Lifting the metal latch, she pushed the door open and walked into the mission church. Her footsteps echoed on the stones in the cavernous space. Candles burned in forged metal stands as light softly illuminated the altar from the two small windows near the ceiling. Above her head, enormously wide wooden beams held the ceiling above the wooden pews, and the statues of the Blessed Virgin and Jesus. The walls glowed golden in the candlelight and light of the morning.

Kneeling before the host at the altar, she bent her head in prayer. God had delivered her safely to New

Mexico – God, and his wayward angel Mr. Keene. Her prayers were answered. She closed her eyes and gave thanks to God for His gifts, all of them, from Colonel Chandler and Sister Agatha, all her beloved family, Jonathan Keene, and his gift of money.

And before she opened her eyes, she asked whether it might he His will for her to meet the mysterious man again, someday.

*****

"Miss Cleary, the gentlemen who was in your company upon your arrival, what is your relationship to him?" the abbess asked as she peered at Alice.

Alice sat in a plain wooden chair in the office of the abbess, Sister Cecilia. She had not been expecting a direct question first thing in the morning, before her coffee. Sister Cecilia had found Alice in the corridor when she was making her way to get some breakfast after visiting the chapel. That was half an hour ago. Alice's stomach grumbled as she sat uncomfortably. Her back ached from the journey, and she longed for a day in bed, some hot food, and a bath – none of which would be forthcoming any time soon.

She looked across the wooden desk set in the room that was nearly as austere as her own bedchamber. There was a shelf of books and papers and a small adobe fireplace in the corner; this room was very spartan in its decoration.

The abbess was tall, as Alice had noted upon her arrival, and many years younger than Sister Agatha. She wore the black and white habit of her order, and her face was pinched and gaunt but not unpleasant. However, at the moment her features were set in a disapproving frown. Rather than be taken aback by the abbess's inquiry about her former traveling companion, Alice wondered how she could describe who Jonathan Keene was in relation to her. There was not a simple answer, because she knew very little about the man who had escorted her safely to the mission.

Taking a deep breath, she decided to plunge into the answer as honestly as she was able to be, considering how little she truly knew about the man. As her stomach rumbled again, she replied, "He was a kind man who happened to be coming to Santa Maria. I don't know much about him."

"That may be for the best. Here at the mission it is the duty of all the teachers to abide by strict rules of conduct. There is a list of rules that we expect all lay teachers to follow. You must keep your classroom clean, the lamps filled with oil, their wicks trimmed. You must be sure to carry your own wood into the class every morning. There is no tobacco, no drinking, no gambling. You may not wear rouge on your cheeks, or dress in clothes that draw attention to yourself. You must take care not to act in public in any way that would bring doubt on your character. You must not entertain gentlemen callers or meet them in saloons or other places of ill repute. Are these rules understood? We do not entertain gentlemen callers and we do not encourage the attention of men."

Alice's cheeks burned crimson with embarrassment. "He was not a gentleman caller, nor did I seek his attention, if that is what you mean."

Sister Cecilia softened her tone. "These rules may sound intimidating, but I expect you to adhere to them, for your reputation and the reputation of this mission. If you follow them, you shall remain safe and sound. Miss Cleary, in the territory a lady doesn't have to willfully engage in any activity to attract the attention of gentlemen, or shall I say men. There are very few gentlemen in this part of the world. You will discover that this land is quite different than where you came from."

"That is what I'm hoping for, that it will be different."

"Sister Agatha wrote to me of your struggles in Georgia. I did not wish to alarm you with my tone, nor did I wish to imply that you are not a God-fearing young woman. I doubt you did much to encourage the attention of the man who accompanied you here to the mission. It is precisely for that reason that I must urge that you take the greatest caution and care, Miss Cleary."

Alice thought of Jonathan Keene's smile and his confident manner of speaking, and fought the urge to sigh girlishly. "I sincerely doubt that I will ever see him again. He only expressed concern for my safety and wished to be helpful, as I was traveling alone."

Sister Cecilia smiled. "I cannot know his intentions, but if you say they were honorable I have no reason to doubt your word. Sister Agatha spoke highly of your character and good judgment. It is for that reason that I caution you to be on your guard. You will find that the New Mexico territory is unlike anywhere you have traveled before. This land is unsettled. There is violence and greed; the devil would have his kingdom here if it weren't for our efforts."

"That sounds alarming. Is evil so prevalent here? I saw the land, the mountains as a strange place, beautiful and wild. I saw the work of God's hand, and I thought surely this place was blessed."

"Santa Maria does possess its own form of beauty. It is a wondrous place, but it is corrupted by the wills of men who would turn away from God and seek their fortunes through all manner of sinful means. I do not wish to catalog the entirety of depravity that you may encounter but there is bribery, gambling, cattle rustling, and all manner of vice. Men fight each other for money, and then there is the matter of the people native to this land. They are unhappy. There have been rumors of uprisings and rebellion to the north. There is distrust and disharmony among the settlers to this land, the Spanish who claimed it for their own and the Apache, the Dine peoples, and the inhabitants of the Pueblos. You will find there is much work to be done, but you must be always wary."

"I left Georgia because it was torn apart by war. I wished to make a new life for myself far away from the violence and turmoil. I thought I knew what the devil could do to twist the will of men. Have I traded one land of sin and vice for another?"

Sister Cecilia made a clucking sound and shook her head. "My dear, I do not wish to discourage you. I have caused you apprehension, and for that I apologize. It is not in my nature to cause undue distress. I may be a servant of God, but I am a practical woman, as I can see that you are. It is important that you know the true extent of the difficulties we face here in Santa Maria. If you only knew how necessary your efforts will be to the success of this very mission! I am thankful to God that he delivered you safely. I did not mean to cause you any reason to regret your long and difficult journey, but I did not wish for you to remain here without a reasonable understanding of the undertaking you have chosen."

"If you think I am fragile, that I am like a flower that will wilt in this heat, in the difficulties that are inherent in this undertaking, then I have yet to prove my mettle to you. I have crossed the country to be here, and left behind all that I knew. I may not have understood all that I would face when I arrived, but I am up to the task."

"Of that, I have no doubt. You seem like a determined young woman. You are clearly capable of overcoming hardships, and I sincerely pray that you will find what you are looking for here among us at the mission. I pray that you will consider my words carefully as you acquaint yourself with our ways and way of life here. I would be remiss in my duties if I did not prepare you for the work that lies ahead, for all that you may confront in the territory. We are not a state, so we do not fall under the same laws. In fact, this land is lawless – but that is why we are here to offer education to the children, to offer comfort to the sick, to feed and clothe the needy, and to offer salvation for all who seek it. I believe you will find the mission to be a refuge to the godly people of Santa Maria and in some cases to those who are seeking God."

"Yes, Sister Cecilia, I understand, and thank you. Although you may not know it, the mission has already offered me refuge, for I was in want of a new life and you have given me one."

Sister Cecilia rose from her desk. "I am as pleased as you are. Go with God, my child."

The interview had come to an end. As she stood to leave Sister Cecilia's office, a knock at the door announced the arrival of a petite woman with dark hair like her own, and olive skin. Her big brown eyes were bright, and had tiny lines around them. She was a beautiful woman, despite the austerity of her plain brown dress and severe hairstyle.

"Miss Ortega, this is Alice Cleary, newly arrived from the east. Please take her under your wing, as we discussed."

"Yes, Sister," Miss Ortega said as she curtseyed to the abbess. Turning to Alice, she said with an accent that Alice had never heard, "Pleased to meet you, Miss Cleary."

"Likewise," Alice replied.

As soon as Miss Ortega ushered Alice out of the abbess's office and into the corridor, she turned to her and lowered her voice. "Are you hungry? I don't recall seeing you at breakfast."

"I'm famished"

"Come with me. I believe we may find a cup of coffee and porridge for you in the kitchen."

"Thank you, Miss Ortega. That's very kind of you."

"Not at all, call me Joanna. Welcome to Santa Maria."

*****

June 5, 1876
Santa Maria, New Mexico Territory

The mission school was far larger than Alice had expected. She'd assumed it would be little more than a one room schoolhouse attached to a church, but the mission at Santa Maria was altogether different. Joanna and Sister Cecilia both explained that it drew children from ranches and from other towns for many miles in all directions. During the cold months of the year, many of the children boarded at the mission. They would become the responsibility of the sisters and the lay teachers, who were charged with their care.

To Alice, caring for children and teaching them was almost the same as having a large family, or being a part of one – a memory she cherished from the days before the war came and sent her own sisters and brothers scattered among relatives, and separated her from everyone but Will. As she looked down at the book that lay open on her desk, she thought of her brother, and wondered how he was faring at Louisa's farm. With a sniff, she realized he was very far away, that New Mexico was much farther away from him than she had supposed it would be. He might as well be back in Georgia, she thought, blinking away a tear.

"Don't let Sister Cecilia worry you. She is happy with your progress even if she doesn't always say so. She can be stern, but she is fair and compassionate. She isn't quick to give out compliments, but she has spoken to me of your progress."

Joanna and Alice sat in a schoolroom that was as austere as the rest of the mission school, at the end of a warm afternoon. Joanna was writing a letter at the teacher's desk. Alice sat in a plain desk at the front of the room, on a hard wooden bench. Her back ached and her head was swimming from the lessons in the book that sat on her desk, open. The words were all in Spanish, a language she was struggling to learn.

"I didn't know becoming a teacher would be this hard. I miss my brother, Will. I'm not sure I shall ever remember all the rules that I must follow to live here at the mission. There is so much I must learn, and so many things I must do. Between my chores in the garden and my turn in the kitchen, how am I supposed to learn Spanish and study for my examination?" Alice said as she closed the book.

Joanna smiled benevolently. "Spanish is not so hard; I know it well. It is my native language. I was tutored in English, French, and German. Do you know Latin? You learned French, is that so?"

Alice frowned and admitted, "No. I don't know French, and I barely know any Latin at all."

"Oh, you are not educated?" Joanna said with barely concealed astonishment, looking at Alice as though she had just announced that she was considering a position at a saloon.

"Educated? Yes, sort of. *Well* educated, no, I wouldn't say that. I'm good at figures and arithmetic. I read well, and my writing is satisfactory. I hope I didn't give the impression that I was very well educated. I never meant to."

"You were not taught Latin?"

"My aunt and uncle took me out of school to work. They expected me to earn my keep. I was an orphan living on their charity, so I had to help out and do my share of the chores. I was taught some Latin, but not a lot. What I do know I was taught by Sister Agatha, or learned myself."

"Yourself? You taught yourself? That is commendable."

"I read every book I could find in my uncle's study, which wasn't very many. Book learning is not thought valuable for women where I came from, and neither is Spanish. Why must I learn Spanish? I thought Sister Cecilia insisted that all the lessons are taught in English. The Indians' languages are discouraged, and so I thought Spanish was as well."

114

"Oh, but it *is* discouraged. She wants you to learn it because when you do become a teacher you may find it useful to know what some of the children are saying until they can be taught to speak English. Some children who come to us from the ranches and the farms do not learn English until they begin school."

"Well, what about the Indians? Do we learn their languages too?"

"That would be impossible; there are too many languages to learn and each one is as difficult as the others to grasp. From my experience, you will not see many Indian children at the mission school. There have been some conversions, but they cling to the old ways. Don't trouble yourself with their native tongue. When would you use it?"

Alice thought about the Indian city that was not far from the mission, the pueblo. She wished there was some way she could walk among the houses, to see what it looked like. But she kept her thoughts to herself and reopened her book. The Spanish words were just as difficult to understand as ever before. Sighing, she said, "I wish there was a different way to learn this language. Reading these words in a book doesn't seem like a good way to learn how to say them."

"Are you asking for my help?" Joanna put her pen down.

"I don't want to be a bother. I feel like I'll never grasp how to say these words or what they mean. I don't want to disappoint Sister Cecilia or Sister Agatha back home. I have to learn somehow."

"I'll teach you when I have time, but you will have to study very hard."

"I will study, I promise," Alice replied.

"Good. Perhaps you don't mind doing something for me?"

Alice nodded, eager to help. "Tell me what you would like me to do. You have been so helpful to me, I can hardly say no."

Joanna blew on the letter to dry the ink before she folded the paper. "Can you see that this letter gets posted?"

"Yes ma'am," Alice said as Joanna gave her the letter. "If I hurry, I can catch Thomas before he leaves for town."

Joanna nodded as Alice slipped the letter into the pages of the Spanish book. Dashing as quickly as she dared down the corridor to the abbey, Alice met an older, hunched man in the courtyard. His kind eyes were sunk deep in his wrinkled face. His clothes were worn, and threadbare around the cuffs of his pants. His shoes were as old as his clothes, but he didn't seem to mind his impoverished appearance – or much else – as he hitched a horse to a wagon.

Thomas was one of the few men permitted onto the mission grounds. He was not a priest or a monk, but a kindly farmer who often delivered food and other parcels to the mission and found work doing odd jobs. When she met him, Alice had liked him immediately. His kind demeanor despite his threadbare appearance reminded her that happiness could be found in a life of service and austerity.

"Miss Cleary, how are you this afternoon?" He said in low voice as he patted the chestnut mare with a gnarled hand, smiling softly.

"I am well, thank you. I have a letter to be posted; do you have time to see that it gets to the post office?"

"I do have the time. I was on my way to the market and the general store for supplies. I can post it for you, or would you like to come with me? You could go run your errand, and check to see if the mission has any letters or parcels. You ride with me, and keep me from growing tired on the road."

"Will I get into trouble, do you suppose?" she whispered.

Thomas smiled. "Trouble? Señorita, stay close to me and you will not have any trouble; Thomas will take care of you. We are going to Santa Maria, not the pirate holes of the south seas."

"You know the south seas?" Alice said in wonderment as she gazed at the elderly man. "Isn't that on the far side of the world?"

"It is on the edge of the world, far away from God-fearing folks. I used to a be sailing man a long time ago, back in my sinning days. Now come along, Señorita. We mustn't tarry."

"Oh Thomas, you are too good a man to have ever been sailor. You're telling me a yarn," Alice fought the urge to laugh.

"Maybe I am and maybe I'm not. You can never tell about old Thomas," he said with a wink.

Alice recalled that Sister Cecilia said she should not venture into Santa Maria alone. For the sisters of the mission, it was forbidden they should leave the mission except in the company of another sister or a teacher. Alice was neither a sister or a teacher, at least not yet. While she doubted Sister Cecilia would be pleased if she went to town, she didn't recall there being any rule explicitly against it. Especially in the presence of a kindly old man like Thomas.

"Señorita?"

"Yes, Thomas," Alice replied, turning her attention to the man who stood beside her, offering her help up into the buggy. "I can give you a hand with the supplies if you like when we get to Santa Maria."

"I'd like to see myself ask for help from a lass such as yourself. No, just keep old Thomas company."

With Thomas's help, she climbed aboard the narrow wooden seat of the buggy, the book and the letter in her hand. In her pocket she had a few pennies, enough to buy postage and maybe a length of ribbon from the general store. Joanna had been so good to her, she wished to give her a gift.

"We'll have to hurry; we don't want to be on the road very late. If you miss your dinner, Sister Cecilia would not be happy with me."

"Then we'll hurry. I'm ready."

Thomas climbed into the seat beside her with a grunt. With the reins in his hand, he made a clicking sound. The chestnut mare walked forward. Alice smiled at her companion, wondering if she might sneak to Mama Rosa for a warm tortilla. As she thought about Mama Rosa's, she remembered Jonathan Keene. She thought of his handsome smile, the mischievous look in his eye. She turned away from her elderly companion, blushing. She wondered how she would react if she actually saw Jonathan in the flesh.

"Señorita? You promised to talk, to keep me and my old horse company."

"I did, forgive me. I was just thinking."

"Thinking? That never did anyone any use; I advise against it. We have a ways to go before we get to town, tell me anything – where are you from? Somewhere back east I'd say, judging from the way you talk."

As Thomas listened politely, Alice told him about Augusta and her family, and how she came to be in Santa Maria. When she talked about her brother Will, her voice caught in her throat as if she was on the verge of crying. Will, her dear brother. She missed him so much. This was the first time in their young lives they had been truly apart, and it had been nearly a month since she last saw him. She wished Kansas was a lot closer. She prayed that God would protect him. Changing the subject, she spoke about her sister Louisa and her farm, and about Pastor Newland. They seemed so far away.

As she spoke about the people she loved and even her new acquaintance with the young pastor, she was careful to leave out the parts of the story that included Jonathan. Even as she did it, she wondered to herself what that meant. Was she embarrassed at her own behavior when it came to the dashing man she'd met on the train, the same one who had escorted her safely to the mission? Why did she savor those memories, carefully holding them close to her heart, cherishing them like mementos? Did she not wish to share these memories with anyone else for fear that if she spoke of them, they might not be as wonderful as she recalled?

As the town of Santa Maria loomed in the distance, she thought of Jonathan. He was only going to stay for a couple of days, and it had been nearly two weeks. In her heart, she knew she would never see him again – not in a town this small. He was too cosmopolitan, too worldly to remain somewhere deep in the territory.

Turning to Thomas, she chided him. "Thomas. I had heard you were a soldier who fought in Texas. Earlier, you told me you were a sailor. Which one is it? You know lying is a sin."

"Maybe I've been both. Never can tell. When you've lived as long as I have, you too may have a bit of fun with the young'uns. Mark my word, there's no sin in a good story."

"You can't be that old to have fought in the Texas Revolution," Alice replied as she tried to forget her own sorrows.

"I was a young man back then, not much older than you. It was a long time ago. Enough of my tales, my old horse has heard them all. Why is a pretty young señorita like yourself out here in the territories? Don't seem like a place for the likes of you."

"So I've heard," Alice said with a nod, "I think Sister Cecilia would agree with you. She made me swear to have nothing to do with any man who did not go to our church."

"Did she? She's a wise woman for her age. Sister Cecilia is tough as shoe leather. Maybe you ought to heed her words. This can be rough country for a dainty little thing like you. It's not the kind of place to be looking for a husband."

"Me, dainty? No, not me. I've spent my life working too hard to ever be dainty. I'm here to work, to do my share. I want to teach reading and writing to the children and do whatever is needed. I'm not here to find a husband or seek romance. Thomas, I doubt I will ever be married at all."

Thomas laughed out loud, his whole body shaking. "Señorita, if you don't take the vows to become a sister, I'd say you were going to be hitched inside of a year. You listen to me. Best you don't fall in love with any of the locals who don't go church, just like Sister Cecilia told you. There's trouble brewing in these parts. If you ask my advice, you'd be safer back in Kansas."

"What kind of trouble?" Alice asked as she recalled Sister Cecilia's warnings and admonishments

about the hardships and challenges of life in Santa
Maria.

"There I go shooting my mouth off. None for
you to worry your pretty little head about. Never you
mind what old Thomas has to say, I was just spinning a
yarn. While we're in Santa Maura, don't go far, you
hear? Go to the post office and come right back. I'll be
at Garson's. He's the smithy in Santa Maria, right
around the corner. You'll be safe enough in the post
office while I'm gone. I've got to get some nails but I
won't be long. Meet me at the general store, and don't
you go wandering off, mind, or you'll get us both into
trouble with Sister Cecilia."

Alice planned to heed his words, although she
did look longingly at Mama Rosa's when the buggy
came to a stop. Jumping down from the seat, she was
careful not to catch her dress on the rail. The air was
scented with Mama Rosa's cooking; the tantalizing
aroma of beans and spices filled the air as she stood
watching Thomas ease the horse into a slow walk. As
he turned the corner, she realized she was all alone in
Santa Maria. Feeling the same sensation of excitement
and fear she felt when she'd boarded the train in
Kansas, she rushed into the post office.

*****

September 12, 1876
Santa Fe, New Mexico Territory

Alice Cleary was nervous. Her hands were sweating and her head was spinning. She wondered if asking for smelling salts would disqualify her from her exam as she tried to focus on the math question on the page in front of her. New Mexico was a territory, but she was taking the standard examination for teaching expected of all teachers within the states. Perhaps, being in a territory, Sister Cecilia would still permit her to teach if she should happen to fail? She tried to recall what she spent all month studying. Looking up, she felt the harsh, hawkish stare of Mr. Lowden, an itinerant representative of the board of education for the territory. His task, he had explained without so much as blinking once or cracking a smile, was to see that the children in the territory received as proper an education as each of the rural communities could afford. New Mexico would one day become a state and he wanted to ensure that when it did, the teachers were properly prepared.

Personally, Alice thought that the certification of teachers was the least of the concerns for the citizens of New Mexico. There was lawlessness here on a scale she was unaccustomed to back in Augusta, or had ever witnessed during her short sojourn in Kansas. Cattle were stolen. Guns blazed and shootouts were regular occurrences, often happening in daylight on public streets. The disputes, she had heard, were usually over gambling and cards. Drinking was a problem everywhere, and men spent more time at saloons than they did in church. Whether or not the children were taught to read and write by a certified teacher was a trivial concern, she thought to herself. She halfway considered sharing her views with the unsmiling Mr.

Lowden, but she thought better of that idea. She had met the occasional zealot in her day, and there could be no doubt that he was a crusader for progress and modernity – even if progress may seem futile in a place like Santa Maria.

"Miss Cleary, pay attention. This test is timed, and you must complete the questions," Mr. Lowden said as he looked down his nose at Alice.

Alice had three more pages of questions to complete before she could be free of this terrible man and his unwavering scowl. She reminded herself that Miss Ortega was sitting outside the examination room, waiting. What a treat it was to come to Santa Fe in the company of her fellow teacher. Perhaps they would go to the market and take in the sights and sounds of the town before they returned to the mission the following morning.

"Miss Cleary, do you intend to daydream for the reminder of your examination?" Mr. Lowden said as he rapped on the desk with his knuckles.

Sighing, she wrote the answers to the questions, taking care not to let her mind wander. Santa Fe was an exciting place, much bigger than Santa Maria. There were hotels, general stores, and all manner of food and dry goods for sale. Even if she did nothing but walk along the streets with Joanna, Alice would be content. It was thrilling to be somewhere different for a day, even if she was cooped up inside a dark, sweltering and airless room with a man who insisted that her eyes remain on the page of her test.

With the last of her answers scrawled on the paper, she rose from her seat at the wooden table. Reaching out to hand the test papers to him, she didn't say thank you, or make any comment. She turned to leave, as she was certain she must have failed. Maybe if she studied hard, she would do better in the future. She resigned herself to the terrible truth; the examination was difficult. She would know what to study the next time.

"Miss Cleary, where are you going? Do you not care to know the results of your examination?"

"Oh. Should I wait?"

Mr. Lowden made a grumpy harrumphing sound as he dropped the test papers on the table. Opening a book, he sat down and aimed a frown in her direction. Slowly, methodically, he reviewed each page of her test, while she felt faint with anxiety. He snorted, scribbled with his pencil on her papers, and made a clucking sound from time to time. If she had failed, why didn't he tell her? Why did he insist on prolonging her misery with this display?

She perched on the edge of a bench, biting her lip, her fear getting the better of her. She watched as he closed his book, stacked her papers into a neat pile and said without a trace of joy, "Miss Cleary, it is with no small degree of astonishment that I must inform you of your results."

"Mr. Lowden, tell me where I failed. I shall improve upon my performance the next time."

"If you would be quiet! You are as unruly as any child I have ever taught. Is this how you intend to behave in your own classroom? Is this the example you wish to set?"

"My own classroom?"

"Yes, you have passed the examination. You exceeded my expectations in the English portion of the test. Your math could use some attention, but you have still passed. I offer you my congratulations; you will receive your certification. I declare that you may now accept the position of teacher at any school that will have you."

"Mr. Lowden! I've passed? I'm a teacher?"

"Yes, you are a teacher."

"My word, that is magnificent news!" Alice said as she fought the urge to embrace the stone-faced man who was peering at her in a rather alarming way.

"Miss Cleary, I do not believe that in my time employed in this position I have ever witnessed a more enthusiastic expression of joy at the news of a successful examination." With the faint hint of smile, Mr. Lowden motioned for her to go.

"Did you pass? Are you a teacher? Why am I asking such a silly question? Everyone in this building knows by now that you are. I heard you through the door."

Alice laughed and embraced Joanna. "I passed. How remarkable that I should have students of my very own in the autumn."

"Oh yes, my dear, you shall have students of your own. I will remind you when you have faced a classroom filled with squirms and crying, when you have weathered an outbreak of infection or cold, that you were overjoyed."

"Joanna, you're teasing. Shall we celebrate my good fortune? I don't have much money, but I may be able to buy us something delectable, perhaps a cordial if we can find a place that sells them?"

"I have a better idea. My family's home is here in Santa Fe. Come with me, and we shall eat as rich as kings. My mother's *mole* is better than any food you have ever eaten."

"*Mole*?" Alice asked. Her stomach rumbled even though she had no idea what they were talking about.

Joanna laughed. "It's spicy. I hope you like chilies."

"Chilies? I adore them, as long as I have plenty of water and tortillas."

"You shall have plenty of tortillas at my family's house. My mother makes them fresh for every meal."

Alice smiled. Everything was going splendidly; she had passed her examination, she was in Santa Fe, and she was going to meet Joanna's family. Even if her brother (or perhaps Jonathan Keene) had been there to share her joy she couldn't have been any happier than she was in that moment.

127

*****

The reception at the Ortega house was not a
joyous one. Mole was not cooked in anticipation of
their arrival, nor were tortillas. Nothing had been made
in the kitchen at all.

Instead, they found an older woman, who Alice
assumed was Mrs. Ortega, in the parlor of the adobe
ranch house on the outskirts of town. Alice assumed
that a terrible tragedy must have befallen the family that
day as Joanna, her mother and her father spoke rapidly
in Spanish, her mother weeping and her father shaking
his head. He was immobile in a chair, a shawl covering
his legs despite the heat of the day, a cane at his side.

A young girl looked from the foyer into the
modest but comfortably furnished room. She was joined
by a boy who looked to be younger by a few years.
Alice thought of herself and Will, and remembered
wondering what the adults were talking about when she
was little and her fate was being decided.

"Jorge, Anna, this is no conversation for
children," Joanna said in Spanish that Alice could
understand.

The children quickly disappeared as Alice
inched self-consciously toward the door of the parlor,
thinking she should not be present for whatever
disaster was befalling the Ortega family.

Joanna threw her hands in the air in a demonstration of disgust as she turned to Alice. She made a few remarks in Spanish before speaking to her companion in English. "This is dreadful, dreadful! What a day to have come to visit my family."

"Joanna, what's happened? Has there been a death?"

"It's worse than a death. I only wish it were a death, so we might have a funeral, and then maybe we could hold our heads up, and not lower them in shame. Oh, what is to become of my sister little sister Anna? She shall never find a husband, not now. What of my sister Flor? This shame shall follow her like a curse. What is to become of me if Sister Cecilia should find out?"

"What's the matter? What curse?"

Joanna regarded Alice thoughtfully. "I can trust you, can't I? Alice, you won't tell a soul what I'm going to share with you?"

"You have my word. I will never tell a soul, not one."

The older woman spoke to Joanna, her words coming fast between the tears, as she gestured wildly and made a sign of the cross. Joanna turned to her mother, spoke to her again, and then held Alice's hand tightly in her own. "My mother is ashamed that you are a guest and you must be a witness to our misfortune."

"There is no shame in misfortune. I was an orphan; I know full well what's it's like to be treated poorly because of unfortunate circumstances."

"Then perhaps you can help me, help my family. You must understand that Sister Cecilia can never know what I'm about to tell you. If she suspects that any member of my family is fallen is beyond the grace of God, then I may be turned out of the mission. I am a teacher and I do not wish to do anything else, but that is not important. What is important is my sister."

"The little girl I just saw, the one in the doorway just now?"

"No, that was Anna, my youngest sister, I am speaking of my sister who is your age, Flor."

"What happened to her? Has she taken ill?"

"I wish that was all! She has run away. My parents fear she has fallen in with bad company."

Alice's eyes opened wide. "Bad company? Do you mean she has eloped? Has she run way with a young man?"

"No, if it were an elopement I would not feel ashamed. My parents fear she has found work…I don't wish to say it, but I have no other choice, in a saloon. She wanted to be a singer, a performer on the stage. What a disreputable way to make a living, but she would not be convinced of that. She has been gone from home for a short while, only three days. If she is here in Santa Fe we may yet find her and bring her home."

"A saloon? Here in Santa Fe? Would she have gone somewhere else?"

"We will pray that she remains here in town. My mother tells me one of the ranch hands saw her at the Shamrock, but he was reluctant to tell my mother anything other than that. I don't know what else to do. We may go to the sheriff, but there may be little he can do, as this is a family matter. I wish I knew what to do. If my father were well he would have already seen to it. My brothers are in Durango and will not be home for a week. My mother is worried that my sister may already be lost."

"We can't go to a saloon. If anyone should see us there, we could lose our certification and be expelled from the mission," Alice whispered.

"I know, but what else can I do? I can't leave Santa Fe not knowing whether my sister is ruined, not when I might be able to help."

"No," Alice replied. "You can't do that. I will go with you; you can't go into one of those places alone. It wouldn't be safe."

"I'm not sure it will be safe for both us together."

"We are on a mission of righteousness. We shall ask God to watch over us," Alice agreed, reflecting on her own life. If she had been turned out of her aunt's house, what would have happened to her? If a young girl was in danger of ruin, how could Alice judge her, or her circumstances? Especially if that young girl was Joanna's sister.

Tearfully, Joanna replied, "Thank you, my dear friend. How can I ever repay your kindness?"

"There is nothing to repay. Let's find your sister. Maybe we won't be too late to save her."

"Miss, you do not have to go to a saloon. I am ashamed my daughter has asked you," Mr. Ortega said in perfect English.

"Sir, it is my honor to help your family. Your daughter Joanna has been very kind to me. We shall be safe with God's protection."

"If you must go, take my pistol. It's in in the desk drawer," he gestured to the writing desk.

"Papa, do you think we'll need it?"

"I pray that you will not. Maybe we should wait for your brothers," he replied.

Joanna was insistent. "No, it may be too late. We shall go now. God will watch over us, you shall see."

"Daughter, tell Flor when you see her that she shall be forever dead to us if she does not come home! Tell her!" Mrs. Ortega wept.

"Come, Alice, there is no time to waste. The stagecoach leaves in the morning for Santa Maria. If we're going to save my sister, we have only a few hours of daylight left to do it. They are lawless enough during the light hours, but when the sun goes down I cannot be sure we will be safe. I fear the people who frequent those places at night." Joanna walked across the room to the desk and opened the drawer. She withdrew a pistol that looked far too big for her little hand. Determined, she shoved it in her bag.

"If anyone in Santa Fe has any sense, they'll fear us. Do you know how to shoot that thing?" Alice asked.

"Of course I do. Papa taught me."

"I feel much better about our chances if you are certain you can fire that gun."

"I can fire it. I can even hit what I'm aiming for, from time to time. Have no fear, we shall have no reason to use it, I promise," Joanna declared.

"I pray you're right." Alice nodded goodbye to the Ortega parents and followed her friend out of the sitting room and through the front door.

When she passed the examination to become a teacher, she'd had no idea that a few hours later she would be jeopardizing her chances of ever becoming one. Recalling the list of rules to be followed by a teacher as outlined by Sister Cecilia, Alice knew that entering a saloon or any such sinful place was on the top of that list. Praying for herself as well as Joanna and her sister, she followed her friend down the dusty road towards Santa Fe, hoping that they didn't wind up dead – or worse, face the ruin of their reputations.

*****

"Are you certain there is no other way? Marching into the Shamrock sounds terribly dangerous now that we're here and on the verge of doing it," Alice said to Joanna as they stopped on the street corner outside the establishment.

"You don't have to go inside. I know it's reckless of me to go in, but I have to. Flor is so young and naïve. She has no business in a place like this, but that's not the only reason I feel I must go. She is a beautiful girl; how long will an innocent young girl last in a den of sin like the Shamrock? You're not from Santa Fe, you don't know how dreadful these places are. What they sell inside is more than whiskey and a chance at cards."

"You don't think…?" Alice whispered.

"I don't know what to think; it's far too horrid to contemplate. How could she be so foolish? What I do know is that if I cannot save her, she will be lost forever to my family. She will be dead to us, and I cannot let that happen."

"Neither can I. If she has become the prey of evil men, then I too shall risk my life to save her. We shall go inside together. Have your pistol at the ready," Alice murmured.

"I have my hand upon it as we speak. If you are ready, so am I. May the Holy Virgin guide us and our Heavenly Father protect us," Joanna said as she made the sign of the cross.

Alice said a quick Hail Mary and stepped forward. In the doorway, they were nearly run down by a pair of smelly, drunken men.

"Watch out there, ladies. Where are you going in such a hurry?" one of the drunken men said as he raised his hat to Joanna and Alice.

"Alice, don't speak to anyone, do you hear me? Let me do the talking," Joanna said.

Alice nodded. Ignoring the drunks as they shambled past, she kept her face turned straight ahead and vowed to avoid looking at anyone.

They were in an enormous long room that had a bar running the length of one wall. Tables and chairs were stuffed into every space on the floor as men drank and played cards in the afternoon heat. Alice could feel the stares of the patrons, the men behind the bar, and the women who were dressed like the lady she recalled seeing on the stagecoach when she first arrived in New Mexico. She blanched and tried not to let her gaze fall on any one person, but she was horrified by the revealing clothes and the painted faces of the women. Some of them were languishing with their arms draped on the shoulders of men who were smoking and drinking.

Alice swallowed and tried not to look as terrified as she felt. Joanna strode purposefully to the bar, leaving her behind. Alice, wearing her plain gray dress with a collar that came to just under her chin, didn't need anyone to tell her she looked out of place in the Shamrock.

"Lost your way, little lady?" a man said from a table in front of her. He was dressed in a clean jacket with a fern green waist coat. He was cleanshaven and amiable, which was a surprise to Alice.

She shook her head and quickly joined her friend at the bar.

"I don't want any trouble. I just want to find my sister. Her name is Flor Ortega, and she was seen in your establishment. I want to see her," Joanna demanded as she stood her ground at the bar.

"Ma'am I don't know who you're talking about. If you want a drink, I'll pour you one. If you want to play cards, have a seat. I don't know who you are or who your sister is."

"Somebody here does. I'm not leaving until I find her."

"You're going to leave if I say so, understand?" the bartender said as he leaned over the bar, narrowing his eyes at Joanna.

"Hank, leave her be. What's the matter?" the clean-cut man at the table said to the bartender.

"Have it your way, Bryce." The bartender turned away and poured a shot of foul-smelling liquid into a short glass, downing it in one swallow.

"Allow me to introduce myself. I'm Bryce Pendleton. You ladies aren't here for a drink, are you?" the man asked with a disarming smile.

Joanna scowled. "No, we're not. It's no business of yours what we're here for, sir, now let us pass."

"Is that any way to talk to a new friend? Look, I don't want anything from you. I can see you have no business being here, and neither does your friend," he said as he nodded to Alice. "Do you want my help or not? Take it or leave it; it's no bother to me."

"Joanna, why not let him help us?" Alice nudged her friend.

Joanna softened her tone. "I doubt a man like yourself will have any care for the welfare of my sister but if you must know, I'm looking for her. She's young, far too young to be in a place like this. She wants to be a singer, and I have heard she was seen in here."

"A singer? Hmm, maybe I have seen her. What does she look like?" he asked.

Joanna described her sister to the man, while Alice glanced nervously at her surroundings. She felt uncomfortable in the saloon, in the presence of gamblers, drinkers, and women who plied their trade. She prayed that they would find Flor soon, because Joanna looked like she might pull the pistol from her bag at any moment.

"I don't think I have seen her. Maybe one of the ladies who work here may have," suggested the man who went by Bryce.

He gestured to a tall blonde who was sporting enormous red feathers tucked into her hair, and they were joined by a woman who Alice assumed entertained men for money. She was wearing a tight red gown with a low-cut bodice which showed a generous amount of her bosom. Her cheeks were red with rouge and her lips were as crimson as her gown.

"Bryce, what do you want? Who are these two dried up prunes, a couple of missionaries who lost their way to church?" the woman draped her arm across the man's shoulder.

"Not quite. They're looking for a woman. If you're helpful I may give you a gift," he said as he reached into his vest pocket, retrieving a gold coin.

"You always play better than any other gentleman I know," she said with a wink. "Who is this someone?"

"It's my sister. Her name s Flor." Joanna described her sister to the woman.

"Hmm, I don't know any Flor. That name doesn't ring a bell; can I have my gift now?"

"Not yet. You haven't been honest, have you? You may have the gift, but only if you tell us the truth. You know everything that goes on here at the Shamrock, tell us the truth, will you, dearest?" Bruce cooed at the painted woman.

"I may know something, but I want more than a gold coin."

"How about two and a bonus if I win at cards tonight?" Bryce said with a wink.

"You have a deal, there was a girl, I don't know her name; she didn't matter to me. She didn't stick around here long. She left when she found out singing and dancing ain't what we do here."

"Do you know where she went?" Joanna asked, her voice strained.

"Lady, how am I supposed to know? I barely remember her at all, but she was a pretty young thing. She was silly to think she could make an honest living of singing in a saloon. I don't know where she is or where she went. There's a dozen dance halls and saloons in this town. Check around, I don't care. That's all I know. Bryce darling, can I have my money now?"

Bryce paid the woman before sending her on her way. "I'm sorry I could not be more helpful to you both," he said with a gallant bow.

"Sir, I wish to pay you for your kindness and generosity; that was a lot of money you just gave her. I'm only a teacher but if you would give me your address, I can send you the money," Joanna explained.

"There is no need. If I may offer you some much needed advice. The Shamrock is classy compared to the other businesses you will find in Santa Fe. Neither one of you has any business walking into a saloon. Allow me to accompany you."

Joanna shook her head. "No, we don't dare bother you, but thank you, sir."

"It's no bother. I insist," he said with a smile as he reached for his hat from the table. "It's not safe for a pair of ladies such as yourselves to be wandering the streets of Santa Fe alone."

Alice quickly smiled at him, thinking to herself how fortunate they were to have found him. Feeling much better about their prospects of finding Flor, she left the Shamrock behind.

In the company of the pleasant Bryce Pendleton, Joanna and Alice went to nearly every single saloon and bar in Santa Fe. Alice had never seen so many painted women and drunk men in her life. Joanna was discouraged, and Alice was convinced that she would never drink in all her life. She had seen men (and some women) in every terrible state of drunkenness she could ever have imagined. Some were passed out, others were awake with red faces and glassy eyes. Some were belligerent, and some were lusty, staring at her and Joanna as if they were fallen women. Alice was beginning to despair of ever locating Flor when they walked into a rough and seedy place with a dusty sign nailed above the door suggesting to the public that this saloon was known as the Lucky Ace.

"Listen very carefully; neither of you leave my side for even an instant. This is no place for naïve young ladies such as yourselves. I rarely frequent it, but I stand a far better chance of coming out alive than either of you," he said as he reached for their arms, guiding them in the door.

Alice's eyes took a moment to adjust to the gloom and the smoke inside the Lucky Ace. It stank of beer, whiskey, and sweat. With Bryce's fingers wrapped around her arm, urging her forward, she had a feeling that she and Joanna had entered a devil's bargain. They didn't know him, yet he was being charming trying to help them locate a missing girl. Why did he wish to help them? She tried to put those thoughts out of her mind as they stood on either side of him.

Bending down, he whispered, "Stay here. Don't move."

Alice and Joanna glanced nervously at each other as they both stayed rooted firmly to the floor where Bryce told them to stay. He made his way to the bar, nodding to the bartender, who pointed to the back of the saloon.

With a grave look on his face, he rejoined them, his voice low. "The bartender says the owner of the Lucky Ace hired a girl that fits your sister's description; she was in here a day ago. Come with me, we'll talk to the owner together. It's not safe for you two to be standing in here unaccompanied."

"We can't wait here for you?" Alice asked as she looked at the patrons in the saloon. "Or outside?"

"No, this fine establishment you're standing in isn't known for its card games."

Joanna gasped. "My sister is here, she's *working* here?"

"Perhaps not. She may not be working yet, if you take my meaning. There's no time to lose, come with me." He led them past tables filled with men who were drinking and leering openly at them. The women in the Lucky Ace looked gaunt, and some of them sported bruises. They were as glassy-eyed as the men they were sitting with. Alice felt her skin crawl as she thought about what it was these ladies did to make a living.

"Alice, if Flor is here we have to save her, but my mother will disown her. She's ruined. It would be better if she had died."

"I have a terrible feeling about this place. I pray Flor isn't here," Alice said to her friend.

"What was that?" Bryce turned to them. "You aren't losing heart, are you? Be brave, my friends. We shall speak to the owner and resolve your concerns."

Despite her discomfort, Alice couldn't help but notice they were walking towards the back of the bar, the back of the saloon. There was a dark corridor back there, and very little else. She didn't see a man who looked like he might be the owner of the business. Drunken men looked at her and her companion in a way that made her flesh crawl and chills climb up her spine. A terrible feeling was growing in the pit of her stomach as they walked farther back into the saloon.

"Joanna, I don't know about this," Alice whispered.

"If Flor is here…" Joanna whispered back as they reached the end of the bar. She didn't finish.

"Mr. Pendleton, you said we were going to see the owner. Where is he?" Alice asked as she became aware that they were deep inside this smoky dark room, too far from the street to be heard if they should call out for help.

"He's this way; he has an office down the hall. Come with me, you're perfectly safe as long as you stay by my side."

Alice tried to ignore her misgivings. Bryce Pendleton was being a gentleman. He was trying to help them find Joanna's sister. Why shouldn't she trust him, except she didn't know him or anything about him. As she looked around the saloon, the hollow faces of the women bore the evidence of their despair under their heavy make-up. Alice had a sudden feeling that she wanted to get as far away from the Lucky Ace as she could get. If she hadn't vowed to help Joanne find Flor, she would never have stepped foot into this horrid place.

"Right this way; here's his office," Bryce said as he opened a door for them and shoved them inside an office that was dim, with only a tiny window.

Alice felt her blood run cold as she looked into the face of a man she had seen before. It was the gaunt man from the stagecoach – the one Jonathan Keene had warned her about. He was seated behind a desk. A cigar burned in his mouth, and there was a glass of whiskey in his hand. It was at that moment that Alice had a terrible suspicion that Flor was not there, nor had she ever been. Turning to look at Bryce, she saw the same charming smile, and got a wink as he patted her on the back.

Bryce addressed the gaunt man. "Johnson, look what I brought you. A pair of doves, what do you say?"

"Doves? They look like nuns. What do I want with a pair of old spinsters?" The man chewed on the end of his cigar.

Alice felt sick from her own fear and the smell of the cigar.

"One may be a spinster, but have a look at his one," he gestured to Alice. "She's young, ripe and ready to work for you. I wager she's worth a fair price."

Alice recoiled in horror from the thin man as he rose from behind his desk and came towards her. He studied her with his beady eyes and scowled. "You look familiar. You're a prize; I'll say that for you. You'll do very well here at the Lucky Ace. I may even let you work for me at the Shamrock." Turning to Joanna, the man continued. "You've got some age on you, but your features are comely. If you have all of your teeth I might use you here. Some men aren't nearly so picky about their choice of companions."

Alice was waiting for Joanna to whip her gun out of her pocket, to threaten to shoot these men dead. She was surprised to hear Joanna's voice, steady and even. "I'm here for my sister, Flor. She looks like me, but younger. If you don't want any trouble, I say you give her to me."

"Flor? What do I care for names?"

With a sudden swishing sound of something gliding past her skirt, Joanna's gun was out of her bag and pressed against the thin man's face. "Where is my sister. You'd better pray you haven't hurt her."

"You'll hang for this," the man said without flinching.

"You'll be dead. I won't mind facing death for killing a man like you."

"You don't want to do that – you won't make it out of this office alive," Bryce said as he removed a gun from a holster around his waist. With the same disarming smile he had used to gain their trust, he said, "No one will hear either of you scream if I shoot you or your companion. Put the gun down and no one will get hurt. Well, not very much," he said, leering at Alice.

"There, you see how ridiculous you're being. There's no escape for you or your friend. If you put the gun away I won't break any of your limbs," the gaunt man said with a cruel smile.

Alice could see Joanna was confused. If she put the gun down they would both be killed, or worse. If Joanna pointed the gun at Bryce, the thin cockroach of a man may pull a gun from his pocket as well, making their position even worse. She didn't know if Flor had ever truly been at the Lucky Ace, but right now she and Joanna were facing a terrible fate of their own.

"We're going to walk out of here, do you understand?" Joanna said forcefully.

"No, you're not. Put the gun down and we won't hurt you," Bryce said as he shoved his gun closer to Alice. "Keep being stubborn and I swear to you, I will kill your friend, even though I would much prefer to get better acquainted with her. What a waste that would be."

A sudden loud, incessant knocking at the door broke Bryce's attention. As he turned his face to the noise, the wooden door slammed open, hitting him and knocking him against Alice. Joanna screamed as the man she was threatening grabbed his cigar out of his mouth and sunk it into the flesh of her hand, burning her. She dropped the gun. Alice screamed and kicked

Bryce, and then scrambled for Joanna's gun. She wrapped her fingers around the pistol, but she wasn't sure who to point it at, the man with the cigar, Bryce, or whoever was coming into the office.

"Colleen, you should be more careful." Jonathan Keene's smile was as handsome as ever.

Alice pointed the gun at the cockroach man as Jonathan placed the tip of his pistol on Bryce's temple. "Put your gun down, Mr. Pendleton."

"Why? So you can shoot me in cold blood?" Bryce asked as he held his gun on Alice.

"If you harm her, I will not be so lenient as to kill you with one shot. I will be sure to fill your gut with lead, so it will take three days for you to die in agony. Understand?"

"You're outgunned here, Keene. We got able-bodied men in the saloon that will never let you leave," said Johnson.

"Able bodied, that pack of drunkards? Bryce, let them go. You don't owe any loyalty to Johnson. Come on, nice and easy," Jonathan said as he stared at Bryce.

Bryce hesitated for a second. He looked at the man with the cigar, and then he looked back to Jonathan. In that one split second of hesitation, Jonathan knocked Bryce out cold with a punch to his jaw. Alice screamed but held onto the gun in her hand. Joanna elbowed Johnson in the groin with all her might. He let out a yelping sound and collapsed, and she fled out of his reach.

"Colleen, my dear, shall we be leaving now? I lied about the men outside. We may have a bit of trouble."

"Here, Joanna, take the gun. If we're in trouble I trust you with it."

"I wouldn't be so quick, my hand is burned," Joanna said as she held up her burned hand to Alice. "You'll have to hold it. Just remember pull the trigger only when you're certain you want to shoot."

"Come on, you two. Colleen, my love, you didn't tell me you had a sister. Who is this?" he said in his Irish accent.

"*Colleen*?" Joanna asked, looking confused as she planted a swift kick in Johnson's ribs. "Where is my sister, you monster?"

He only grunted.

Jonathan replied, "He doesn't have her. I checked with the bartender, and he hasn't seen a girl come in here that looks like her. Your friend Bryce lied to you about that."

"I can't go home without her," Joanna said as she glowered at Johnson again.

"Ladies, we can discuss this when we are safely away from this establishment. I want to thank you both for bringing an end to my gambling career here in Santa Fe, it was prosperous while it lasted."

"You'd better not show your face in this town ever again," Johnson spat from the floor.

147

"That's enough out of you," Joanna said as she kicked him again. "God forgive me."

Jonathan gestured to the door with his head and held his gun pointed towards the dark hallway. "Come on, there may be a back way out of here. Let's go, just in case his men aren't as drunk as I think they are."

Alice was shaking as she held the pistol with both hands. She was at the back of the small band as Joanna followed closely behind Jonathan. Without any further trouble they were out of the dark corridor, walking past rooms that were not empty.

"Joanna, this is awful. These poor girls; I wish we could save them," Alice said as they shuffled forward.

"Try not to think about it, and I won't either. We shall pray very hard that these ladies find a way out of this life," Joanna replied.

"I hate to tell you the truth, but some of them are too far gone to save. It's the devil drink that has many of them, that and laudanum. Let's keep quiet, we aren't out of here yet," Jonathan whispered.

Alice prayed and Joanna wept as they followed Jonathan to a back passage leading to a door. As they exited the building they were met by a large, burly man who staggered a little at the sight of them.

"Where're you going? Ain't slipping out without paying, are you?"

"Yes, I am, and I'm taking these two lovely lasses with me. My appetite is insatiable!" Jonathan remarked as he motioned for Joanna and Alice to stand behind him. He held his gun on the large hulk of a man.

"You don't scare me, gun or no gun." The man came towards him.

Alice, in her terrified state, closed her eyes and pulled the trigger. A bullet went whizzing past the enormous man as she felt the recoil of the gun. The powder burned her hand.

"How about now? Does she scare you?" Jonathan said to the terrified hulk of man.

"You could have killed me, Miss! What's the matter with you?"

"I've had enough of drink, smoke, and cheap perfume. I've had QUITE enough of saloons for one evening. Unless you want me to try my luck again, you'd better let us go!" Alice declared, her voice squeaking with agitation.

"Leave, sir! Take those women with you. I wish you no luck with them – no luck at all."

"Come along, Colleen, we mustn't tarry," Jonathan said as he urged Alice and Joanna out of the alley.

"Run. Don't look back, do you understand?" he ordered them when they were on the street.

Joanna and Alice ran as fast as they could beside him, dodging drunks, ruffians, and ladies who were dressed as scantily as any saloon girl. The sun had set and it was dark. Alice's hand hurt from the burns. Her wrist and shoulder ached from the recoil of the gun she carried in her other hand. She was afraid to slip it in her pocket. Would the warm barrel burn a hole in her only good dress?

As they reached the town square, Jonathan slowed down and pulled them aside. "Where to, Colleen? I'm not leaving you out here on these streets alone, not after the trouble you two have caused in every saloon in town."

"Mister," Joanna panted, "I don't know who you are, but thank you. If you would be so kind as to escort us back to my family's home I'm sure they will want to thank you as well."

"I don't need gratitude, but I will accompany you to your house and see you safely inside. Lead the way; we can stop to do introductions when we're all safe."

Alice looked around the square anxiously. She felt certain they were out of danger, but she didn't wish to remain on the streets of Santa Fe another moment. It was a beautiful town during the day; the shops were inviting, and the people were friendly. But tonight she had seen the seedier side of life in the territory. She understood now why Sister Cecilia had so many rules for her to follow. This place was treacherous. As she glanced at Jonathan she smiled. Once again he had saved her from a terrible fate. How could she ever repay him?

*****

"I love her, and I am grateful to God that she is alive, but I'm going to kill her!" Joanna snapped as her mother dressed the burn on her hand. In the kitchen of the Ortega's house, Joanna gritted her teeth as she sat at the table, her mother tending to the cigar wound.

In the corner of the kitchen a young woman sat on a stool, inconsolable, her face wet with tears. She was beautiful, nearly as lovely as Joanna, but she was younger. To Alice, the girl looked small and scared. It was hard to tell that she and this young woman were nearly the same age.

Mrs. Ortega spoke Spanish to her daughters and then with a kind expression she spoke in English to Alice. "Make a pot of coffee for the man who saved you. There is cake in the pie safe. Take it to him, hmmm? There is a tray in the pantry, cups on the shelves. Quickly now, you mustn't keep him waiting."

Alice looked down at her own bandaged hand. She had a small gunpowder burn, but it wasn't as terrible as the cigar burn on Joanna's hand. Preparing the tray, she yawned. It was late in the evening, and it had been a long day. It was hard to make sense of everything that had happened. With a look towards Flor, who appeared to be stuck in state of humiliation and fear, she was thankful the girl had not ended up at a place like the Lucky Ace.

Joanna and Alice had not saved her, exactly, but they were responsible for her coming home. Flor was at the Bull's Head saloon when she saw them walk in. They didn't see her, but she overheard them. She didn't realize how much trouble and sorrow she had caused her family until she saw Joanna in tears, looking for her. Now, at home in their kitchen, her mother could barely look at her. Alice didn't know what would become of Flor, but she was home safe and sound and that was what mattered.

Alice tried very hard not to drop the tray laden with cake and coffee. In the sitting room, she smiled. Jonathan Keene was all alone beside the fireplace.

"Where is Mr. Ortega? I brought cake for him," Alice said.

"He was feeling unwell, and has retired for the night. His son, Jorge, is it? He seems like he is a nice young chap, helping his father walk. What a sweet boy. Is that coffee for me? I could use a cup of something strong after the evening I've enjoyed in your company, Colleen. I thought you told me you were a teacher? For a teacher you lead a dissolute life."

"Are you teasing me?" she asked as he reached for the tray.

"Let me have that; you have burned your hand. You've done quite enough for one evening."

Alice didn't argue with him as she sat down by the fire. She was glad for the warmth as there was a chill in the air. Gazing at him, she smiled as he poured a cup of coffee for her, setting the cup and saucer on a table beside her chair. "Use your good hand for the coffee, better let that burn heal."

"Mr. Keene, I have a question. It's been on my mind since you burst into the office at the Lucky Ace."

"What is that? Why a handsome gentleman such as myself was in place like that?"

"Well, yes. Frankly, it didn't seem to be your sort of place."

"What sort of place do you think I belong?" he asked.

"I don't know, just not there. Maybe on one of those fancy river boats?"

"A river boat? Where do you get your ideas from?"

"You haven't answered my question."

"I know. If we really were married, I wouldn't have to continue to save you from villains."

"Married?" Alice asked, uncertain she heard him correctly. "Do you mean that?"

"Hold on, Colleen. I'm not the kind of man who can be married. My life is too unsettled for a wife and children. I didn't mean that. I meant why do you find yourself in harm's way? What do you do when I am not around to save you?"

"Joanna had a gun. We were trying to save ourselves," Alice explained.

"I commend you and Joanna on your courage, but you two were no match for scallywags like Bryce and Johnson. I shudder to think what may have happened to you both if I didn't see you leaving the Shamrock."

"You were at the Shamrock? I didn't see you. Why didn't you come to speak to me?"

"That wouldn't have been polite, not when you ladies were being so friendly to good old Bryce. I thought there was some reason you were walking on the street in his company."

"I wasn't being friendly," Alice said as her face turned crimson.

"Bryce is a handsome fellow, and he's the worst sort of man. I followed you on a hunch that he may be up to no good. I see that my instincts were correct."

"I'm glad you did follow us. We should not have gone into those saloons. If Sister Cecilia finds out where we were and what happened, she would see that Joanna and I never teach again." Alice put her head in her hand.

"There's no reason to worry yourself. Who's going to tell her? Not I. I doubt Joanna will say a word about your adventures. Your secret is safe with me."

She yawned. "I'm so tired. My hand hurts, and I don't know if I ever want to leave the mission ever again. It was horrid what we saw tonight, horrid! I can't get it out of my mind. We nearly died, and so did you!"

Jonathan kneeled in front of her, coffee and cake forgotten as he looked into her eyes, his hands on hers. "Show me your hand."

He held her hand in his, gently cradling it as he kissed the part that wasn't burned. Alice gasped at the sweetness of the gesture, how his lips felt on her skin.

"You were brave tonight, my dear Colleen. Not many women would have been as brave as you. I'm in awe. If I was the marrying sort I would propose to you, but I am not the kind of man who can make you happy."

Alice gazed into his eyes, lost for a moment in their dark tumultuous depths as she leaned close to him. "You could make me happy, if you wanted to."

"After tonight, my life is going to be interesting. The saloons of Santa Fe are closed to me, my dear. That may be for the best, but I have nothing to offer you – nothing but myself, and I'm a sinner. Shall we part as friends, after you give me one kiss?"

"How can I kiss you if you are my friend and not my husband?" she asked as she felt her breath growing shallow, her skin tingling where his lips had touched her hand.

"With your permission," he said as he leaned close to her. He gently lifted her face towards his.

"Yes," she murmured.

She closed her eyes, overwhelmed with the emotion of the moment as his lips touched hers. She wasn't sure how long they kissed, until she became aware that she was no longer breathing. A gasp and the sound of footsteps from the hallway reminded her that they were not alone.

Jonathan rested his forehead on hers. "We have been discovered. Goodnight, Colleen, stay out of trouble. Promise me you will."

Alice stood, her body trembling. "Tell me this isn't goodbye."

"I can't make any promises," he said.

"Neither can I," she murmured as she gazed at him with a mixture of passion and regret. Why couldn't he stay? Why couldn't he declare that he loved her? As she watched him leave, he turned and smiled at her. She felt tears welling in her eyes as the door closed behind him.

Chapter Six

November 7, 1876
Santa Maria, New Mexico Territory

A letter from the young Pastor Newland of Tucker Springs sat opened but unanswered on her desk as she finished teaching a grammar lesson to a classroom full of children from the surrounding ranches and nearby towns. They ranged in age from six to ten. Alice found the class challenging, as many of these children were learning proper English for the first time.

Sister Rafaela walked down the corridor ringing a bell, signaling that classes were at an end for the day. Alice dismissed the children, knowing many of them had long walks home in the chill of the autumn. Some of the children would be staying at the mission, their homes being too far away to reach by foot every day.

"Good work. Older students, study your rules very carefully. And you younger students, please practice your verbs for next time."

"Yes, Miss Cleary," the children called out in unison as they left.

"Eloisa, Joseph, don't forget your lunch pails. Geraldine, your bonnet is untied. Diego, your shirt is untucked. Wear your coat," she chided them as they filed past her.

Standing in her doorway, she listened until she could no longer hear their footsteps on the stone floor of the corridor. How odd it was to have her own classroom, she thought as she leaned against the door.

Her reverie was interrupted by Sister Rafaela. "Miss Cleary, have you attended to your duties? Is your classroom prepared for tomorrow?"

"Yes, Sister Rafaela," Alice said as she mimicked the same singsong tone of her students. She felt like a student more days than she felt like a teacher. She was the youngest woman at the mission who was not wearing a habit. Sometimes she felt like a child herself, as she had much to learn about teaching a classroom filled with active (and sometimes unruly) children.

Walking back to her desk, her gaze landed on the letter. It was only two weeks old, a record in the territory. The letter felt strange to her. She barely knew the pastor, had only spoken to him once, during her brief stay at Louisa's farm back in Kansas. She recalled giving him permission to write to her, but that seemed so long ago. In his letter, he expressed an interest in her future plans, asking her if she was considering remaining a teacher and making it a career.

The question was harmless, but why would he ask such a thing? Joanna had shared her opinion – it seemed perfectly clear to her that the pastor was close to declaring his intentions for Alice. Wasn't it obvious? Joanna asked, with a gleam in her eye.

Was it obvious? Alice wasn't sure what to do about the pastor. He was the sort of man she *should* want. He was handsome, compassionate and lived his life as an example to his congregation. His kindness touched her; she remembered it well, but she didn't know how she felt about him. How should she answer him? Should she encourage him, or tell him the truth? Her mind was filled with Jonathan now.

It had been two months since she saw Jonathan, since they'd talked and shared a stolen kiss in the Ortega's sitting room. Raising her fingers to her mouth, she could still feel the weight of his lips on hers, still smell the scent of his skin. She couldn't forget about him, even though she hadn't heard a word from him since he'd said goodbye. Why did he have to be so handsome, so heroic? He'd told her was he wasn't the marrying sort, but did he intend to never see her again?

She knew she didn't love Pastor Newland, but where did her future lie? If she returned to Kansas, she would be safe and loved. She would be near her brother Will for always. She did admire and respect the pastor. He was a good man, and honest. He cared for the people in Tucker Springs, and he seemed to care for her as well. In his letter he congratulated her on becoming a teacher, told her how her brother and sister were doing, and expressed hope that he would see her again at Christmas.

Opening the drawer of her desk, she pulled out a piece of letter paper. Without a second thought, she picked up her pen, dipped it into the inkwell and started writing. Pastor Newland wasn't asking her to marry him; he was only asking her about her future. With confidence, she answered his question. In a few moments she was finished, and she folded her letter and slipped it into an envelope. If she hurried, she could send it out this afternoon. With any luck he would have his answer by Thanksgiving.

As she rushed from her classroom she thought about Will and Louisa. She didn't have much money, because she sent nearly every penny to Louisa, but Alice was certain she had enough to go to Tucker Springs. If Sister Cecilia gave her blessing, she may find a way to see her family and Pastor Newland in December. This plan made her smile with anticipation. Christmas in Kansas! She couldn't think of a better way to spend the holidays – unless Jonathan Keene suddenly arrived and asked her to be his wife. Then she could be completely happy.

Giggling at her own foolishness, she rushed to catch Thomas, praying that she hadn't missed him.

*****

December 10, 1876
Santa Maria, New Mexico Territory

"Dress warm, and don't forget your gloves! It's cold out there!" Joanna said to Alice as Alice scrambled to wrap a scarf around her neck.

"I'm ready," Alice grabbed her winter gloves.

Sliding her gloves on her hands, she shivered involuntarily. The rooms at the mission were heated, but just enough to ward off the worst of the cold – not provide comfort. The sisters were accustomed to deprivation as they lived austere lives, eschewing comfort in nearly every form, but Alice was not like them. She wanted to be warm, to sit in front of a raging fire with a nice cup of coffee or tea. With a glance at the small fire dying in the fireplace in her room, she knew that a bigger one was out of the question.

She was colder than she ever remembered being in Georgia, a strange thought when she considered the mission was built like a fortress. Even with the thick stuccoed walls, cold seeped into the cracks in the windows and under the doors. It radiated up from the stone floor and got into Alice's bones. She never expected New Mexico to be cold; her imaginings of the desert was that it was hot all year round. But December in Santa Maria was much colder than she had expected.

"How do the sisters live like this?" Alice asked Joanna as she considered slipping on a pair of mittens over her gloves.

"They're used to it. They all took vows of poverty, remember?"

"I do, but they have to feel cold. They are still people."

"Come on; we're going to be late if we don't get going!"

Alice shoved her gloved hands in the pair of mittens she'd knit for Will. He wouldn't mind if she wore them, not since she desperately needed them, she decided. Besides, he had never cared for Christmas presents, not since he was a boy. During the war, there weren't any presents and after the war ended an orange or a bag of candy was considered cause for celebration. He would be happy to see her arrive for Christmas, whether she came with presents or not.

As Alice followed Joanna through the labyrinth of corridors and hallways of the mission, they passed Sister Rafaela and Sister Cecilia. Slowing down, Joanna and Alice walked past the two sisters solemnly, concealing their excitement. Alice stifled the urge to giggle as she always felt like one of the mission students when she was around the sisters at the school. She was also ready to burst with happiness, especially when she thought about seeing her brother. Will had been her best friend and closest ally since they were children. Correspondence kept her abreast of what he was doing, how he liked his new life in Kansas, but letters would never be the same as hearing his voice, as seeing him in person. In a few days, she would be on a train heading to Tucker Springs by way of Fort Monroe, and to a Christmas she hoped would be a good one.

"Hurry, we don't want to miss the start!" Joanna whispered as they turned the corner and picked up speed again.

"The start? I thought we were going to Mass at the church in Santa Maria. We're not late for that," Alice replied as they burst through the doors of the mission and into the bright sunshine and the cold.

"Alice, have you not been paying attention? Mass is at the end of the procession; we must first walk along the streets of Santa Maria, then we go to mass."

"Walk? We're walking to town, then we walk some more? I'll be frozen!"

"No, you won't! Come on; you're tough. Remember, I've seen you in a saloon!" Joanna laughed.

"Oh no, don't say that out loud! What if Sister Cecilia hears you?"

"She won't hear me. Stop worrying about it; that was months ago! Flor is safe, and we're still alive – which is why we're doing this. The Virgin protects sinners and she protected us in our time of need. I still have nightmares about what may have happened to us if she hadn't sent your friend to our aid."

Alice immediately had a flash of a memory, a powerful one that made her blush. She could feel Jonathan's lips on hers, his hand on her cheek. "She sent a sinner to our aid, is what you mean," Alice said playfully as she wrapped her arms around herself.

"She is merciful to sinners, even the ones who steal kisses," Joanna smirked.

163

"Joanna!" Alice exclaimed in mock indignation as they walked through the courtyard.

"Ladies, good morning! Where are you two going so early on a Sunday morning? The sun is barely up and it's freezing cold out here." Thomas greeted them as he exited the barn.

"Thomas, good morning! We're going to the procession to honor the Virgin," Joanna replied happily.

"Ahh, be careful. There's still some folks in town who haven't forgotten about Texas."

"There hasn't been trouble like that in a long time," Joanna answered.

"That's not the only kind of trouble that worries me. I would take you ladies to town myself if Sister Cecilia's horse didn't need me to stay with her," Thomas said as he stamped his feet in the cold.

"Sister Cecilia's horse? The one you bought for her last month?"

"The same one; I call her Delia. She's a pretty little mare, strong of heart and ready to do any work you need," he said as he lowered his voice. "Let me tell you a secret about our newest addition to the mission. She's about to…well, there isn't a polite way to say this to you unmarried ladies, but she's with child, to quote the Bible."

"That's wonderful news. The man you bought her from didn't know it?" Joanna looked shocked.

"He's an old friend of mine, Jasper Faro. Let me tell you another secret: he's a good man with a heart of

164

gold. If he knew the horse he sold me was in the family way, he probably figured the mission could use more than one horse."

Alice thought about the long walk to town. If they walked fast maybe it wouldn't feel so cold. "Thomas, we're going to be just fine. I promise! You worry about Delia, she needs you."

"I expect she does. She's a young mare; this may be her first time."

"Thomas, what would we do without you?" Joanna asked she gave the old man a hug.

"Just be careful. There's been trouble brewing in town for a while, and I worry it's not safe for any of you ladies to go there without someone with you. Maybe I'm being old and crazy, but I've got a bad feeling about it. Just keep a lookout," Thomas said with a frown.

Alice and Joanna agreed to do as he suggested. They left the mission and headed for Santa Maria. This wasn't the first time Thomas had warned them of trouble. For months, he had been saying that there was something going on in town, that the women of the mission should be careful. As Alice walked down the road beside Joanna, she wondered if Thomas was just being cautious.

"Joanna, do you think Thomas is right?"

"About the procession?"

"About any of it." Alice watched the smoke rising from the pueblo, wondering what it would be like

165

to sit by one of their fires and talk to the people who lived there. Turning her attention back to Joanna, she continued, "He's been telling me that there's trouble in town for a long time, I think ever since he met me."

"I wouldn't worry. What's going to happen during a religious procession? Almost everyone in town goes to the church or attends Mass here at the mission."

"Remind me again about this procession. We didn't have anything like it in Augusta. It's not sacrilegious, is it?" Alice asked, the pueblo forgotten.

"It's not sacrilegious! If it was, we wouldn't be going to Mass afterwards, now would we? I'm not surprised you don't know what it is. I don't think there are many Spanish people in Georgia."

"No, there aren't. Not one that I've ever met," admitted Alice.

"The procession is in honor of the Blessed Virgin, because she appeared to a shepherd five hundred years ago in Mexico. It's to celebrate her message of love and compassion and to celebrate that she chose a plain man, a man like our Thomas, to share that message. Isn't that beautiful?"

"It is beautiful. It gives me hope. What's Thomas worried about, then?"

"He's referring to the new settlers in the area, people like you who are from back east. I don't mean people just like you, Alice. I mean people who are German, Irish, English, or whatever it is you are. They're not all bad, but some of them are. You're not – well, I mean you're not against anything. Some of the settlers don't like anyone Spanish, or Mexican, or Indian. Do you understand? How can they not like any of us? We were in New Mexico before they were. We built the towns."

"I think I do understand what you mean. I admit that I don't know the history of the territory very well, but I don't hate anyone except the Yankees who destroyed my family and burned my parents' house to the ground. I keep trying to forgive them but it's hard."

Joanna spoke with tenderness. "That's because they gave you a reason to be angry with them. Keep praying that you can forgive men for the evil they do. It's how I manage to forgive those who think that my family and I should leave Santa Fe. Why should we do that? One of my ancestors was a founding father of the town, but that was a long time ago, before anyone spoke English in New Mexico. If I was to be honest, New Mexico should be part of Mexico, or Spain, not the United States – but that's another matter altogether. We shouldn't worry about such things today. Nothing is going to happen; you have my word."

"How can you be certain?"

"It's Sunday morning. Who wakes up on the Lord's day and wants to cause trouble?"

Alice nodded in agreement. "I suppose you're right. Besides, it's almost Christmas!"

"Almost Christmas? My dear, it's already Christmas in New Mexico. After the procession we have *Las Posadas*. That begins in four days."

"Las what? What do you mean, it's Christmas? Christmas isn't for another two weeks!"

"Not in New Mexico, You have a lot to learn about Christmas here."

Alice agreed she had a lot to learn about a great many things in New Mexico, while in her mind she was thinking of the Christmas celebration that was waiting for her in Kansas. She wasn't going to be in New Mexico for Christmas to find out what *Las Posadas*, or whatever Joanna had said, was about or what it was. She was going to be at her sister Louisa's house, gathered around a warm fire with her brother, her nieces, and her nephew. Smiling, she thought of the gifts she'd made for her family and how she still needed to buy one or two small things for the children. Maybe she could go to Santa Maria this week to purchase candy at the general store.

As she walked along beside Joanna, her thoughts drifted (as they often did) to Jonathan Keene. Where was he? She hadn't heard from him in a long time. When she remembered him, she thought about their kiss, and their goodbye. Then her mind darted toward someone else: Pastor Newland. She would see him at Christmas; there could be no doubt about it. Was she ready to see him? Was she any closer to knowing what she wanted from him, if she wanted anything at all? She remembered the letter she'd sent to him in November, the one that she still felt slightly guilty about writing. She hadn't encouraged him, but she hadn't discouraged him, either.

When he asked her about her future plans in his letter to her, she'd answered that her future was not planned, that she was willing to do whatever God willed, and so she had no future neatly arranged. Perhaps she should have written that she had no plans to marry anyone but Jonathan Keene, but she knew that wasn't true either. He had no intention of marrying her, isn't that what he'd said? If he wouldn't marry her, maybe she would never be married, or maybe she would marry a nice, respectable man like Pastor Newland and keep a house for him.

"You're quiet, Alice."

"I'm sorry. I was just thinking about Christmas with my family in Kansas."

"Is that why you were smiling?" asked Joanna with a smirk.

Alice didn't realize she had been smiling. She wondered why the thought of Jonathan made her smile, even when he was responsible for breaking her heart.

*****

December 15, 1876

Alice was not going to spend Christmas in Kansas. Sighing as the day's lesson went on, she tried not to think about being away from Will for the holiday.

169

"Miss Cleary, why are you sad?" a voice piped up for the front row.

"Rose, I'm not sad. It's not polite to say such things," Alice reminded one of her younger students, a small girl who was prone to speaking out of turn.

"Sorry, but you look sad. Why?" Rose persisted.

"Stop it, Rose. Teacher told you to hush!"

"No, she didn't."

"Yes, she did!"

"Didn't!" replied Rose to her classmate, a blonde girl who like to boss the others around.

"Rose, Katie, that will be enough. You are both speaking out of turn. One more outburst and I will be forced to punish you," Alice said to her squabbling children.

"Yes, Miss Cleary," the little girls said in unison as Katie glared at Rose.

"It's your fault I got in trouble with teacher," Katie whispered to Rose as she pulled the girl's braid.

"Ouch! Miss Cleary!" Rose squalled.

Alice could feel her patience dwindling. "Katie, apologize this instant! Rose, stop crying. There's no need to cry. Everyone else, eyes straight ahead."

"Miss Cleary," Sister Cecilia said suddenly from the door. Alice jumped and the children suddenly sat up straighter in their chairs. Rose wiped away her tears and Katie smiled as the other children stared straight at the blackboard like perfect students.

How long had Sister Cecilia been standing there? Not that Alice had done anything wrong, but she didn't want the abbess to think she couldn't keep discipline in her class. Turning to the children, Alice said, "Study the verb tenses on the board, and be ready to recite them when I return."

"Yes Miss Cleary," the children said as Alice joined Sister Cecilia in the hall outside her classroom.

Alice expected the older woman to criticize her for the incident involving Katie and Rose. If Alice was a better teacher, perhaps the children would have listened to her the first time she told them to behave, but that wasn't always the case. At Alice's young age, with her soft voice and tenderness towards the children who boarded at the school for most of the year, she knew the children regarded her as more of an older sister. It was her youth and her compassion for the children which made them see her as less strict a disciplinarian than the other teachers in the school. Bracing herself for the inevitable criticism, she waited for Sister Cecilia to speak.

"Walk with me a moment. I don't think your class will get too out of hand, do you?" Sister Cecilia asked in her stern but calm voice.

Alice murmured her agreement, and watched her feet while they walked a short distance down the hall. The hall was colder than her classroom, and Alice tried not to shiver in front of Sister Cecilia. She wished she had taken her shawl.

"I've spoken with Miss Ortega, as I'm sure you have." Sister Cecelia said. "Her father has taken a turn, I'm afraid, which has led to her hasty departure at first light this morning."

Alice knew about Joanna's father, Mr. Ortega. He had developed a fever that Joanna's mother was convinced could be the end of him. She'd sent a letter to Joanna, begging her to come home to be with her family, as this may be her father's last Christmas. Joanna cried when she shared the news with Alice. Alice cried too, worrying about Mr. Ortega as she helped Joanna pack for the trip home to Santa Fe. With Joanna's departure, Alice knew that her own plans had changed, although she didn't say so to her friend. Joanna had too much else to worry about to think of Alice's hopes to go to Kansas.

"Yes, Sister Cecelia, I know about Joanna's father. I pray he recovers his strength."

"As do I, but there is the matter of her responsibilities here at the school."

"Are you asking me to stay during the Christmas break? Is that what you wish to discuss with me?" asked Alice.

"Why, yes, it is. I see you have already concluded that Joanna will be sorely missed at this time of year. With our classes continuing for another week, and Las Posadas beginning tomorrow, I was counting on her to be here. I could not deny her wish to be with her family, and neither do I wish to ask you not to be with yours."

172

"If I'm needed here, I understand. I know that many of the sisters have already been called away to care for sick parishioners from the church in Santa Maria. I also know that Joanna was teaching twice the number of students that I am. Of course, I'm not sure what kind of benefit I can be during Las Posadas, but I will help where I can."

"If you could shorten your trip to Kansas, perhaps there may be a way for you to still see your family? I understand it's very important to you, being that you are quite young, Miss Cleary, and this is your first Christmas away from them."

"The journey is long; it would be over before it began. Maybe I can make the trip in the spring, when the weather is warmer." Alice tried to appear more stoic than she felt about the change in her plans.

"Then you would stay for the Christmas season? I do not wish to cause you any sorrow, but we could use your help."

"Yes, Sister, I will stay. The mission needs me."

"Thank you. I will see to it that you shall have time in the coming year to see your family, if God wills it."

"That is very kind of you, Sister, but what do you want me to do to help?"

"Take some of Miss Ortega's children into your class. You'll be responsible for the children who are boarding with us, but you already help with that. Also, about Las Posadas – Miss Ortega helped with that as well. Do you think you can do her part?"

"What do you mean?" Alice was unsure what Sister Cecilia was referring to. Was she talking about a role, like in a play?

"Miss Ortega was in charge of taking the children into town to go to the Christmas market and to reenact the nativity story. Do you know nothing of Las Posadas?"

"Joanna mentioned it, but I don't think I understand."

"No matter, it's easy enough. You are in charge of taking a group of children into Santa Maria to take part in the festival. There's not much for them to do but carry poinsettias and sing songs. Some of the children in town dress as angels.

"It's the story of the nativity, of Joseph and Mary searching for a place to stay. Each night, people dressed as the holy couple go to a different house, where they are welcomed inside. The festival lasts for eight nights. Miss Ortega seemed to enjoy it, and the children look forward to it every year. It may not be strictly in accordance with our doctrine or the rules of our order, but it is a religious festival condoned by the bishop. If he approves, there can be no harm in celebrating the birth of Christ, now can there, Miss Cleary?"

"No, there can be no harm in that. Sister, what am I to do? Take the children to town, is that it?"

"Yes, Thomas may accompany you with the wagon. Just be sure the children are bundled up warmly against the cold and that you don't lose any of them.

Sister Rafaela usually helps Miss Ortega. I don't think she will mind taking care of the children for a night or two, so you don't have to go every evening. Then you'll help? The children are counting on going; it would break their hearts not to go."

"Won't we be keeping the children up well past their bedtime? Alice wondered when she would finally grasp all these new and strange traditions.

"There is no need to worry about bedtimes."

"What about the children? Is everyone going, the entire school?"

"We are responsible for the children who board with us and going to Las Posadas. The children who live locally may go with their families."

Alice wasn't sure if she could endure several nights being outside in the cold weather, trying to account for a group of excited children, but she would try. After all, she was in the New Mexico Territory – this was their home and she would abide by their traditions. What better way to experience the ways of her new home than to accompany schoolchildren to Santa Maria every night of the festival while praying none of them caught their death in the freezing air?

"What about sickness and fever? Aren't you the slightest bit concerned about illness?" Alice asked sister Cecilia.

"Miss Cleary, you sound like an old woman. Have I chosen the wrong teacher for this task?"

"No, sister you haven't," Alice replied, feeling embarrassed.

"Good. See that the children dress warmly. We've been taking the children to Las Posadas ever since there has been a town and a mission. We haven't lost a single one yet and no has become ill. No harm has come from a missed bedtime. Let's hope that our good fortune holds this year, Miss Cleary," Sister Cecilia said as she peered at Alice, her eyes twinkling, before she left her standing in the cold corridor.

What had happened to Sister Cecilia, Alice wondered. Where was the stern abbess she knew, and who was this strange woman dressed in her clothes?

*****

December 16, 1876

The weather was unseasonably warm for December, or so Alice had been told by her students. After feeling cold for two weeks without relief, she was surprised that on this Saturday so close to Christmas she didn't need her coat. her long-sleeved dress made of heavy cotton was sufficient to ward off any chill she might have experienced as she walked along the main street of Santa Maria.

The streets were crowded. The general mercantile was busy for a late Saturday afternoon, bustling with people who were buying candy, penny toys, and many gifts for Christmas. But the store wasn't the only place in Santa Maria that was bustling with trade. A new store had opened just up the block and past that, the Christmas market filled the town square in front of the church. The market was a busy, cheerful place full of the exotic but welcoming aromas of fresh foods and baked goods. There were people selling baskets, carved wooden animals, ornately colored clay pots, and every manner of thing anyone could wish for at Christmas.

Alice was drawn to a colorfully decorated stall manned by a group of women who displayed their knit and sewn items. Her eyes settled on a brightly knit shawl with a rose design in its pattern. The workmanship was lovely, and the price wasn't so very much. Touching the material, she told herself she could always use a shawl, especially in the chill and cold of the mission, but she felt guilty. She knew it wasn't the cold that made her wish for the shawl. In her plain navy dress with a prim white collar, she longed for a little color, something pretty to make her feel fashionable. Sighing, she wanted to try the shawl on, but she told herself she shouldn't. She couldn't spend money on herself. It was Christmas, after all, and she should be charitable.

After the deprivation of the war years and the poverty she'd endured at the hands of her aunt and uncle in Augusta, Alice wasn't accustomed to having money in her pocket. The few coins she could spare for Christmas gifts felt like a fortune to a girl like her, who'd never had very much. Maybe she could buy this shawl for herself, spend money just this once on something she wanted? How often did she buy anything, she asked herself wistfully.

"Senora, el chal es bonita, si?" an old woman with kind eyes spoke to Alice from behind the table as she gestured to the rose shawl.

The shawl was red and green, with white thread worked around the edges. It was bright and cheerful and reminded Alice of the gardens in Augusta.

"Si," Alice answered, translating the woman's words, the shawl was beautiful. Was the price negotiable?

"Cuanto? How much?" Alice asked, knowing that the price of the shawl was marked with a small slip of paper pinned to it. Fifty cents.

The old woman smiled and pointed at the price written in a careful script. Alice had a dollar in her pocket, enough for dinner at Mama Rosa's and few small items for Christmas for Joanna and the students who boarded at the school, especially the irrepressible Rose. She knew the shawl was worth more than fifty cents; the work must have taken whoever made it hours to complete. She was being selfish, there was no way she could spend that amount of money on herself.

"Gracias," she said to the older woman as she shook her head, no.

Alice cast one last look at the shawl and smiled, regretting she couldn't purchase it. She had started to walk away when she caught sight of the person in front of her. Not two feet away was Jonathan Keene. He was smiling at her and shaking his head.

"That shawl would look really nice on you. It suits you."

"Mr. Keene, I don't know what to say. I haven't heard from you in months and now here you are, offering me advice about what to purchase?" Alice said to the handsome man who was smiling softly at her.

"You can't walk away from her; it's rude. Look at her face, you've disappointed the woman," Jonathan said as he glanced at the woman at the stall, who carefully rearranged the wares with a frown on her face.

"I don't have the money to spend on myself, not at Christmas. It wouldn't be right."

"Then don't. Stay where you are." He addressed the woman in Spanish, speaking so quickly Alice couldn't make any sense of it. With an enormous smile, the woman unpinned the paper bearing the price and folded the shawl, together with a pair of knit gloves. She handed them to Jonathan, and he gave her a dollar coin. He spoke to her once again in Spanish. From what Alice was able to translate, he'd said, "Keep the change, Merry Christmas."

"Mr. Keene, what are you doing?"

"Buying you a Christmas present. Here, I want to see how that looks on you."

"I can't accept it, you know that. It would be improper to accept gifts from a man who is barely an acquaintance," Alice said, breathless as she tried to understand how he was standing in front of her offering her a present.

"No, it wouldn't be improper. You've kissed me, remember? I'm pretty sure we know each other well enough for you to permit me to buy you something now and again."

Alice blushed and looked back at the woman in the stall. The old woman beamed at her. "Es que to esposa?" she asked Jonathan.

Alice blushed as she slid the shawl around her shoulders. "Did she ask if I was your wife?"

"She did. Should I tell her the truth?" he asked with a wink.

"Tell her what you like," Alice replied.

"Si, gracias, senora," Jonathan said, tipping his hat to the woman.

"I know what you said to her. Now we're married again. Why? You do that on purpose. I shouldn't accept this gift from you, or anything else. Why do you do this? You appear like an apparition out of thin air, you make terrible jokes about us being married, and then I don't hear from you ever again."

"You can't say ever, can you?"

"I nearly can; I haven't seen you in months. Didn't you buy a pair of gloves? Who are they for? Some other poor girl like me, whom you have enraptured with your charm?" Alice demanded as she admired her new shawl.

"Never you mind. We're not married, after all."

"No, we're not!" she huffed.

"Is that how you intend to thank me for your present?"

"Maybe I should return it, so you can give it to the woman who is getting those gloves."

"If you want to know who's getting the gloves, I suggest you come with me. I'm feeling mighty peckish, as they say in these parts." His smile charmed Alice more than she liked to admit.

"I had plans to go to Mama Rosa's for dinner," Alice explained.

"That sounds like what I planned to do. Come with me, then. You can explain to me what you're doing all alone at the market in Santa Maria."

"Maybe you can explain what you're doing in Santa Maria. How long have you been in town, and when were you going to tell me you were here?" She frowned at him.

"My dear Colleen, that shawl looks good on you, much better than that matronly dull blue dress you're wearing. Who makes your clothes for you? The sisters?"

"Mr. Keene! I'll have you know this dress cost me a pretty penny. It's plain, I admit that, but it's made of good sturdy cotton and will last for years. It may be dark and not very stylish, but I'm not allowed to wear anything fashionable at the mission. You know – vanity, pride, those sins?"

"Oh yes, Colleen, I know all about them," he said with a gleam in his eye. "Come along to Mama Rosa's. I'm famished and I'm buying."

"Wait, I can't be seen in public with a strange man."

"I'm not a stranger, remember?"

"But I'm a teacher at the mission. What if word gets back to Sister Cecilia that I accompanied you, and then ate food with you? I could lose my position."

Jonathan Keene took her hand and tucked it in his arm. "We're going to be sitting in a respectable restaurant in town. No one will think anything improper, I assure you. Even if they did, it's Santa Maria, the territories. No one will mind what we do."

Pulling her hand away from him, she walked beside him instead, allowing him to lead the way to Mama Rosa's. Why did she fall into the same old pattern of arguing with him and wishing he would kiss her all at the same time? What kind of hold did he have on her? Wishing she could figure it out, she pulled her shawl around her shoulders, feeling like the prettiest girl in the market even if she was in the company of a scoundrel.

*****

Mama Rosa's was a cramped restaurant that had seating for only about twenty people. The dining room (if it could be called that) was a small space stuffed with tiny rough-hewn tables and equally rough chairs. But the wood of the furnishings glowed from being cleaned and polished, gleaming until it was nearly reflective. On the walls, ceramic plates and strings of dried chili peppers shared space, and the room had a delectable spicy smell that wasn't from the cooking alone.

An older woman wearing an immaculate white apron over a calico dress held out her arms to Jonathan. Alice knew who Mama Rosa was; she had snuck into the restaurant every chance she could to enjoy the unassuming fare that was unlike any food she had ever eaten. She didn't always understand what Mama Rosa or her staff said, and she wasn't always sure what she was eating, but she knew it would be delicious – hearty and spicy enough to bring tears to her eyes.

Mama Rosa spoke to Jonathan and gestured to him to have a seat anywhere there was a place. Alice looked around the crowded restaurant before her eyes rested on a table near the window. There was nowhere else to sit, so she headed towards the table. She heard a laugh as warm and welcoming as Mama Rosa herself, and she turned to see Mama Rosa wiping her hands on her apron and examining the gloves Jonathan had bought, before trying them on. She looked happy with her present. Alice smiled.

"Mama Rosa is going to bring us a meal worthy of a king. I hope you like pozole for starters, tamales, and sopapillas for dessert," Jonathan announced as he held out the chair for Alice.

"I honestly don't know what you just said, but I'm willing to eat anything Mama Rosa puts in front of me," Alice admitted. "I can't remember being so hungry."

"Aren't they feeding you at that mission of yours?" Jonathan asked as he sat down across from her. "It looks like you've gotten too thin. I'm going to have to see that Mama Rosa sends you a hamper of food once a week."

"They feed me, they do, but the sisters have a rule about gluttony and excess. You would know about that if you were Catholic."

"Don't think I'm not Catholic, just because I don't go to Mass every week," Jonathan said in his best Irish accent.

"You may be Catholic, but you don't act like it," Alice chided him as a young man brought over a pitcher of a milky drink that smelled vaguely like cinnamon and vanilla.

"What is this? It smells like dessert," she asked.

"There are many names for it, but I think you'll enjoy it. Try it," Jonathan said as he poured the thick beverage into a glass.

The drink was surprisingly soothing and refreshing, with a hint of sweet flavor and a touch of spiciness. Alice temporarily forgot she was angry with Jonathan as she drank it down quickly. "Oh, I forgot to ask, there weren't any spirits in that, were there? I'm not supposed to drink spirits."

Jonathan chuckled. "Mama Rosa isn't going to be serving spirits here; she doesn't believe in them," Jonathan explained as the young man brought over two bowls of thick hominy stew. They ate in companionable silence for a while.

"Colleen, my dear, you haven't told me what you were doing in the market all alone on a Saturday afternoon. I didn't think you were permitted to go into town by yourself?" Jonathan peered at her over two steaming bowls of pozole.

"I didn't ask for permission. That was wrong of me, I know. I should have waited for Thomas or Sister Rafaela to go into town, but the weather was so beautiful, and I longed to have a few minutes on my own. I've been taking the children to Las Posadas nearly every night, and teaching during the day. Wait, why am I telling you this? I'm angry with you."

Jonathan's dark eyes sparkled in the light that filtered through the window. "You have the oddest ideas. Why stay angry at me? The truth is you can't. I've never lied to you. I've been honest even if the truth wasn't what you wished to hear. I'm charming and I speak more than one language. The odds are stacked against you, I'm afraid. If this was poker, I would have the winning hand."

"Oh, you think so, do you?" Alice glared at him, her soup uneaten. "Just because you're honest about not wanting to marry me, that gives you permission to come and go as you please without so much as a letter or an explanation? You could have been dead. I didn't know if you were alive, or sick, or if I would ever see you again."

"My dear Colleen, is that what's bothering you? Don't worry about things we can't change. We're here together, and there are no little Ortega children to interrupt us. There's no one shooting at us or chasing us. Can't you appreciate that we have this restaurant, this good food, and good company?"

"I would appreciate if it was with anyone else. I don't know how you live so unpredictably."

"Admit it, that's why you adore me," he said in a roguish voice.

"Adore you? How can I adore someone who isn't here? You still haven't told me what you're doing in Santa Maria or how long you've been here." Alice demanded. Their eyes met and held, and she sighed. "Forgive me. I sound like I have a reason to expect to know your whereabouts. Since we're being honest with each other, you don't owe me any reason for your actions, and I don't owe you my loyalty."

"My, you are stern today. Doesn't Mama Rosa's soup seem perfect for a December day? Wait until you try her tamales," Jonathan changed the subject.

Alice stared at him and temporarily admitted defeat. "Very well, we can talk about her entire menu of dishes if you like, but you haven't answered my question. If you aren't going to tell me how long you've been in town, at least tell me why you're here. For a man like you in your profession, I wouldn't think the saloons of Santa Maria would offer you much temptation."

"I can make a modest income for a few days at the saloon here. But that's about all. If I tell you what I'm doing here you have to promise not to try to talk me out of it. That's another reason I don't have a wife. I don't need anyone telling me what I may or may not do, especially when it comes to how I earn my living."

"It's against the law, isn't it? You're a smart man, but I have a terrible feeling that you like to fancy yourself an outlaw or a cowboy. Is that why you insist on making your living playing cards and doing I'm afraid to imagine what else?"

"For a teacher at a mission, you possess an extraordinary imagination. In your eyes, I'm a swashbuckling villain, a cowboy, an outlaw wanted for my lawless ways. Is that the only reason you flirt with me?"

If Alice wasn't swallowing a generous spoonful of the pozole, her jaw would have dropped. Nearly choking, she replied, "Flirting? Did you imply, sir, that I have been flirting with you?"

"You sound like a southern belle when you're angry with me, did you know that? We have been flirting. Call it whatever you wish, but that is what we've been doing," he said as he casually ate his soup.

"If I wasn't sure I would insult Mama Rosa by leaving before I finished this meal, I would leave you alone to do all the flirting you wished with any woman but me. I have not been flirting with you. I'm not the

187

kind of woman who flirts with men," she whispered furiously.

"There, there, Colleen. There is no need for all that anger directed at me. I told the truth; you just didn't like what it was. If your version of the truth is slightly different then I suggest you call what we've been doing whatever you like. I'm not suggesting you're the kind of woman who flirts with men, just the kind of woman who flirts with me."

"Oh, you are incorrigible and arrogant to think I'm flirting with you at all."

"I am not arrogant. If you'll stop acting like you're auditioning for top billing at a vaudeville show, I'll tell you why I'm in town," he changed the subject as their bowls of soup were whisked away and plates of tamales were set in their place by the smiling young man.

Alice looked down at the corn husk wrapped around something that smelled even better than the soup. "I've never had these before. These are tamales? I've heard about them."

"I knew you couldn't stay mad at me. Here, I'll show you how to eat them," he said as he deftly unwrapped his tamale and ate it with a fork.

"I should stay mad at you. I should refuse to ever see you again, but I can't do that, not in Mama Rosa's."

"About Santa Maria," he said as he lowered his voice, "I shouldn't tell you this in this restaurant, but I trust Mama Rosa and I recognize most of the men in here as being honest ranch hands and cattlemen."

Alice studied her handsome companion and waited for him to continue. She raised one eyebrow.

"If I tell you, you have to promise not to worry about me, or pray for me, or anything of that nature. I don't want you to waste even one day worrying about me. Do I have your promise?"

"Please don't tell me that you rob banks or trains," she said as she shook her head.

"Colleen, my dear. Have you been reading the wild west stories in the newspapers? Where do you get those ideas? No, it's nothing like that, not at all. It's actually honest, by my standards. Do you know that new store that opened on Main Street, the general store?"

"You work there? Behind the counter?" she said as if she couldn't believe it, "That doesn't seem like the kind of work a man as well dressed as you are would choose."

"I'm not a counter clerk; you know that much about me. There's more to it than that. That store is run by a fellow named Garcia. His father owns a ranch outside of town. You won't believe what I have to tell you, but there's a war going on in town and we're in the middle of it."

"A war? Is this a story you would tell to amuse children?"

"It's not a story. The Garcia family are old territory money. They've been ranching and farming here since the first conquistadors divvied up the land. The store is a venture Javier wanted to try – he's the youngest son and unlikely to inherit much of the ranch. That goes to Juan, the elder brother."

"You mentioned a war?"

"The family that owns the other general store, the one that's been here for two generations, are the Caseys. They're not happy about the new store, or about the Garcias' recent purchase of new land for their cattle. The new land belonging to the Garcia family sits next to the Casey's property, which is also large. What you have here is a dispute between the new blood and the old families."

"The settlers from the east against the Spanish ranchers, is that it?" Alice asked she looked around the room. "You're sure it's safe to talk about this here?"

"Safe as anywhere else. I'm on Garcia's side. I'm a hired gun, you could say, me and a couple of other men he pays to watch the border of his land, and keep an eye on his store."

"Does he expect trouble? Thomas at the mission has been saying there's going to be trouble for months, but I haven't paid much attention to him, I'm sorry to say," Alice confessed.

"You should listen to the man; he knows more than most people do. There is trouble coming to Santa Maria. I don't know what it will look like, but something is bound to happen. The Garcias want to own as much land as they can, and they're buying it when it's available. They opened a store. In time they want to build a hotel, and who knows what else. The Caseys aren't having it, not when they're going to see their profits from the store start to fall. That isn't the only reason the Caseys aren't too happy about this arrangement. Word has it, they used to let their cattle graze on this land purchased by Mr. Garcia. Old Mr. Casey feels like the land belongs to him, even though he didn't pay a dime for it."

"Why do you think there's going to be trouble?" Alice whispered.

"We have guns, and the Caseys have guns. They hired a few sharpshooters, and so has Garcia, just to keep things even. It's an old fight, the settlers versus the Spanish colonists. It bubbles over every so often like boiling water on the stove; it's bound to happen again."

"Why do you have to be here for it when it does?"

"I told you to promise not to worry. I've been looking out for myself for a long time."

"I thought you left New Mexico. Why are you here, doing this? It sounds dangerous."

"I was going to leave New Mexico when Javier told me he and his family needed help. The pay is good, and the rations and the sleeping arrangements aren't too terrible. I figure I'll make sure everything ends peacefully here, make some money, and head west. Maybe I might try my luck in California, what do you say? Doesn't that sound like paradise on earth,

California? A man has room to breathe in place like that."

"I thought you liked New Mexico. It's lawless here, you told me when I first met you."

"I love New Mexico, but a man like me has got to do something with his life other than gamble and live by his wits and his gun. In California I could do that, or maybe up in Montana. With some money in my pocket, I'll be free to go anywhere I want to go and be anyone I choose."

Alice thought about what he said; he was leaving as soon as this dispute was settled. Did that mean she would never see him again? She tried not to dwell on that, while Mama Rosa approached the table with the young man who was holding a tray of fried bread dough drizzled with honey. Alice could only surmise that this must be the sopapillas.

"Senor Keene, Senorita, how is the food today?" Mama Rosa asked as she smiled broadly at her guests.

"Delicious. You make the best tamales I've ever eaten!" Jonathan replied.

"I make the only tamales you've ever eaten. Where does a man like you find good home cooking like mine, hmmm?" The older woman said as she glanced at Alice.

"I'm in no need of home cooking when I have you to keep me as fat and happy as a hog," he answered.

"This is my grandson; he wants to learn the business," she said as she put her arm around the young man's shoulders. "Family is important, isn't it? Maybe you should think about one of your own." Mama Rosa's English was heavily accented.

"Maybe I should," Jonathan winked at Alice.

Alice was infuriated. What made him delight in teasing her about making a future together as man and wife, when he had absolutely no intention of doing anything like that?

"Senorita, you teach at the mission, si?" Mama Rosa asked as she spoke to Alice.

"Si," Alice replied.

"You should make haste to go back. The sky, it doesn't look so good," Mama Rosa said as she peered out of the window.

"Don't you worry about the senorita over here, I'll see that she gets back to the mission," said Jonathan as he reached for a sopapilla. "Did you make these fresh? They smell better than heaven."

"Eat your sopapillas, and don't waste any time. The sky doesn't look good. You don't want to get caught in the rain, not tonight." Mama Rosa cleared their plates and left with her grandson on her heels.

Alice stared out of the window. She couldn't see anything different about the sky except for a few clouds that looked harmless to her. "Why was Mama Rosa worrying about the sky? I don't see anything out of the ordinary."

"Don't let her worry you. It's common on days as warm as this in winter for Santa Maria to get a few drops of rain. Eat your sopapillas before they get cold."

Alice didn't argue with Jonathan because the dessert was as delicious as everything else she had consumed. Did it rain in Santa Maria in December? She could remember a small rain shower back in October, and then another one in November, but they were over so quickly she barely noticed them at all.

*****

"I need to stop by the general store for a few things before I return to the mission. If I hurry, I should be back before sunset," Alice said as Jonathan paid for their dinner. She intended to leave him at the restaurant, but he didn't seem to hear her.

Walking out onto the street, Alice could feel that the wind had picked up, but only slightly. There was a chill to the air, which made her even more grateful for the shawl wrapped around her arms. Holding out her hand to Jonathan, she said, "This is where I say goodbye, I can't be seen with you in the general store. I've been far too bold to be seen with you walking down the street and having dinner."

"Go to Garcia's store. His prices are better and he has more merchandise. If he sees you're with me, he might give you a discount," Jonathan said as he steered her towards the new store at the end of the street.

"I appreciate the dinner and the gift of the shawl, but I'm not *with* you. You've made that clear. I don't know what you want with me, but I wish you would decide."

"I know what I want, but you're not the kind of woman who wants to live like I do. I can see it in your eyes. You want a house, a good man, and children. That's not me, Colleen. Why can't you be content with being with me just as I am? We have fun together, don't we, you and me? You know how I feel about you and I know how you feel about me. Isn't that enough?" he looked at her with a faint frown.

But a second later the frown was gone, and he was the same Jonathan she knew so well, smug, handsome and always smirking. "Come on, that's enough talk about that. Mama Rosa was right, you need to get back to the mission before nightfall. It's going to rain. It may be one heck of a storm; the territories are due for a good gully washer."

"I won't be long at the store. With Las Posadas all week long, I don't know when I'll have another chance to sneak away from the mission," Alice explained, choosing to ignore the frustration in Jonathan's voice when he spoke about the two of them.

"If you hurry, I'll see you get back home before you're drenched like a drowned rat. Come on!" he ordered her and she offered no resistance as she followed him through the thinning crowds of people.

When she reached the storefront, she looked at the market, which earlier in the day had been a bustling place filled with people. It was less crowded now, as

195

the stalls and tables were being cleared of the items that didn't sell and the townspeople were heading home for the day. Alice felt a small twinge of apprehension. Did the people who were raised in these parts anticipate a bad storm?

Inside the store, she felt calm, like nothing could happen to her, whether it was a storm or anything else. The other general store was large and filled with farming implements, but this store was different. There were farming tools hanging from the ceiling and the walls, but there was also an astonishing amount of cloth, ribbons, and every manner of button a woman could wish for. Candy lined the shelves in glass jars, penny toys were displayed in baskets. Pencils, slates, and ledgers sat beside all manner of household goods. Most delightful was the vast amount of food and dry goods that was offered. Alice inhaled the aromas of coffee, flour, spices, and sugar.

"How is business today?" Jonathan greeted a small man in his thirties, who stood beside a woman who appeared to be roughly Joanna's age.

"Very good, my friend," the man replied, as he glanced around nervously. "But we've had some bad luck."

Jonathan directed Alice to finish her shopping as he accompanied the man to the back of the store. Alice was curious what was going on, but she did as he suggested, picking out a bag of peppermints, a bag of lemon drops, and several bright ribbons and buttons. She also saw a small carved horse that she was sure one of the children at the mission might like, so she added it and a few other penny toys to her purchases. By the time Jonathan reemerged, she had amassed a small pile of goodies.

Jonathan was right about Javier, he did give her a good price. Alice thanked him warmly as he wrapped her purchases in paper.

"Gracias," Javier said to her as she followed Jonathan out of the store.

"You need to get back to the mission. I don't know what might happen here in town tonight, but it's probably not where you or the children from the mission want to be. Javier told me that someone tried to set fire to the store today while there were customers inside."

"What? Fire? I didn't see any sign of a fire."

"It started out back, in the store room. He lost some merchandise, but he managed to put it out before it could spread. Luckily for the Caseys, my horse wasn't harmed. At least they had the sense not to set fire to the barn out back. The Caseys don't want Javier in business, so I fear that this is only the beginning. Javier's father won't be content to let this insult go, but it's not him I'm worried about. If the Caseys were willing to do this in broad daylight, what else might they try?"

"Jonathan, are you certain it was the Caseys that started the fire?"

"Javier is certain of it. He's been getting threats for some time, warning him to close his store. If I know his father, he'll want to retaliate."

"You don't mean that you're going to do anything to hurt anyone, do you?" Alice asked as she looked at him warily.

"No, that's not the kind of man I am. I'm here to protect the Garcias and their property. I'm not here to start any kind of trouble. I may be a hired gun but I'm no outlaw."

"I don't think we have to worry about the children being in town tonight," Alice said as she gazed at the sky. The white clouds from late in the afternoon had turned a dark gray color that appeared even darker on the horizon. The wind whipped around her dress and she saw a drop fall to the dusty ground in front of her. Rain was coming to Santa Maria, and she was far away from the mission.

Jonathan looked at the clouds. "Colleen, it appears that you have three choices. You can stay here in town for the night. You may return to the mission on your own two feet and be soaked through to the bone – though you may catch a chill and your packages will be ruined. Lastly, you may allow me to take you home."

"I can't stay here; I'm not even supposed to be gone. If I were out past dark, Sister Cecilia would send me packing! And you can't take me home, not to the mission. You can't just deposit me at the door, what will Sister Cecilia say?" The wind picked up, and with it the rain.

"I can take you near the door, how about that? You can run the rest of the way if you must, but decide, because the storm is coming," Jonathan held out his hand.

Alice knew she didn't have much of a choice. Even if she ran back to the mission she would be drenched. Placing her hand in his, she ran behind him as he led her to the lean-to that served as a barn. A tall black horse pawed the ground as he turned his enormous head to look at Jonathan.

"Whoa, there, Goliath. Whoa." Jonathan untied the horse from a hitching post.

"I can't ride with you on a horse! That would be indecent!" Alice exclaimed as she sheltered under the roof of the lean-to. The rain was coming quicker now, splattering against the ground outside.

"Indecent? It's about to rain hard – harder than it has in a long time. People are inside their houses, not standing on the streets gawking. No one will see you; I give you my word. Once we get out of town, there will be even fewer people to see you. Do you want my help? I can stay here, if you prefer."

Alice bit her lip, unsure of what to do. She couldn't stay in town, she couldn't ride with a man on a horse, and walking back would be horrible. She didn't have much of a choice, she thought to herself.

"Colleen, I'm willing to face catching my death to see you safely home. Come on, give me those packages and your hand," he said, ordering her in a stern voice.

Alice didn't hesitate any longer. She handed him every package she had, and prayed that she and Jonathan wouldn't be seen. The wind wailed under the roof of the lean-to, causing the horse to shake his head in apprehension as Jonathan shoved the presents into a pair of saddlebags before he held out his hand to her once more. "Climb up and hold on," he said.

The horse was tall, taller than any horse Alice had ever stood beside. Jonathan folded his fingers together, making a step for her and hoisting her up. She tried to smooth her skirt, but there was simply no way of making this predicament proper. Climbing into the saddle behind her, he wrapped his arms around her and held on to the reins. The horse backed away from the lean-to and headed towards the street.

Chapter Seven

Goliath galloped swiftly, flying over the ground as Alice leaned against Jonathan. His strong arms encircled her, and she gripped the saddle horn with all her might. She was aware of his body behind hers in the saddle, even through the corset and the layers of crinoline under her skirt. She could feel his body heat radiate from him as his chest pressed into her back, his thighs snug behind hers. Riding like this, so close to him, was indecent, as her thoughts soon became. She was glad Jonathan couldn't see her blushing as Goliath galloped to the edge of town, carrying them swiftly along the dirt roads that were becoming creeks.

The storm was growing worse by the minute as the rain fell in torrents. Alice could barely see in front of her as the rain hit her face. Leaning back against Jonathan, she felt a twinge of guilt. She should be sitting straight as an arrow, as far away from him as she could get. That would be the decent thing to do, but she didn't want to be decent. She wanted to wrap her arms around him, she wanted to kiss him, to feel his lips against hers as they held each other.

Shocked that her thoughts were taking such a sinful turn, she tried to block Jonathan out of her mind, but she couldn't. He was too near, his masculine scent all around her as she leaned the back of her head against his shoulder.

"Hold on, the road looks likes it's almost washed away," he said as he gripped Goliath with his powerful thighs and she felt the muscles flex in his arm as he urged the horse over the rivers of water flowing over the road.

"It's a good thing you didn't try to walk back to the mission," Jonathan leaned down and said to her, his mouth near her ear. "You could have been washed away."

Jonathan urged Goliath on as the storm continued to dump enormous amounts of rain on the desert. Dry creek beds sprang back to life as water flowed through them again. The road was becoming treacherous. Jonathan urged the horse to jump over the worst of the washouts. Alice closed her eyes and held on. She could hear the roar of water rushing along the road, and the wind around her skirts as they rode furiously towards the mission.

"You can't get back to the mission from here, the road is too dangerous," Jonathan said as he steered his horse from the roadway and into the countryside.

"Where are you taking me? I can't be seen with you," she said desperately.

"No one will see anything, not in this weather. Do you trust me?" he asked, his breath hot against her cheek.

"I trust you," she said, even though she knew she shouldn't. What choice did she have? The road was dangerous, the countryside was flooding, and she wasn't back to the mission yet.

Jonathan urged Goliath around rocks and through raging water, but it was a while before Alice could see the outline of the mission ahead. She was drenched and exhausted. She prayed that none of the sisters would see her sneaking back in through the garden, but she wasn't just worried about herself; she was worried about Jonathan and his horse.

"Over there, do you see the wall? That's the wall of the garden; it connects to the courtyard and the barn," Alice said, trying to be heard over the pouring rain.

"I see it," he said.

Goliath seemed to sense the urgency as he raced towards the mission, being reined towards the garden wall by his master. Alice held on, praying that they would arrive safely as the horse's feet slipped and stuck in the soggy ground.

"There isn't anywhere dry to set you down, Alice," Jonathan said to her. The sound of her name was almost as startling as the harrowing ride through the rain-soaked desert.

"I'll soon be dry, but what about you and Goliath? It's too dangerous to go back to town."

"We'll manage. That pueblo might give us shelter, if not…" he didn't finish the sentence.

"Promise me you'll wait for me on the other side of the barn. Do you see it?" Alice asked as Jonathan urged Goliath to the garden wall, beside a low wooden door.

"What are you thinking? You're not going to suggest anything improper, are you?" Jonathan slid down from the horse and reached for her.

She felt his hands on her waist as he helped her down, his grip through the wet clothes that hung from her body. She looked up at him, even as the rain fell into her eyes. Without warning she leaned up and kissed him, forgetting about being discovered or any other dangers she'd thought she cared about.

He pressed against her, his body against hers, and kissed her harder than he had at the Ortega's house. There was an urgency in this kiss, a feeling she hadn't known existed. She wanted more, but first she had to get him and his horse out of the storm. Forgetting about her presents, she rushed inside the low wooden door, thankful it was unlocked.

Racing through the garden, past the rows of vegetables, she dashed into the barn. She found the double wooden door facing the outside of the mission to be heavier than she expected as she removed the board bracing them and opened them to the weather. Jonathan and Goliath were on the other side, both as drenched as she was. They walked through the doors into the dry barn that held the sheep, goats, and horses of the mission. Jonathan closed the doors behind himself, bracing them as he looked around the dark space. Alice felt her way along the wall until she found the lantern.

"Do you have a way to light it?" she asked.

"I do, Colleen," he said, returning to the name he had given her. "What are you doing?"

Alice didn't know exactly how to answer that question. She thought about it while he lit the lamp and handed it back to her.

"I believe you know where this goes," he said.

In the falling temperature his breath hung in the air, visible in the faint light of the lantern. She was risking everything by bringing him inside the grounds of the mission, by hiding him and his enormous horse in the barn. He was a stranger, a man Sister Cecilia didn't know, and the same one she'd asked about when Alice first arrived at the mission.

"I don't know what I'm doing, but I can't let you and Goliath drown because of me. I shouldn't have snuck away from the mission today. You didn't have to buy me a gift or dinner, and you didn't have to bring me home. I don't know what would have happened to me if you hadn't brought me back. I can't let you go back out there, you might be killed," she said as the rain hammered against the tiles of the roof overhead and the wind shook the great wooden doors.

"I can't let you ruin your life or your reputation because I was reckless. I didn't have to bring you home. I knew the roads would be bad; I should have insisted you stay in town. It's not your fault that I made a bad decision. If I leave now, maybe Goliath and I can make it to the pueblo."

"You don't know if they'll take you in, do you?"

"It's Las Posadas, isn't it? Me and my horse, seeking shelter?" he laughed.

"You're wet through and shivering and you're still incorrigible. Stay here, at least until the storm ends. As long as you're quiet, no one will ever know you were here. Sister Cecilia doesn't come out to the barn very much. It's normally up to Thomas to take care of the animals, and me and sometimes Sister Gabriella, but she's been tending to the sick."

"Are you suggesting that I stay the night? Here in a barn?" Jonathan asked as he stepped closer to Alice, causing her shivers to turn to tingles of anticipation.

"I'm suggesting that you and Goliath have a safe place to stay until you can go back to Santa Maria, and nothing else."

"Is that why you kissed me outside, because you don't want anything else?" His eyes sparkled in the lantern light.

Alice swallowed. She wanted more than a kiss, even if she wasn't sure what that was. She knew she wanted to feel his arms around her, the scent of his skin filling her senses, but she resisted the temptation she found mirrored in his eyes.

"Forgive me, Colleen. I didn't mean to say that. It was your kiss. That kind of kiss makes a man wonder about...well, about a lot of things best left for another conversation. I can't stay here. You're a teacher, you can't be caught offering me shelter. It's not proper; I'll go," he said as he opened his saddlebags and removed the presents. They were damp, but not drenched.

"Here. These are yours," he said as he handed her the packages. "If you give Goliath some water and hay, we'll be on our way before anyone even knows we paid a visit to the mission."

"No. Jonathan, listen to me." She set the parcels down on a wooden bench nearby. "I can't bear to think of either you or your horse out there tonight. I've heard that wagons, horses, and cows get trapped and drown in these floods. If you drowned I would never forgive myself. Stay a little while at least, for my sake. If Sister Cecilia wants to punish me, let her. I will not have your death on my conscience. Offering shelter to someone in need is not a sin. If she doesn't understand that, then maybe I don't belong here."

Jonathan stared at her, his expression unreadable as he gathered her in his arms once more. Instead of kissing her lips he held her, his lips grazing her forehead. "You care about me, don't you?"

"Yes, I do. I thought you knew that."

"I knew it, but you would risk everything you've worked for, for me?"

"It's not just for you, it's about what I know in my heart I should do. How can I turn away the man who may have saved my life tonight, and who saved my life in Santa Fe?"

He sighed. "If you insist, Colleen. I suppose my horse and I could stay for a while," Jonathan said as he rubbed her shoulders. "You're soaked, and you're going to catch your death if you don't change into something dry."

"You too," she said. "You're going to be sick, all because of me. Wait here. I'll see what I can find."

"Where are you going?" he asked.

"To the mission," she said as she gathered the presents. With a peck on his cheek, she was gone.

Alice retuned an hour later in a plain brown frock, bearing a basket that was nearly as wet as she was when she arrived at the barn. She found Jonathan tending to his horse in an empty stall, and she watched as he gently whispered to Goliath, comforting him as the storm raged outside. She knew that she would be in terrible trouble if he was found, but how could she ask him to leave? She was always so concerned for what may happen to her if she should be thrown out of the mission, but Jonathan wasn't like that. He didn't think twice about putting himself or his majestic steed in harm's way for her. She could be more like him, if she only tried. If she was more daring and less worried about what may happen. Maybe that's what he meant when he said she wasn't the kind of woman who could live like he did.

"How long have you been standing there?" he said in a slight Irish accent.

"I love that accent, when you say words that sound Irish," she whispered as she walked towards him.

"You should hear my Gaelic to appreciate what real Irish sounds like, Colleen," he said with smile.

"Say something in Gaelic," she murmured as she found a place on a pile of clean, fresh-smelling straw in the stall to sit on and unpack the hamper.

"You won't understand a word I'm saying, will you, lassie?"

She shook her head. "That doesn't matter. I just want to hear your voice; say something, please."

"Tá tú álainn, mo dhaor. Is breá liom tú," he said as he walked towards her.

"What did you say?" she asked, her eyes locked on his.

"That you are beautiful," he said as he sat beside her in the straw.

"Is that all that you said?" she teased.

"No, but I'm not going to tell you the rest, not yet."

"I brought some coffee from the kitchen. There's a slice of bread as well, it's all I could manage," she explained as he drew near to her while she poured a cup of coffee, giving the cup to him.

"This is fine, something hot to warm my bones. Thank you, Colleen," he said as he reached for the cup, sipping it as the steam rose. "You make a fine thief, don't you, my dear little outlaw."

"I wasn't being a thief! I have a right to drink coffee and eat bread, and I'm sharing my portion with you. I brought a blanket. It may be slightly damp, but it's all I could spare."

"Thank you for the hospitality, I can't remember when I've ever spent a more comfortable night in a barn," he said.

"How do you know Gaelic and Spanish? You seem too well educated for a hired gun and a gambler," she replied as he handed the empty cup back to her.

He laughed. "It's a wonder to me, your notions and ideas. Calling me well educated when I speak Gaelic. That's not how the English see it, not at all. In Galway, where my family is from, they were punished for speaking it, and called ignorant. Spanish? That's the language of the territories. I picked it up here and there, but the Gaelic, my own mother spoke it to me since I was a boy."

"Where do you come from? You told me once, up north somewhere, wasn't it?"

As she packed the coffee cup back into the hamper, Jonathan slid off his jacket, revealing a vest and shirt that were soaked and sticking to his muscled chest. She gasped at the sight as he ran his fingers through his dark hair. "Don't you go fainting on me."

"Why would I faint?" she asked, knowing full well that if he took anything else off, the sight of his arms and his rippling chest would be more than enough to send her into a fainting spell.

"I'm sure a woman like you wouldn't faint; that would be improper. Talk to me, why don't you? I've told you enough about me. I want to know about you," he said as he lay down on the straw, the blanket folded under his head, against her leg.

She had never been this close to a man who was laying down. She reached out, tentatively at first, and stroked his hair. His hair was thick and wavy. From his hair, she caressed his brow as she spoke to him. His eyes closed as he murmured occasionally as she told him about her life until at last he was asleep.

Leaning down, she kissed his forehead and watched him sleep on her lap. He was handsome, and dashing, and he had a streak of the hero in him that made him more than a scoundrel. He wasn't going anywhere that night, not as the rain pelted the roof. Every part of her wanted to remain at his side in the barn. She wanted to close her eyes and lie down next to him, nothing more, just to feel the comfort of knowing he was near to her and safe. Her lips softly touched his forehead again, as she whispered good night to him.

She would leave him, so he could sleep and so that she could return to her place at the mission. She had a feeling he would be gone by first light. Kissing him again, she whispered goodbye, not knowing when, or if, she would ever see him again.

*****

December 18, 1876

Alice was not expelled from the mission. She was not sent packing, nor was she asked to leave. She was, however, heavily censured, her behavior was questioned, and she was thoroughly scolded for sneaking out of the mission without permission even if it was to purchase Christmas presents for the children. Standing in Sister Cecilia's office on Monday afternoon before dinner, Alice felt like she was a child once again.

"I am astonished at your behavior! You should have told me where you were going. What were you thinking? It's a miracle you arrived safely back when you did, do you know that? You could have been killed."

Alice listened to the lecture stoically as she remembered what *else* she was guilty of that Sister Cecilia didn't know about. She silently listened to every rule she had broken as Sister Cecilia continued her tirade. To Alice's way of thinking there weren't many rules of being a teacher at the mission that she had left unbroken, from socializing with a strange man to bringing a man onto the mission grounds. She deserved to be barred from the mission, but she didn't tell Sister Cecilia any of that, which was a lie of omission. Perhaps she would confess her wrongdoing one day.

"You're supposed to be a role model to the children. You're supposed to be leading a godly life. Is breaking the rules of the mission and violating the trust I placed in you leading a godly life?" Sister Cecilia glowered at Alice.

"No Sister Cecilia, it's not." Alice looked down at her feet, just like the children in her classroom did when they were being scolded.

"I am aware that your heart was clearly guided by generosity to the children in your care, but that does not excuse your behavior. Not at all. I am counting on you to take charge of the children for Las Posadas. Am I to worry that you will sneak away and not return at the proper hour? That you will leave the children to fend for themselves in the cold?"

"No, Sister. You may rely on me."

"What about during your class time? Am I to expect that you will sneak away when you should be teaching?"

"No, Sister Cecilia."

"Miss Cleary, I do not wish to reprimand you. You have proven satisfactory in your position as a teacher here. I am grateful that you have traveled a long distance to come to the mission to take up the mantle of teaching and you have done well up until now. I have often been impressed by your maturity. Was my trust mistaken?"

"No, Sister Cecilia. I will do better. You have my word."

"Very well. I expect you to go to confession. You will want to unburden your soul of your wrongs and sins. For me, I expect that you will add the job of cleaning the kitchen in the mornings and at night to your tasks."

"How am I to do that, when I already see to the stables and help with Las Posadas?"

"You will find a way. You are also strictly confined to the mission except on mission business until further notice, do you understand?"

"Yes, Sister Cecilia," Alice replied.

"Consider this a lesson learned. Report to the stables to see if Thomas or Sister Gabriella needs any additional help, and then go to the kitchen when you return this evening before you retire."

Alice nodded and turned to leave the office of the abbess. She wasn't sure how she would ever fit in the additional tasks, but she would find a way. Feeling slightly sorry for herself, she was surprised to hear Sister Cecilia call out to her.

"A letter arrived for you from town," the abbess said as she slid open a desk drawer and pulled out a letter, which she handed to Alice. "One more thing, Miss Cleary. Use the time you are confined to the mission to pray, to ask God to forgive you. You will find that He will lift the burden of sin from your heart if you show repentance."

Alice slipped the letter into her pocket as she left the office, closing the door behind her. On her way to the stable she stopped in a quiet alcove of the corridor, a place where a statue of the Virgin was beautifully decorated with flowers and lit by a narrow window in the stone. It was a peaceful place, a place where Alice didn't think she would be de disturbed, as she was overwhelmed with curiosity. The letter wasn't from her sister or her brother, and it wasn't from Joanna. It was from Pastor Newland.

Carefully opening the envelope, she almost dropped it as she heard someone walk past her. Looking up, she saw the stern features of Sister Rafaela, who frowned at Alice as she passed. Alice nodded to the sister and concealed the letter behind her skirt until she was alone again.

In the envelope, she felt something cold and metallic. Peering in, she saw the glint of silver. Slowly, she slid the letter out. With it came a silver cross. The cross was small, as was the chain it was attached to, thin and braided but delicate, she thought, as she held it up to the light. Glancing at the letter she read the message that accompanied the jewelry.

Pastor Newland had sent the necklace two weeks ago, before she knew she wasn't coming to Kansas for the holiday. She remembered asking Will and Louisa not to mention her plans to anyone in case the distance or the money for the ticket were out of her reach. They must have kept their secret, because Pastor Newland clearly didn't get the message that she was supposed to have been in Kansas.

The necklace, he wrote, was a Christmas gift. He hoped she liked it and would wear it as a reminder of her savior and his own devotion to her. Reading his letter, she was astounded at his presumption. She had met him once and written to him a few times, but that was all. He should not be sending her presents, least of all jewelry or anything of a personal nature. It raised the question in her mind, what did the pastor want from her? Did he wish to marry her?

Looking at the necklace in her hand, she admitted she was grateful for the gift. She couldn't accept it, yet she was afraid to send it back through the mail is case something should happen to it. It would be better to return it in the spring, when she saw the pastor in person. By then she would know what she wanted to do; whether she wanted to 'settle down with a good man' as Jonathan said, or continue to wait until she found a man like Jonathan, only without the dissolute life.

Slipping the necklace and the letter into the envelope, she slid it into her pocket and walked out of the mission to the barn. She found Thomas in the stables, tending to the horse who looked like she could give birth at any minute.

"Thomas, I was told to come see you and ask if you have additional work that you need done," she explained.

"Not a thing. You do too much already, if you ask me."

"I have to do more. I got into trouble."

"I heard all about it, Senorita. Running off to Santa Maria, when a storm came in. You could have been drowned, or worse. There was trouble in town that night, just like I've been telling you."

"There was? I heard about a fire at a store," she said vaguely as she tried not to look at the stall where she last saw Jonathan.

216

"More than that. There was gunfight and a murder."

"What? Did you say a murder? When? On Saturday?"

"On Saturday. Even with all that rain, folks still found a way to shoot up the main street of town. The sheriff rounded up every man that fellow Garcia hired. He says they're going to hang."

"Hang?" Alice asked, riveted. "What for?"

"Why, murder of course. One the Caseys wound up dead, and the ones that survived say the Garcia fellows were trying to steal horses, which is a hanging crime. Then there was the gunfight and a killing, all during that big old storm. The sheriff is going to hang the whole lot of them. I heard it while I was in town picking up the mail. Best if you stay out of Santa Maria for a while. Don't even take the children until it's over."

"Did you say the sheriff is going to hang the whole lot of them? *Every* man who worked for Garcia?"

"Every one of them. They rounded them all up this morning – seems the last one was hiding in the back of Mama Rosa's."

Alice didn't need to know the rest. She had a horrible feeling that Jonathan was the man who was found at Mama Rosa's. He couldn't be guilty of horse stealing and murder, not when he was here at the mission. She didn't know what to do, except to head into town and find out the truth. Was Jonathan arrested?

Was he going to hang? Remembering Sister Cecilia's order not to go to Santa Maria, Alice knew she had no choice. If Jonathan was going to hang for a crime he didn't commit, she was going to provide his alibi.

*****

Alice was terrified. Was Jonathan going to hang for crimes he didn't commit? Standing in the barn, she wept from fear. Was Jonathan the last of Garcia's men to be arrested? She didn't know, but she had a terrible suspicion he was in trouble. If Thomas was right about all Garcia's hired men being rounded up, Jonathan could not have escaped unless he left town. Praying that he had managed to slip away, she knew that it was little more than a dream. He was not the kind of man to run away from a fight or be disloyal to men he respected, like the Garcias. She had to do something, and that something was defy Sister Cecilia.

"I shouldn't have told you about the trouble in town; I've gone and upset you." Thomas frowned.

"I'm grateful that you told me what happened."

"Grateful? You don't look it to me. You're crying. I should have known a story like that would be a shock. I forget sometimes that I'm talking to a lady. There, there, no need for you to cry. The sheriff has the town safe and sound; no need for you to worry about a thing."

"You dear old soul, Thomas, I'm not worried about me," she replied as she wiped away her tears.

"You worried about the children? There's not a thing in the world for you to fear; I'll have the horse and wagon hitched by the time you finish your dinner. I'm going to be with you tonight, and no one's going to mess with old Thomas; you have my word. Delia here will be fine without me while I'm gone to town with you, won't you girl?" he asked as he gently patted the pregnant horse.

Alice sighed, exasperated. "I can't be worrying about las posadas tonight – I have to get into town. You said those men who worked for Garcia are going to hang. Isn't there a trial? Don't they get a jury?"

"You ain't been in the territories very long, have you? Around these parts, the sheriff does what he likes. Nobody around here is going to say much about it. Who in Santa Maria is going to side with a horse thief? Justice will come to those fellows, no matter what the law books say."

Feeling faint, Alice reached for a bench as Thomas rushed to her aid. "You feeling alright? You look like you're liable to faint."

"I'm fine, Thomas, but I have to get to town. If the sheriff is going to hang these men there isn't a minute to lose."

"Whoa, hold on there. No one is getting hanged tonight; it will be dawn when he does it. What are you doing? You're already in a heap of trouble for going to town by yourself. You nearly died the last time you done it, and you want to go and do it again?"

"I have to."

"Sister Cecilia won't have it, no ma'am. You're in trouble enough as it is. You about to go turning your nose up at what she done told you? I heard she told you to stay put in this mission. If you go to Santa Maria she's going to be madder than a wet setting hen!"

"I know," Alice answered, hanging her head. "You're right, I know."

"You listen to old Thomas," he said to her, pointing a crooked finger in her direction. "You're a good woman and a darn fine teacher, but you ain't got the common sense God gave a mule sometimes. I don't mean no harm by telling you that, but it's God's own truth. Listen up; you best be doing as Sister says or there'll be hell to pay."

"If it were up to me, I would listen to Sister Cecilia and do just what she says, but this isn't about me. I have to see the sheriff. There's a life at stake."

Thomas peered at her with a wary look in his eye as he rubbed his grizzled chin with his gnarled fingers. "I don't know what kind of foolish notion you got in that pretty little head of yours but I can see you've dug your boots in. You're a stubborn sort, aren't you? I can see there ain't no use trying to tell you any different, is there?"

"No, there isn't. I just hope I'm not too late, is all."

He sighed. "Well, then. If you're set on going to town, don't go against Sister Cecilia's wishes. Wait until after you and the children have had your dinner. We were going to town tonight for the young'uns to have their part in las posadas. Might as well go into town like you planned. If you want to go see the sheriff then, I'll make sure get there."

"Thomas!" Alice exclaimed. "You would do that for me?"

"Don't tell a soul, or you'll get us both in a heap of trouble. I'm doing it for you, senorita, but there's a lot you ain't telling me. If you're dead set on seeing the sheriff, I reckon there has to be reason."

"You dear man," she said as she kissed him on the cheek. She drew back, reddening. "I'm sorry Thomas, I didn't mean to do that."

He laughed. "No need for saying sorry. It's been a long time since a pretty woman gave me a peck on the cheek. Dry your eyes and don't cry no more; I can't take it. I got enough to worry me with Delia here about to be a mother and you scheming to get yourself in trouble. I don't know what you intend to do at the sheriff's office but you better be sure about it. He's not like me – he's a hard man and he don't take kindly to anyone questioning him."

Alice's smile faded, but her resolve didn't. After dinner, she and Thomas were going to town in the company of a wagon load of children heading for las posadas. She didn't know what was going to happen, but she was feeling hopeful – and more than a little frightened.

*****

The children sang songs and marched in the
procession as Alice nervously looked toward the main
street of Santa Maria. The jail was not far from the post
office or Garcia's general store. She suppressed the
urge to run towards the building, not stopping until she
opened the door and told the sheriff that Jonathan was
innocent. She had a terrible feeling that he was in there,
awaiting his fate with the rest of Garcia's men. Stealing
horses in a storm, that didn't make any sense to her, not
at all.

"Thomas," she whispered as they walked behind
the children, "Did you say the men were stealing
horses? In that storm? They couldn't have got far if
they did, not with the flooding."

"That's what I heard. I didn't say I thought they
had good judgment. What kind of man steals horses just
to see 'em drown? I can't figure it out, but that don't
mean one of the Casey boys didn't wind up dead as a
doornail."

"What about the fire? Was there anybody
arrested for setting it?"

"What fire? You mean the one that started at
that store, the one run by the Garcias?"

"That's the one. Was anyone arrested for it?"

"I haven't heard a word about it. I'd be
surprised. Casey and the sheriff are good buddies, like

brothers. They go way back. Best I can tell, the sheriff took old man Casey at his word. No question there was shootout on the street – everyone in town heard it –but we best not be talking about this here in front of the young'uns. Don't want to give 'em the frights."

"Neither do I, but I'm scared that some of the men in that jail didn't do anything wrong. I know one of them is innocent but there might be more than one innocent man who's going to die. Why would Mr. Garcia send his men to steal horses in the middle of a flood? Why would he want to stir up that kind of trouble when he just bought more land and his son opened a store?"

"Senorita," Thomas said, "What you're saying makes sense to me, but I ain't the sheriff and I ain't Garcia. Who can say what he told his men to go and do? Revenge and anger make men act mighty peculiar."

"Peculiar? Maybe, but that doesn't strike me as the kind of thing a man who wants to build his business goes out and does, stealing horses from his neighbors. That's ridiculous."

"You might be right, but that's the crime they're accused of, that, and shooting one of the Casey boys. Heck, it don't amount to a hill of beans difference what you and I got to say about it. The men Garcia hired are going to hang, and that's all there is to it."

"Not if I've got anything to say about it," Alice replied.

"Hold your horses. We'll get these young'uns herded up and back in the wagon first before you go running off to the jail. You're stirring up trouble if you ask me, a heap of it by the looks of it."

Alice patted Thomas on the shoulder. He was old, thin, and wiry but he wasn't frail. There was a sturdiness in his presence, in his voice, that she appreciated. She felt safe around him, and she was grateful he'd told her the truth, no matter how unpleasant. She knew he was risking Sister Cecilia's ire for taking her to the jail after the las posadas that evening.

Alice was more worried than she had ever been in her life, but not for herself. She was worried about Jonathan and the other men who'd been arrested. She wished she knew what had happened – they couldn't all be guilty, could they? As she walked beside the children, she tried to be cheerful for their sake. She knew her student Rose was watching her, keeping an eye on her, should she be sad. With the biggest smile she could muster she winked at little Rose, satisfying the girl's insatiable curiosity and instincts to mother Alice. Rose was going to be a smart, strong woman one day, Alice mused. She didn't miss a thing.

Alice wondered how many of the men sitting in the jail waiting to be hanged without a trial were fathers. Were they married? Were they going to leave children and wives behind? Shuddering, she tried not to think about that. She needed to get to the jail and see the sheriff. Praying for patience and God's mercy on anyone who was innocent, she walked beside Thomas, keeping her smile planted on her face. The children didn't need to know that inside, she was frantic.

An hour later, Thomas lifted the last of the children into the wagon. Rose tucked the blankets around herself and helped some of the other children her own age as Alice climbed into the seat. She was nervous, scared out of her wits at what she might find at the jail. Thomas cracked the reins and the old mare started walking forward.

What was she going to say? What would happen if the sheriff didn't believe her? She tried to push that possibility from her mind and stared straight ahead.

True to his word, Thomas stopped near the jail. He leaned close to Alice. "You best be quick about whatever it you're going to do. These young'uns will be mighty curious if you ain't back soon, you hear me?"

"Thank you, Thomas, thank you with all my heart," she said to him as she hopped down from the wagon seat.

Alice marched to the doors of the jail and took a deep breath before she tried the door. In the cold, her breath hung in the air as reached for the handle, illuminated by the warm lamp light coming from the window. The door was locked. Frantically, she knocked. Someone had to be there; the sheriff had to be there, she thought to herself.

"Hold on, don't break the door down," she heard a man's voice coming from inside. The door opened wide enough for her to see a young man's face peering out into the darkness.

"Who are you? What business do you have out at this time of night?" he asked. A badge on his vest glinted.

"Sir, please, if you let me in I can tell you."

"Let you in, to a jail? Do you have a crime to report?"

"Not a crime," she stammered.

"If you don't have any business here, why don't you run along? The streets aren't safe after dark for a woman by herself."

"I'm not by myself, please let me in. I will state my business but I have to know if you have a prisoner here, Jonathan Keene?"

The young man narrowed his eyes as he studied her. She felt the seconds slow down as if time were standing still as she watched him weigh his decision in his mind. With a scowl, he said, "Suit yourself; I can't have a woman freeze to death on the doorstep. Come in, but you best be quick about telling me why you came here."

Alice stepped inside the door, thankful for the warmth that came from a small iron stove in the corner of the sparsely furnished room. A desk sat in the middle of the floor, a few chairs lined the walls, and a chest of drawers was shoved in the corner opposite the stove. A coffee pot sat on the stove, giving the room the unmistakable smell of coffee, which she found comforting.

"Sir, are you the sheriff?" she asked, thinking he was young for such a venerable position.

"Not me," he chuckled. "I'm his nephew, Horace Dalton. Tell me what brings a lady like yourself to a jail late at night."

Alice stared at him, unsure where to begin. "Do you have prisoner here, a man by the name of Jonathan Keene?"

"Ma'am, I don't rightly know who all I have in this here jail. It ain't my job to keep up with their names, I just keep an eye on 'em and make sure they don't run away. If you want to take a peek and see if any of the men are the one you're looking for, I'll let you take a look – but I'm warning you, these ain't churchgoing men. I can't account for what they might say in the presence of a lady like yourself."

"Thank you, Mr. Dalton," Alice said as he reached for a lantern. Lighting it, he motioned for her to accompany him.

Alice had never stood inside a jail. She nervously followed him past the desk and into a gloomy hallway. Away from the cast iron stove she was cold again. There was no heat in the jail, nor was there any light. Horace Dalton held the lantern high as he led her to the jail cells. Alice shivered to see so many men housed in the cramped space. Heavy iron bars were all that stood between her and them, some of whom were likely criminals. For all she knew, she might be looking at murderers when she gazed into the darkness searching for Jonathan.

"If he's here, you'd best find him in a hurry. It's a cold night and I'm not hankering to be away from the stove for too long."

Alice studied the men in the cells. Many of them were laying on narrow cots, turned away from the light. She heard coughing coming from one of the men as she searched for a face she recognized, the face that belonged to Jonathan. She didn't see him. Maybe he'd escaped from Santa Maria before the sheriff found him? How could she tell if he was here, she wondered, when so many of them were huddled against the walls of their cells, turned away?

"Jonathan?" she called out. "Jonathan, are you in here? Please answer me."

"Put that light out," an unfriendly voice called from the darkness.

"I'll be Jonathan, Miss, if you're aiming to see me," another spoke to her with a chuckle.

"Leave her alone. Alice, is that you?"

Alice knew the sound of the voice in that last cell, farthest away from the office and the cast iron stove. Feeling her insides bunch into a knot of cold fear, she stepped away from Horace Dalton and immediately grasped the bars of the cell. Jonathan stood on the other side, his face pressed against the bars.

"Colleen, what are you doing here, you silly girl?"

"I'll ask you the same thing. What are you doing here? You didn't have a thing to do with anyone getting shot, so why are you in jail?"

"No one wanted to hear the truth. I should have made a run for it, but I couldn't. You see, Mama Rosa's nephew got arrested the day before they found me at the restaurant. I was trying to figure out a way to get him out of trouble when the sheriff came barging in. I ended up here. But Colleen, you don't need to be here, to see me or these men in jail. If you care about me, get going. Leave, and don't look back."

"Miss, you found him. You saw him; he's here. What more do you want? We don't have what you call visiting hours," Horace Dalton complained.

"Just a minute, Mr. Dalton, please," begged Alice.

"I'll give you a minute and that's all," Horace said in a huff.

"Colleen, if you won't take my advice and leave, can you do something for me? I have a letter I wrote to my mother; can you mail it for me? I don't want her to waste her life worrying about me anymore. If she doesn't know what happened to me she might spend years waiting for me to come home – when you and I know I'm not ever leaving Santa Maria."

Alice could feel the hot tears running down her cheeks. Her voice trembled as she took the paper he pressed between the bars. "Jonathan, don't talk like that. We both know you're innocent."

"We know it, but it doesn't matter to the sheriff. Half these men are innocent, but he doesn't seem to care. Look, that's not important. What's important is that I got to see you again. I can go to my grave knowing that I saw your face one more time, Colleen."

"You fool, don't say that. Not when I came to save you."

"You can't save me, but you're a brave girl for trying."

"I won't let you die for something you didn't do. It's not right," she replied, as she wiped away her tears.

"Colleen go on home and don't worry about me. I made my peace with the Lord. Know that I love you, and that I always have. You were the one girl I could have married."

"Jonathan don't talk like that, like you're going to die."

"I'm surprised it didn't happen before now. I've had an interesting life and there were some close shaves. I'm glad to have met you, my dear Colleen. Go now; I don't want to see you crying over me, not for one minute."

"Jonathan, I love you!" she sobbed.

"Come with me, miss. You've had your minute." Horace Dalton gripped her arm.

"Jonathan?" Alice called out but Jonathan had shrank away from the bars, into the darkness where she could no longer see him.

Alice dutifully followed the young man back to the office. Gathering her courage, she said, "Your uncle is the sheriff."

"Yes ma'am, he is."

"I have to speak with him. I can vouch for that man in there, and anyone related to Mama Rosa."

"Vouch for him? Unless you can give him an alibi, your vouching for him don't mean much. I can't bother my uncle with some hysterical woman, not when he has an early day tomorrow. Good thing you came by and said your piece, these men are going to hang tomorrow bright and early, mark my word."

"Mr. Dalton, I can provide an alibi."

"I bet you would say anything to get your man out of the hangman's noose, wouldn't you? Go home; there isn't anything you can do but mourn him. Be grateful I let you say goodbye to him."

Alice could see that Horace Dalton wasn't interested in hearing another word about alibis or vouching. With a heavy heart, she thanked him for allowing her to see Jonathan. Tomorrow morning would be too late and she had run out of time. When she returned to the wagon, she hung her head, crying silently. The children were tired and cold. Thomas would take her and the children back to the mission and she would find her way back to her room. Jonathan and the other innocent men would die in the morning, and there wasn't anything she could do about it.

Chapter Eight

"Sister Cecilia is going to be mad as fire I let you talk me into this. I don't know what good it's going to do. I need to be back at the barn with Delia, and you need to be back at the mission instead of out here in the cold. We're both going to catch our deaths if we ain't careful," Thomas said as he shook his head.

The children were returned to the mission and tucked into their beds. It was late, and the temperature was dropping as Alice and Thomas sat huddled together on the wooden wagon seat. Ahead on the dirt road was the town of Santa Maria. Alice had one more chance to save Jonathan. Thomas knew where the sheriff lived, and that was where they were heading. Alice felt slightly less guilty about defying Sister Cecilia now that the children were back home in their warm beds. If she was lucky, maybe Thomas would be back in the stables before Delia needed him.

"I don't know how I let you talk me into this," Thomas repeated. "It's a foolhardy notion, anyways, waking up the sheriff in the middle of the night. That ain't the way to get a man to listen to you."

"Thomas, what choice do I have? Those men are going to hang tomorrow; if I wait until then it will be too late."

"That's why I'm here, talking you back to town. I think you're plumb crazy but I know you would have gone back to town whether you had my help or not. Might as well let me take you so you get home safe."

"It won't matter if I'm safe or not. What am I going to do about the men who don't deserve to hang? The sheriff is going to be just like Horace Dalton, he won't listen to a thing I have to say, will he?"

"I can't say for sure what he's likely to do when you wake him out of his sleep. He might shoot us both for trespassing, never can tell."

Alice didn't disagree with Thomas as the sound of the horse's hooves on the dirt street echoed in the quiet town. Alice was desperate, frantic that she wasn't going to be able to save Jonathan. She didn't care what happened to her if he died; she would never forgive herself for not being able to save him.

Three blocks from the main street of the town, a row of wooden houses sat prim and proper. Fences surrounded yards just like they did in towns back east. If it wasn't for the lack of trees, Alice would have wondered if she wasn't in Georgia as she peered through the inky blackness of the night, searching for any sign that the sheriff might be awake at this hour.

Not a single light shone from any of the windows in the houses. Everyone must be asleep, she thought to herself as the wagon came to a stop outside a two story white clapboard house set between two nearly identical houses on either side.

"Let me hitch the horse, and then I'm coming in there with you, do you hear me? You don't have no place waking this man up but he might be a sight more forgiving if he sees you're with me."

"Yes, Thomas. I'm glad you're going to be with me, but I hope you won't think any less of me when you hear what I have to say to the sheriff."

"Senorita, you can't say a word to give this old heart a shock," he replied.

Alice steeled herself for disappointment as she and Thomas walked up the front steps of the sheriff's house. The air was cold as ice, freezing her through her coat and bonnet as she fought to keep her teeth from chattering.

"It smells like snow. It wouldn't surprise me none at all if we didn't get an early snow this year, seeing how cold it is," Thomas said as he reached his hand to the door to knock. "You sure about this? When we get this man out of his bed you best have something to say to make it worth his while."

Nodding her head vigorously, Alice answered, "Go ahead. I'm ready."

Thomas knocked on the door. The sound carried in the cold night air, echoing from the front porch of the sheriff's house and down the street. Alice was convinced that every person on the street must have heard the knock and would soon be wide awake.

"He must not have heard it," Thomas said as he stood on the porch, his hand raised to the door.

"Knock again. I have to speak to him, and you know it can't wait."

Above the porch, Alice heard the sound of a window being slammed open.

"What in tarnation is going on down there?" a man said from the second story of the house.

Thomas stepped down off the porch and out into the yard. Addressing the irate man who was leaning out the window above, Thomas spoke plainly. "Sheriff, how about you let me in and I'll tell you why I saw fit to wake you at this ungodly hour?"

"Thomas? Is that you? Have you taken leave of your senses? What in the name of God could be so darn important it couldn't wait until tomorrow?" the sheriff demanded.

"Just open the door. It's cold as a…well you know how that one goes, sheriff. I can't say it on account of I've got a lady with me."

"You got a lady with you? This better be good cause if it isn't I'm going to arrest you for disturbing the peace. Your lady friend, too."

"Come on down and arrest us both, then, Angus. Just open the cotton picking door," Thomas said to the sheriff.

Thomas joined Alice on the porch and gave her a stern look. "It looks like we've gone and done it now. I hope you got something good to say. If we ain't careful we might end up in jail with Garcia's men."

Alice was going to reply but she didn't have time to think of an answer. The door opened to reveal a short man wearing a robe over his long underwear. Alice blushed but didn't comment on the sheriff's lack of decorum.

"Come in; I'll get the fire going. You look half froze to death."

"I am froze. This cold gets in my bones, makes my joints ache something terrible. My horse ain't doing much better. We'll say our piece and be on our way." They followed the sheriff into the parlor.

"I don't care how long you're staying. I'm getting a fire burning then you can set a minute and tell me what brought you to my house in the middle of the night," the sheriff answered.

Thomas gestured to Alice. "This lady is who brung me to your door. She has something she needs to tell you."

"Sit down, both of you." The sheriff bent down in front of the fireplace. Alice watched as he started a fire, thankful that she would be warm while she was telling her story to the sheriff. She didn't know how much good it was going to do, but she had to try.

The fire blazed to life, the light glowing and illuminating the features of the sheriff's face. He was frowning, his face set in deep wrinkles and his eyes peering at Alice. "I don't know who you are but you better have a darn good reason for coming to my house."

"Sheriff Dalton, this here is Alice, Alice Cleary. She's one of the teachers at the mission. You probably seen her at church; she's here to talk to you about one of the men you got in the jail, one you arrested who worked for Garcia," explained Thomas.

"Miss Cleary, I'm not in the mood for any tearful pleas for mercy. I've heard my fair share all afternoon and I'm not going to hear another one. Those men are guilty of horse thieving and shooting a man. You might as well save your breath because I've made up my mind," the sheriff said coldly.

Alice knew she was in trouble; she also wondered how many people had been to see him. Maybe Mama Rosa was among them? There wasn't time to think about what she had to say anymore.

She spoke quickly. "Sir, sheriff, I'm not here to make a tearful pleas. I didn't wake you up for that kind of nonsense. I'm here to tell you that Jonathan Keene was not in Santa Maria Saturday night. I am here to provide an alibi for him."

"An alibi? What kind of alibi can you give for man who's guilty of horse thieving? Are you his wife? Do you love him? I bet you do. A school marm and an outlaw – what kind of lies has he been telling you to come here and save his hide? I don't have time for this, Miss Cleary."

Alice's cheeks burned. "I'm not his wife and he didn't tell me what to say. He was at the mission on Saturday night. He saved my life, carrying me home through the storm. He stayed at the mission all night…with me."

A log snapped in the fireplace as the sheriff stared at Alice. Alice knew there was no turning back.

"At the mission, with you? I wasn't aware that Sister Cecilia was in the habit of allowing sin under her roof."

"Sheriff Dalton, I didn't say he stayed in my room! How dare you suggest it; I'm not that kind of woman. He slept in the barn, he and his horse took shelter in the barn during the storm," Alice replied angrily. "Nothing else happened but it's no darn business of yours. All that matters is that he wasn't in town."

"Says you. Who else saw him in the barn? You want me to believe that, don't you? That he slept as innocent as a babe in the barn? You've wasted my time enough for one evening. Unless you have a witness that wasn't a horse or cow, you best be going now before I arrest you."

"Hold on one moment, Angus." Thomas rubbed his chin. "I didn't know who the fellow was at the time, but I went to the barn late that night and sure enough I saw a man sleeping in the hay, his horse hitched nearby. I didn't say a word because of the rain, mind you, or else I would have had plenty to say to him. It didn't seem Christian to throw him out in that kind of weather. She's telling the truth; he was there that night and he was there in the morning. I watched him head out at first light."

"Thomas, you don't know it was the same man. It could have been any stranger passing through, saw the barn and took shelter for the night," the sheriff replied.

"I'll know him if I see him again. You take me down to that jail and we'll just have a look see, won't we?"

Angus appeared disgusted as he shook his head. "Thomas, you better not be lying to me, so help you."

"When have I ever lied to you? Sheriff, this lady is telling you the truth. Even if I ain't seen the fellow with my own eyes I wouldn't have reason to doubt her word. She stands to get into a heap of trouble for telling you what she did. She didn't have to do it, but she did. I think you owe her an apology for saying what you did about her sinning at the mission. And what's more, how are you going to sleep at night when you hang a bunch of men who ain't done nothing wrong?"

Alice gasped. She hadn't been expecting Thomas to stand up for the innocent men in the jail.

The sheriff rounded on Thomas. "Thomas, I'm willing to let this fellow – what's his name?" the sheriff looked at Alice.

"Jonathan Keene."

"That man. I'm willing to let him off the hook if he swears to leave Santa Maria and never step foot back in my town ever again, but you're going too far."

"Are you sure about that? You want to be known as a hanging man? Folks in these parts won't forgive you for killing a bunch of men for no good reason."

"I know you got a lot of people who will listen to what you got to say, but I don't have to be one of them. You better steer clear, you hear me?"

"Angus, you're a reasonable man – at least you were before you got that badge pinned on your chest. You know as well as I do that there wasn't no one out at the Casey place that night fixing to steal no horses. It rained so much it looked like the flood was coming just like in the Bible. The roads were running like rivers, the creeks were full up – it wasn't no night for robbing horses and you know it. I can't say what happened on Main Street, I can't tell you how that Casey boy ended up dead, but I bet you every cent I got that not half those boys in that jail are guilty of anything more than working for Garcia."

"I don't want to hear another word, you hear me? Not one more word."

"That don't matter cause you're going to hear it. That Garcia fellow may not mean much to you but he ain't no ordinary rancher. He's got friends in other places, in Texas and Oklahoma. You go through with this, you won't be a sheriff no more, and that's the truth. You might even up in jail. What happened to you? Did the Caseys get to you? That no-good lying cattle rustler, he ain't no more than a two bit hustler. You ain't forgot that, have you, sheriff?"

Alice found a strength deep inside her she didn't know she possessed. She stood beside Thomas and said, "Sheriff, listen to him. You know he's right. There won't be any good to come of this. You may hang all these men, but you'll just be causing trouble in town and making more yourself. I may not be anyone important, but I swear I will make it my business to see that you are brought to justice. That isn't a tearful plea, that's a promise."

"What's to stop me from arresting you both and running you out of town on a rail?" demanded the sheriff.

"I'd say you'd have yourself a heap of trouble. I heard that you got Mama Rosa's nephew in that jail alongside the rest of the men. You know her. You know that family, ain't a single one of them would hurt a fly. What have you got against the Garcias, anyway? They're good folks, and they work hard for what they got. What's got you so against 'em all of a sudden?" Thomas leaned against the mantle.

"I got to do something. Folks in this town are demanding I do something about the trouble. There was a shoot-out. One of the Caseys is dead. The public needs to know I got this town under control."

"By taking the Caseys at their word and rounding up the whole bunch of men who work for Garcia? Who else you going to round up? His hired hands, the clerks at his son's store? The Garcias never caused no trouble before, and they haven't done it yet.

Looks to me like old man Casey's got you doing his dirty work for him. That don't look like no kind of way for a sheriff to get respect, not in the territories. What's he going to have you doing after you hang all these men? You going to start taking orders from him? Because you might as well. There won't be a Spanish man or woman who will ever give you the time of day, ever again. You can bet that won't be the end of your troubles."

Sheriff Dalton was no longer seated; he was standing and he was face to face with Thomas. Thomas wasn't flinching and neither was Alice as the sheriff glowered at them. "Thomas if you were any other man, I would beat you until you couldn't stand no more, do you hear me? That ain't no kind of way for you to be talking to me, and in my own home."

"Angus, I've known you since you were a boy. You're not this man, you don't want to hang the lot of those men. I ain't saying *someone* didn't shoot Casey's man. But it wasn't all these men, and I bet you every penny I got and my whole farm that those Casey horses weren't touched. Do yourself a favor. Figure out who killed that man, and keep 'em locked up till the marshal comes. Have a trial but do it right; send the rest of those boys back to Garcia. You ain't got to do what no man says – least of all, me – but you know what's right and one day you got to answer for it, same as the rest of us. If Casey can't stand it that's his business, but be a sheriff, not some hired gun for the wrong man."

"Get out of my house, Thomas, and take her with you. Get going now before I arrest you." The sheriff glared at Thomas.

243

There was a terrible silence as Alice realized that Jonathan and the rest of the innocent men were going to hang.

"Sheriff, please, let Jonathan Keene go. Let those innocent men go!" she pleaded.

"Get out of my sight."

"Come on, we best be going," Thomas spoke to her as he wrapped his arm around Alice.

"No! Sheriff, listen to us, you can't do this! It's not right and you know it," she cried.

"We best be going. Come on, we can't do no more here. The rest is in God's hands." Thomas pulled Alice out of the house and down the stairs. She wept as she allowed the old man to lead her away. She wept for Jonathan, for Mama Rosa's nephew, and for the injustice that she knew she was powerless to stop. She wept until she climbed into the wagon and promptly fainted.

*****

December 19, 1876

Dawn came as Alice lay in her bed, weeping in the early morning light. She couldn't recall much about the wagon ride back to the mission. At some point, she woke after fainting. Thomas had taken his ragged old coat off and wrapped it around her, trying to keep her

244

warm as he froze in the icy wind. She had stumbled to her room, but she was still dressed in her coat and wearing her gloves when the sun came up. She didn't have the strength to leave her bed or venture out of her room. There was no reason to continue. The man she loved was dead, innocent men hanged right alongside him because of the sheriff and his foolish pride.

If she had ever been in any doubt of her feelings for Jonathan she knew that there was no doubt in her heart any longer. She'd told him that she loved him at the jail and she meant every word of it. And he'd loved her – how often had she longed to hear those words from his lips? He said he loved her, and he meant it, she knew it in her heart that he did. How was she supposed to carry on after losing him?

She left the bed, sliding to the floor, wracked with emotional pain. She flung herself against the bed, her hands clasped together as she prayed to God that he have mercy on Jonathan's soul and her own. How desperately she had tried to save his life, to save the lives of all the innocent men. Crying into her bedclothes, her knees on the cold stone floor, she closed her eyes, letting the feeling of despair wash over her. She couldn't bear to see her students that day, or help with Joanna's class. She couldn't bear to dress or do much else. Jonathan's letter to his mother lay on the bedside table but she couldn't mail it, not yet. But as despairing as she was, she knew there was one person she had to speak to, even if that meant dragging herself away from the cold safety of her small room.

Gathering all her strength, she stood and forced herself to move toward the wash stand in the corner of the room. She washed her face and slowly changed clothes, calming herself as she slid into a dark grey dress. It wasn't black, but it was the closest thing she had to mourning clothes. She touched her hair. She knew it must be a frizzy, knotted mess. She unpinned it, unbraided it, and combed it, trying to think of Jonathan as she had seen him that day at Mama Rosa's, smiling and happy.

When she was dressed, her hair pinned back in a plain austere fashion, she took a deep breath, feeling the pain in her chest like a dull throbbing that she doubted would ever go away. She wondered how many other women felt as she did on this morning. How many other women had lost husbands or sons because the sheriff was a weak man?

She left her room, taking care not to make a sound. It was early; the sisters would be in prayer before breakfast. If she was lucky, she may avoid seeing them at all. There would come a time in the near future when she would have to see Sister Cecilia, but that could wait. She wanted to see one person and she prayed he was awake and about on this cold December morning.

She left the mission, walked through the sad, dead remains of the gardens, and headed towards the barn. With a creak of the rusty old hinges, the heavy wooden door opened. She heard Thomas's familiar murmurings. He was speaking gently to Delia, as was his custom. Alice's heart leapt in relief, almost joy, that he should be there. As she walked slowly towards the stall, she was astonished to see that Delia was not the only horse occupying her usual place. Beside her was a tiny horse; a spindly little foal that was all legs and big eyes gazing back at her.

"Thomas! Delia has had her baby," Alice whispered as she stood beside the wall, not wanting to interrupt the beautiful scene she saw before her.

"She did me proud last night. She gave me no cause to worry. Look at this little fellow, he's as strong as a buck," Thomas beamed.

"I'm so glad you were here, that you didn't miss it," Alice replied.

"I think Delia would have been fine without me, but it made my heart proud to see him arrive all the same. I needed some good news after last night," he answered as he wiped his face with a faded black bandana.

"Thomas, that is why I came to see you. I wanted to thank you for all you tried to do. You were so brave to take a stand for Jonathan, for all those poor men. I will be forever grateful to you for it," she said as she fought back the urge to weep again.

"I'm sorry, Miss Cleary, that it wasn't enough. That sheriff is a stubborn man, but he's going to find out that stubbornness ain't no kind of excuse for not doing what's right, no sir. Mark my words, I know the good Lord teaches us to forgive and forget but I ain't fixing to forget no time soon – and neither will the folks in this town. You wait and see; he's going to get what's coming to him," Thomas said as he left Delia's side.

"I may not be here to *wait and see,* as you put it. If Sister Cecilia doesn't send me away I'm going as soon as I can buy a train ticket. I don't want to be here in Santa Maria. I can't bear it."

"Sister Cecilia don't know about what we done last night. Why go off until you have to?"

"I have to leave, don't you understand? I can't stay. When Sister Cecilia finds out about all I've done, she won't have any mercy on me. I don't deserve any; I did everything I promised not to do, and more. I might as well resign. It's what I want to do, to get as far away from here as I can. I can't bear to be here a minute longer."

"What about your friend Miss Joanna? Don't you need to stay here for her sake? Her father is bad off; he may even be dead for all we know. You can't leave, not when she's going to need you when she comes home."

"Thomas, you and I both know I can't stay. Sister Cecilia was adamant about not breaking the rules and I broke all of them, just about. I don't think she's the kind of woman who will understand that I let a strange man sleep in the barn, or that I snuck away to town to wake the sheriff up in the middle of the night. She won't see what I've done as anything but sinful. She won't see it any other way. Besides, I don't think I have the heart to stay. Everything I do, everywhere I go will remind me of Jonathan, and what's worse, remind me that this town is run by a sheriff who is a coward. It breaks my heart to think of those poor men this morning, of Jonathan."

"Before you go running away, pray about it. Will you do that for old Thomas? It's the least you can do. Folks like me, like Miss Joanna, will surely miss you. Those young'uns will miss you too. They look up to you, whether you know it or not. They think something of their teacher."

"Thomas, you've been like a father to me. How can I ever repay your kindness?"

"I know it's going to be tough. It's going to be the toughest thing you've ever had to do, but stay strong. Don't pack your bags, not yet. It's almost Christmas. There'll be folks like Mama Rosa who are going to need a friendly face, like me and all those young'uns who aren't going home this year. You have to be strong for them."

"But if I leave tomorrow I could with my brother at Christmas in Kansas, away from here. I'd be miles away from all this pain and trouble."

"But senorita, if you leave, you'll never be able to look at yourself again without feeling ashamed. You're needed here. Even right now I need you to do me a favor. It seems to me that you were supposed to be helping with the stables. Tend to Delia and this young gentleman here while I head to town. I remember a good horse that night your friend stayed here in the storm. I want to see Garcia about what happened to that horse. He might make a good companion for Delia here, and the mission could use another horse."

"Goliath? You mean Jonathan's horse Goliath? You're going to find him?"

"Yes ma'am, I aim to do that. I couldn't save his master but I bet I can give Goliath a decent home. If

Sister Cecilia don't want him, he would be the star of my own stables. Stay here, see to my Delia. I'll be back before breakfast."

"Thomas be, careful. That sheriff didn't look like he was the type of man to forgive us for what we tried to do last night."

"I ain't worried about him. I ain't worried about no man. He would be a fool to mess with me. I shouldn't be telling you this, but the federal marshal is due to come by any day now. Let's see what he has to say about Angus Dalton then, 'cause I won't mind telling him what I think about what he done to those men."

Thomas adjusted his old felt hat on his head, and slipped his coat on over his worn out shirt. His gloves were threadbare, and so was his scarf. For an instant, Alice remembered the shawl Jonathan had bought for her. She didn't know if she would ever be able to go to town again. With a heart filled with sadness she approached Delia, and sat down in the straw beside the mare. The mare nudged Alice's hand with her nose. Alice petted her, grateful for the company as she prayed to God to grant her strength to get through the days ahead.

*****

"Senorita, what in the name of all that is holy is this? I left you taking care of my Delia and you've gone and fallen asleep!" Thomas exclaimed as he stood over Alice.

Alice blinked. She didn't know where she was for a moment. As she opened her eyes, she looked up at a familiar face. Delia nudged Alice with her nose as Alice realized she had a terrible crick in her neck. She was lying in a pile of straw.

"I must have fallen asleep," Alice replied with a yawn.

"That's what it looks like from where I'm standing."

"I'm sorry, Thomas. I didn't get any sleep last night. I couldn't, not with Jonathan..." she said but could not bring herself to finish the sentence.

"That ain't no excuse, I'm darn near three times as old as you, maybe more. I ain't had a wink of shut eye and I'm raring to go." Alice could hear the smile in the old man's voice.

She rubbed her neck. Her back ached and so did everything else. She sighed as she remembered why Thomas went to town in the first place. "Did you see Goliath?"

"I didn't see Goliath, senorita. He ain't for sale, says a man I met in town. More's the pity, I had my heart set on making a match with my Delia here."

"Maybe Goliath will find a new master, a kind man who will look after him. He's a good horse. He was just like Jonathan, brave and true, they both saved my life that night."

"He don't need a new master," Thomas said as he offered Alice his hand.

Alice put her hand in his. With a grunt he lifted her to her feet. She brushed the straw off her dress and yawned again. She wasn't hungry, but she could use a cup of coffee to chase away the chill from her bones.

"You look like you're awake but I think you might still be asleep. Didn't you hear a word I said?" Thomas asked.

Alice picked straw out of her hair. "I'm sorry. I am asleep. I don't feel like myself. I lost someone, Thomas. Someone I cared about and I don't know when I'll wake from that terrible dream."

"Just as well we got ourselves a good old fashioned Christmas miracle. I heard these things happen once in a while but I never thought I would live to see one."

"A Christmas miracle, are you talking about the horse? The new one here with Delia, or Goliath?"

"Enough about the horses already, the man who owns Goliath ain't in no kind of mood to sell him. Garcia ain't the horse's master – it was some young man, a man I only ever laid eyes on in this here barn."

Alice froze, and stared. She was afraid to even think what she was thinking. "Jonathan is alive?"

"He is alive, is what I've been saying, Miss Cleary. He's alive and so are a bunch of the other men. I heard there's a couple of those fellows still locked up tight, waiting for the marshal to come to town."

"Thomas! What you said to Sheriff Dalton must have worked! God be praised!"

"It wasn't my doing. You put a bug in my ear about those men and that storm. When I got to thinking about it, I knew there wasn't no way any man in his right mind would have gone out stealing horses on a night like that, not working for Garcia anyway. He ain't the kind of man who would have hired men like that. I can't say what happened on Main Street but the men who are still inside that jail know a little something about the Casey man getting shot. Seems to me like the whole thing is over and done with."

"Thomas, you are an angel sent by God. Do you know that?"

"Not me. I just couldn't stand by and let you risk your pretty little neck when I knew what you were saying was right. Maybe now this is all over, folks can go about their lives with no more trouble."

"This is the best Christmas present I ever had. Jonathan's alive and so are all those men. I'll have to ask for forgiveness for every mean thought I had about the sheriff."

"I wouldn't worry about asking for forgiveness. He knew he was doing wrong. It just took me and you to remind him of it. That's why he got ornery about it."

"I don't know what to say. Jonathan's alive! I can face anything now, anything at all."

"Maybe the worst is behind you. Now you go on inside the mission and get you something to eat; you look like you're half starved. I'm here now. I can look after Delia."

Alice wanted to jump, to sing, and to let the entire world know of her happiness, but she couldn't. The mission was a place of quiet, of refuge against the harsh realities of the world. It was also a place run in an orderly manner with rules that bound the sisters and the teachers together. Alice didn't dare express her joy even though she desperately wanted to. Maybe she would hand out the Christmas presents to the children a few days early? She didn't have much to give them, a few small toys and some ribbons, but she did have a bag of hard candy. Yes, that candy would be a treat for them, she thought with a smile. She was planning how to celebrate as she walked into the kitchen and right into Sister Cecilia.

"Miss Cleary," Sister Cecilia said her name like it was poison. "I was on my way to find you. If you would accompany me to my office, I require a word with you."

The joy that Alice felt was nearly destroyed by the gruffness in Sister Cecilia's voice. As Alice looked longingly at the coffee pot on the stove and a tray of biscuits fresh from the oven on the counter, she knew it was no use to argue. She was going to have to face Sister Cecilia sometime. If it had to be that morning, then she was ready.

*****

"Appalled, do you hear me? I am appalled at your lack of respect and your lack of decency. You had a man here at the mission? You were seen in town in the company of a strange man, then you had the audacity and the poor judgment to bring him here? To my mission, a place that is holy and sacred to God. You dared to do that? What's worse, I hear he is a gambler and he was arrested. He was going to hang but you put a stop to that, didn't you?" Sister Cecilia railed against Alice as soon as she closed her office door.

Alice had thought she was ready to face any criticism from the abbess, but not an onslaught like this one. As she tried to figure out how Sister Cecilia knew all of these things about her, she knew that it spelled trouble. Sister Cecilia was a stern woman by nature but on this morning, she was livid. Her face was red, her eyes were narrowed to slits, and she stared at Alice as though Alice was a fallen woman – or worse, a saloon girl.

"I am not prone to anger. Anger is a deadly sin but I have never encountered a woman who so flagrantly violated the principles of this mission. Have you no respect, no decency?" Sister Cecilia demanded as she sat down behind her desk.

Alice didn't quite know what to do. She didn't feel like sitting down. Considering the tone of the conversation, she wasn't sure if she would be in Sister Cecilia's office long enough to sit down. She half expected the abbess to tell her to march out of the mission that very day. It would be terrible knowing she would be leaving without a reference. She may even lose her credentials to teach, but she had done what she thought was right. The knowledge that she hadn't let those men die was enough to sustain her through any hardship. It came to her that there wasn't a thing she stood accused of that she regretted.

"What have to say for yourself?" Sister Cecilia glared at Alice. "You gave your word at our last meeting that you would obey my rules, and you flagrantly disregarded them. Your word meant nothing! I should dismiss you. I cannot allow such wantonness and disrespect for our order to continue. Why have you not answered me? Do you have anything to say in your defense, any reason I should show the slightest consideration?"

In her mind, Alice was already packing her trunk. If she left the next day, she might be in Kansas in time for Christmas. She would miss Joanna and Thomas, and Jonathan most of all, wherever he was. Sister Cecilia was furious, and there was no denying that the abbess had every reason to be angry. Alice had violated Sister Cecilia's trust but she was not wanton, nor was she indecent. If she was going to leave the mission in disgrace, she was not going to be remembered as a woman without principles.

"Miss Cleary, I am waiting for an answer. Are you incapable of telling me the truth? Do you not care to offer any defense at all for your deplorable actions?" Sister Cecilia demanded.

"How is Joanna's father? Have you received word from her? It's only been a few days since she left but I would very much like to know how he is, if he still lives," Alice asked, feeling regret that she would not be in Santa Maria when Joanna returned. Perhaps she could see Joanna in Santa Fe, but she didn't want to intrude on her family during a time of illness and possibly death.

Sister Cecilia clenched her jaw as she answered, "I pray for her family and her father but I have not heard word from Miss Ortega."

"I understand. I have been praying very hard that Mr. Ortega would not die, not at Christmastime. When I think of Joanna and her younger sisters and her brothers, I am overwhelmed with sadness."

"Yes, as we all are, but you have not answered my question. Can you account for your behavior? Can you offer any explanation to me that would explain your immorality? Your position is in jeopardy unless you can convince me that you must remain."

Alice bristled at the word *immorality*. Indignation rose inside her, a feeling that she suspected was only made worse by the righteous glare of Sister Cecilia.

Meeting Sister Cecilia's scowl, Alice replied, "I may have done a lot of things that were not in accordance with the rules of the mission, but I was never immoral, nor did I behave in any way that was sinful. I don't mind what you think of me and my decisions, but I will not allow you to judge my character when I have done nothing to devalue it."

"Have you done nothing to devalue it? You have opened yourself to speculation and ridicule, consorting with a man who is a gambler and a known sinner, and you were seen in a public place with him. You brought him to *this holy house of God* and allowed him to stay a night within these walls. As if your sins were not terrible enough, you dared to leave the mission after dark to seek out the sheriff in the name of this same man. What am I to think? You have called into the question the morals of every woman, every sister who inhabits this mission."

"Sister Cecilia, the man is Jonathan Keene. He saved my life the night of that rain storm, and I could not in good conscience send him and his horse back out into the flood waters to drown. As to my speaking to the sheriff on his behalf, I could not allow an innocent man – or a whole host of innocent men – to die. If your rules, your pride, and your honor mean more to you than the life of innocent people, then there is little I can say. If that is your interpretation of being a Christian, of being a Catholic, then I have no place here at the mission. I shall resign from my position, as I can see you will undoubtedly be asking me to leave. Good day."

Alice turned to leave. Her heart was heavy; she had failed Thomas and the children, but she had no choice. There would not be a reference from the mission, so her days as a teacher were at end. She wasn't sure what she would do with her life now that her teaching days were over, but she decided to go to Kansas. If she was lucky she may have enough money to buy a ticket.

"Miss Cleary, where are you going?" Sister Cecilia demanded.

"To pack my trunk. I'm going back to Kansas."

"I said your position was in jeopardy; I never said I had made a decision. If you repent for your sins, if you are truly humble and sorry for what you have done, I shall consider keeping you as a teacher."

"Sister, I thank you for the position here at the mission, but I will never be sorry, and I won't seek repentance for what I have done. If saving an innocent man's life is a cause to ask for forgiveness, then I shall remain in sin. I will ask God to understand that I did what I thought was right. Perhaps he will be more merciful than you."

"You would allow pride to come in the way of your salvation?"

"No, Sister, it is not pride. Jonathan Keene is a man deserving of a second chance. If I had sent him to drown because of some foolish rule, who would I be? If I allowed him to hang when I had a chance to speak up for him, how could I live with myself? It is not pride, but certainty. I am certain that I acted as my conscience dictated. If you believe that your rules are more important than doing what is right, then pride is not my sin – it's yours. If you will excuse me, I have to say goodbye to Thomas."

"What about the children, or las posadas? We need you here at the mission; your work is vital to us. Will you not repent for them?" Sister Cecilia stood up.

"If I repented, it would be a lie. I would be lying to you and to God. That is far worse than the sins you

259

have accused me of. Can you tell me that what I have done is wrong?"

Sister Cecilia closed her eyes, and sighed. "If you must go, then I pray that you will one day see that you have sinned. I will pray for mercy that you do not die with that stain upon your soul."

"Thank you, Sister. Goodbye."

Alice left the office. The emotions she felt were tumultuous. She would miss the children, Thomas, and Joanna, but she could not lie to God, no matter how much the abbess insisted that what she had done was a sin. She may not have a reference but maybe there were other places in the territories that needed teachers, places that wouldn't dig too deeply into her past. She thought of what her future would bring and her mind drifted to Jonathan. He was alive and he was safe. She didn't know if he was still in town, or the sheriff had made good on his threat to see Jonathan leave for good. Alice longed to see him but she didn't know where to begin to look for him. Maybe Mama Rosa knew where to find him, or Javier Garcia? Would she have time to see them before she left Santa Maria, she wondered as she headed towards the kitchen. Surely she was entitled to a cup of coffee after all she had endured.

*****

Christmas in Kansas may be poor, but Alice was looking forward to seeing her brother, Will. How she missed him. She would tell him all her problems, and

260

he would listen and then offer her advice. She'd never realized how much she relied on him, until now. She wanted to see him again, in this dark moment when she felt all alone in the world.

She thought back to the last letter she'd received from him. He was doing far better in his work as a farmer than she was as a teacher. Maybe she could find work somewhere far away, like California? Or the territories to the north? She had heard of settlements springing up, of small towns that were being settled in the Dakotas. Maybe when she applied for a teaching position no one would mind, or ever know, what had happened in New Mexico.

Alice sat in the kitchen of the mission, hiding from the sisters and from what awaited her. She had to pack and then she was leaving, even though Thomas had asked her to stay. Even though she knew Joanna needed her. She may never see anyone in Santa Maria again, she may never see Jonathan. She loved him, but what was she to do?

By now her class would be wondering where their teacher was. She had come to care deeply for her students during her short time at the mission. She knew she would miss them, but they would forget her in time. There were other children who needed her, somewhere in the dangerous Indian country. She thought about the wild tales she had read in the newspapers, of the violence and the bloodshed. Was she prepared to go to a place even more lawless than Santa Maria?

She didn't really want to, but neither could she repent when she didn't feel sorry for anything she had done, except for lying to Sister Cecilia. By not telling Sister Cecilia what she had done on Jonathan's behalf, she had lied by omission. For that, she felt sorry, but she knew she would have done it again. She also felt terrible that dear Sister Agatha had given her money to come all this way to be a teacher, and she had ruined everything. When she thought of that sweet woman who believed in her she felt like she was nearly as bad as Sister Cecilia believed her to be. Sitting at the long wooden table in the kitchen, she bowed her head. What should she do?

"There you are." Thomas stepped inside the back door of the kitchen.

"Thomas, hello." Alice braced herself. She would need to tell him she was leaving.

"I heard about you, yes indeed. I heard all about you getting in trouble. I warned you that you would get in a load of trouble, didn't I?"

"You did, but how did you hear about it? I just left Sister Cecilia's office a quarter of an hour ago."

"I hear things, don't you forget it. What is this I hear that you're leaving? Didn't I tell you that you couldn't go, on account of me and the children and that young fellow of yours?"

"You said that, yes. And I agreed to it, but Sister Cecilia had other ideas," Alice explained.

"Did she? That's not how I heard it."

"She accused me of being a fallen woman, she demanded that I repent for what I did, all of it. What was I supposed to do?"

Thomas rubbed his chin like he always did when he was thinking. "Seems to me, you don't have to say sorry for *all* that you done. Maybe you could be sorry for some of it? You got to stay, it's Christmas. You can't leave the mission. Sister Cecilia may not have told you, but she needs you. We need you. If you stay, you won't regret it. No sir, you sure won't, mark my words."

"Thomas, if I stay, I'm only doing it because you asked me to."

"Call it what you will but you'll be glad you did, now stop fretting. Go see sister Cecilia. I can't say what went on between you two, but I know she loves them young'uns. If I'm right, you do too. Don't leave your old Thomas here with a passel of crying little ones. You won't do that on the Lord's birthday, will you?"

"What about my brother Will? I won't see him if I stay here. It's been so long since I saw him."

"He'll keep. He's in good health, ain't he? No fearing he might die?"

"The last I heard he's doing well."

"Good, you can go see him come spring. The roads will be better then. Now buck up your courage, go back to that office and tell that woman whatever you have to, to make her happy."

"I don't want to lie."

"Don't lie, God wouldn't like for you to do that, but I reckon he might not mind if you were to be kind of sorry."

"Kind of sorry? I called you an angel today but I may have been wrong, you've got the devil's own charm about you."

"Think of those children and me and your friends. Think of that man you went through all this trouble to save. Get off your backside and get to it, go on, now. Git."

Alice sighed. There was no winning an argument with this man she owed so much to. "If I didn't owe you for taking me to town and getting those men out of trouble I would say you were crazy."

"Do this f

or me, then, and you don't owe me a thing. Like they say in those gambling halls, I'm calling in my marker, and you best be willing to pay it. Get going, those young'uns will be needing their teacher today."

*****

December 24, 1876

Alice was still in Santa Maria. She was still a teacher at the mission, but she knew that her position

264

was far from secure. There existed a delicate understanding between her and Sister Cecilia. The abbess needed Alice. Sickness was widespread at the pueblo and in the countryside, requiring the sisters to administer to the ill who would accept their help. Joanna was still in Santa Fe with her father, who was slowly making a recovery. The mission was woefully understaffed, and so Alice remained. She repented for the wrongs she truly felt remorse for, but not for anything else – although she did not highlight the distinction when she talked with Sister Cecilia.

It was Christmas Eve in Santa Maria. The children were cold and their teeth chattered on this last night of las posadas, but they were happy. Alice worried about them catching cold but their faces were beaming as they sang songs before the procession ended at the Church of our Lady of Sorrows in the square of Santa Maria. Alice followed the children as they walked inside the old church. There was always something magical about a church at night, especially on Christmas Eve. Candles burned on the altar, luminaires lined the steps outside, leading the way. In every sconce candles burned brightly, their golden hue illuminating the red tile and dark wood of the old Spanish church.

Alice and Thomas ushered the children into a long wooden pew, and Alice glanced around the church. Tonight, the sanctuary was filled with people she knew from town. The Garcias were seated near the front. Mama Rosa, her family, and some of her staff were seated one row behind Alice. Families from town and from the mission sat together as Alice felt a moment of sadness for the children in her care.

Many of the mission children were home with their families, but some remained. There were children with her whose homes were far away, and families that were suffering from sickness or poverty. She thought of the candy and penny toys she had in her room. She knew they would be appreciated by these few remaining boys and girls. When she sat down beside them she had to admit that Thomas was right, she was glad she had stayed in Santa Maria for the children. They needed someone to hug them and wish them a Merry Christmas, didn't they?

Seated in the pew, she thought of the letter she'd received from Will. He was well but he wrote how much he missed her. In the spring she would undoubtedly be returning to Kansas, possibly for longer than a fortnight. As the parishioners began to sing a Christmas hymn, she knew in her heart she would miss this town, miss the people she'd met here, the food, the sights, and the smells of a world so far removed from Georgia. This Christmas she would do everything she could to savor all the memories being made, as she was not sure she would ever come this way again.

The mass on Christmas Eve was a beautiful, sacred rite that always left her feeling joy and peace. Despite the hardships she had endured and the brushes with danger she was thankful for her time spent in Santa Maria. She was grateful for all that had happened, both good and bad. Even in the worst of times there had been beauty and love. She remembered Jonathan sleeping in the hay in the barn as the storm raged. She

266

remembered him in jail, saying he loved her. She hadn't seen him since that night and she wondered where he was, as no one in town seemed to know where he went after the sheriff freed him.

The letter to his mother still sat on the table in her room. She'd left it unopened, swearing to return it to him when she saw him again, if she ever did. It contained his last words to his mother, words that he wrote when he thought all hope was lost. She was curious to read it, to learn more about him, but she knew it would be terribly dishonest if she did. So she left it sealed.

Jonathan Keene was the man she loved, and he was also her biggest dilemma. Listening to the parish priest tell the story of the nativity, her mind should have been on spiritual matters, but she found she could not think about anything else but Jonathan. Would she ever see him again? Was he gone to California? This night, a magical night, she should have been filled with love and happiness but there was part of her heart that was not able to find joy – not when the man she loved had disappeared as quickly as he arrived in her life, like a phantom.

Alice was lost in her own sorrow when a gentleman slipped into the pew at her side. The priest led the congregation in prayer as she looked down. She felt the cold from his clothes, and the damp wool against the arm of her coat as a gloved hand brushed the snowflakes from his sleeve. It was snowing, just like Thomas had predicted. She slid closer to the children to make room for the man at the end of the pew.

"You don't have to run away, Colleen," the man beside her whispered.

With a start, Alice turned to take a good long look at the person beside her. She couldn't speak.

"You said I never went to church, but here I am."

She wanted to throw her arms around his broad shoulders and kiss his lips, but not in the middle of Christmas Eve Mass. She didn't know where he had been or what he was doing sitting beside her, but she didn't care. At that moment, her heart was bursting with joy. In the darkness, he reached for her hand. She felt his fingers wrap around hers in a gesture that felt as natural as if they had always been together.

With a gentle squeeze of her hand and a smile, she felt all her worries and troubles drift away. The first few notes of the last hymn of the evening began as she thought she heard Thomas chuckle. Peering at him over the heads of the children, she caught his eye in the dim light. He smiled, and she realized that he must have known all along that Jonathan was going to be at Mass that evening. She wondered what else Thomas knew about Jonathan as she looked at Jonathan once more. His eyes sparkled in the candlelight, making Alice feel warm inside. She was content. This Christmas in Santa Maria would be one she knew she would cherish for all the days of her life.

Chapter Nine

May 16, 1877
Tucker Springs, Kansas

Santa Maria seemed as far away as Georgia, Alice mused as she sat on the quilt spread out under the shade of a tree. Beside her was her beloved brother Will, and the young woman he had taken a shine to, as he put it. Her name was Millie and she was a Tucker, the daughter of the local blacksmith. When Alice looked at her brother, she noticed his eyes were bright and cheerful as he listened to Millie discuss the latest news of Tucker Springs. She had a feeling that it wouldn't be long before the news that would be traveling around Tucker Springs was of a wedding.

Alice's sister Louisa and her husband James were eating cold chicken and apple pie as their children played with the other boys and girls from the little town. Although Alice still thought of Tucker Springs as a village, it had grown by the addition of five more families and a few newly constructed houses in the year that she had been gone. All around her, on other blankets and quilts, were families and townsfolk all laughing and having a good time. This was the first annual Founders' Day celebration and so far it had been a success, at least according to Louisa. Alice was glad to be there, to be with her family, but it wasn't how she had envisioned it. Back in the winter, when she thought of traveling to Kansas to see her kin, she'd thought it would be in Jonathan's company, but that was not to be.

As a couple of boys ran by, she marveled at the change in her nephew Thomas. He had grown into a hardworking and much taller boy in the year since she last saw him, Alice observed with a smile. His name, Thomas, reminded her of a dear friend back in Santa Maria, a man who had treated her like a daughter. She missed him profoundly. She also missed her friend Joanna, the children she taught at the mission, and so much more about the town she'd left a week ago.

Sighing, she wondered if she would return to Santa Maria. Her future was unclear. It was too much to think about, she decided, as the excited whooping and laughter of the children reminded her that here in Tucker Springs life continued to be simple and uncomplicated. Not like her life in Santa Maria.

Her life there *should* have been simple. She'd gone to the New Mexico territory with one goal in mind, to become a school teacher. What had happened in the year she'd spent in that town was unexpected, and it wasn't simple. She had become a teacher at the mission, but she had also grown fond of a man she could never have. Mr. Keene, (whom she affectionately called Jonathan when he wasn't being infuriating) had drifted into her life on the train heading to New Mexico. This past January, he had drifted back out of it, just as quickly and mysteriously as he had arrived.

Louisa pulled a women's magazine out of the hamper. Sliding close to her sister, she flipped through the pages. "Look at those dresses! All those flounces and ribbons, and the size of those bustles? Not many women dress like that in Tucker Springs, I can tell you. How did they dress in New Mexico?"

Alice glanced at the magazine, at the fashionable ladies wearing clothes that were beautiful and undoubtedly expensive. Her own dress was plain. It was her nicest afternoon frock, forest green with a pattern of tiny pale flowers, but there wasn't much to it – just a plain, tiny white lace collar and trim around the sleeves. As she looked around the churchyard, she saw that the other women in Tucker Springs were dressed as plainly as she was, as money and material were in short supply in this tiny town in the heart of the prairie.

"They dressed a lot like they do here, but some of the women wore less," Alice spoke absentmindedly.

"Less?" Louisa asked.

"Well, in the saloons," Alice explained.

"You were inside a saloon?"

Alice winced. She'd forgotten that her sister didn't know all of her adventures, least of all her brushes with death.

Alice untied the ribbons holding her bonnet on her head. It was already warm that afternoon and she didn't care if it was improper to take her bonnet off. She felt like she needed to be free. If she could take off her corset and sit here the shade in just a plain old calico work dress, she would do it. Setting the bonnet down beside the magazine, she answered her sister's question.

"Not exactly. There are quite a lot of saloons in New Mexico. It's because of the cattle ranches and cowboys, they do like a game of cards."

"I'm glad you were at a mission and stayed out of trouble. It sounds like no place for a good Christian woman," Louisa replied.

"There were good people there, and the cowboys and cattlemen weren't a bad sort. Most of the time," Alice said as her memory drifted back, as it always did, to Jonathan Keene – card player, gambler, and occasional hired gun.

"I'm thankful you had the good sense to come back to your family. I understand wanting to see the world and have an adventure but New Mexico seems like a dangerous place."

Alice wanted to say that it was, but since her mind wasn't yet made up about her future, she simply stated, "Santa Maria is a nice town, filled with good people. Not like what you've read or heard."

"Well, you're here now." Louisa reached over and patted Alice's hand. "Things have changed since we last saw you. I should have written and told you about it, but I didn't want you to abandon your dream of being a teacher. Now that you're here with us, I can tell you that things are looking up."

"I'm so glad. You must have had a good year?"

"We did. Last year's harvest was better than we could have hoped. It was the best year we've had so far, and this year's crop looks to be just as good. The war has been over for a decade and people are moving and buying things again. There's a need for corn and wheat, and for all manner of what we can grow in this fine Kansas soil. I know you haven't made up your mind about what you want to do, but if you want to stay here, to lend a hand with the children, I would be happy and so would Will. And I happen to know of one other person who would love for you to stay here with us."

"Louisa, I don't know what to say. That is very generous of you."

"I'm not being generous, it's what I wished I could have done last year. I'm heartily sorry I was unable to ask you to stay. We just didn't have the money. We need Will's help, with Mr. Burke not being able to work as he used to. He earned his keep but there wasn't much left to go around, not even for our own children. All that's changed. We need you home with us, and we need a teacher."

"A teacher." Alice nodded slowly.

"Tucker Springs has grown so much, we need a real, honest-to-goodness teacher. I don't know what the Tuckers will say about it, but if you wanted the position, I'm sure they wouldn't object. Not with your connections to our family…and the pastor's recommendation."

"Do you think he would recommend me?" Alice asked, thinking about the uncertainty of her future at the mission.

"He already did. It was his suggestion that we find someone with experience to see to the children's education. He told me himself that he was thinking about you when he made the suggestion. You've been a teacher at a mission; that sounds like experience to me."

Pastor Newland. Alice's eyes darted around the churchyard, looking for his familiar face. She had come back to Kansas just two days ago. She hadn't seen him yet, and she wondered where he could be. She half wanted to see him and half didn't. Compulsively, her hand went to the collar of her dress. She wasn't wearing the silver cross he had given her, and she hadn't worn it. Not once. Would he notice?

"Is he here? I haven't seen him."

"He'll be along. He has his hands full these days. There's a family of homesteaders, just arrived from somewhere back east. They've been sick with fever for a week, or so I've heard. There a houseful of children and a sick baby."

"Oh, that would explain why He hasn't been to the house since I came back from New Mexico."

"You were looking for him?" Louisa asked brightly.

Alice knew what her sister was implying. She didn't know if it was true or not, or whether she wanted to see him. She thought she would like to say hello, and tell him how forward he was to send her a present, but now that she was back in Kansas, she was having second thoughts.

Jonathan's withdrawal had left her feeling alone and confused, and she didn't know what to think anymore. Her mind was muddled, and she didn't know what she wanted. She wished she could figure that out for herself, but until she decided if she was staying here or going back to New Mexico, she had no choice but to accept that she was going to be confused.

"Alice, are you sweet on the pastor? I had hopes that you might be. He told me you wrote to him while you were away."

Alice didn't want to get her sister's hopes up, not when she didn't know whether she wanted to pin her future on the pastor, or any man. Not after Jonathan.

"I don't love him, if that's what you mean," Alice sighed.

"I didn't say you did, but that doesn't mean you can't still be sweet on him. Falling in love is easy if you like someone, and you do like him, don't you?"

"I like him," Alice admitted.

"He is a good man, generous and kind; you could do far worse than a man like that. I stand by what I said last spring – he likes you and there's no doubting it. He hasn't so much as looked at another woman, not that there aren't plenty of women who are looking for a good husband."

"It's been a year since I saw him; he's probably forgotten about me by now."

"All this year, he's asked about you every time I've seen him. I know he wrote to you."

"I'm sure he writes to a great many people."

"That doesn't matter; he wrote to you. He hadn't forgotten you, take my word for it. I know what a man in love looks like and he looks the part."

Alice knew that Pastor Newland was a good man. He was the kind of person who visited the sick, pitched in at a barn-raising, and did whatever he could for the people of Tucker Springs. She recalled how he came to her sister's farm to help with the plowing. She also knew from Will's letters that the pastor had kept the family from starving more than once before the crop was got in last autumn. He was, just as her sister described him to be, a man of God who would undoubtedly make a caring husband and devoted father.

Alice startled herself by her own thoughts. What was she thinking? How could she consider the pastor, when she loved Jonathan? Even if he didn't love her enough to ask her to marry him. Dismissing the pain that came with the memory of the last time she saw Jonathan, she turned her attention back to the conversation with her sister.

"He doesn't know me; how can he be in love with me?"

"My dear sister, you are so young. It doesn't take much to make a man fall in love with you, not when he's the man God intended you to be with."

Alice didn't think for a second that Pastor Newland was the man God intended her to be with, not at all. She didn't question God, but she did question her sister's judgement – and she knew her own heart. If the handsome pastor of the church in Tucker Springs was the man God intended her to be with, why didn't she feel it in her heart? He was a nice man, a good sort whom she admired, but he couldn't be the man for her, not when she still loved Jonathan Keene.

She wanted to groan, to cry, and to forget about Jonathan as easily as he seemed to forget about her. Instead, she sat on the quilt beside her sister as Louisa recounted in detail all the ways Pastor Newland would make a fine husband. Alice didn't doubt what her sister had to say, but she did wonder why she didn't feel more strongly about him.

"Alice, you haven't heard a word. You must be tired from the journey to Kansas."

"I have heard you, well, mostly. I like the pastor well enough, I suppose."

"Well, you should. You would be settled nearby. You could teach in the school. In a town this small, I don't think anyone would mind if the teacher was married, until you started having children. If they did mind, they probably wouldn't say so."

"Wait, Louisa, you've gotten ahead of yourself *and* the pastor. He hasn't asked me to marry him."

"Not yet, but I have it on pretty good authority that he will and that will be a happy day," Louisa said with a smile. Nudging Will, she said, "Won't that be wonderful to have our Alice here in Tucker Springs with us? Oh Will, you must convince her to stay."

Alice's heartstrings tightened at the sight of her younger brother's face turned towards her. Of all her brothers and sisters, he was her favorite; he was her weakness. She adored him and he loved her. She would do anything for him.

"I'm grateful you're back from New Mexico. I heard stories about that place that made me pray for you the whole time you were gone. I would have gone to fetch you back, but there was too much work to be done and I didn't have the money for a ticket."

"Do you want me to stay?" she asked, waiting for his answer.

"You know I do, but I won't be the one to hold you here. But that ain't saying that Pastor Newland might have something he wants to say about it."

"Pastor Newland? Are you and he getting married?" asked Millie Tucker.

Alice looked at the young woman as if she was speaking a language she didn't understand. This was the first time she had been addressed by her, except at their introduction when Millie complimented Alice's lace gloves, a present from Joanna. To Alice, it seemed a long way from praising her gloves to directly asking about her plans for matrimony.

"No. Maybe. I don't know," Alice admitted. "If you all will excuse me, I was seated on that train for so long, I still haven't gotten over it. I'm going to take a stroll while you all finish the chicken and pie."

Alice stood. She wasn't lying about being uncomfortable sitting down; her knees ached and so did her back. But what she really wanted was to end this conversation before it went any further. Her sister and Millie Tucker would have her wedding to the pastor planned this very afternoon if she let them. She didn't know how her brother truly felt about it, but he hadn't said anything against it either. It seemed like everyone she knew in Kansas wanted to see her married and settled into a life as quiet as their own. As she walked away from the families assembled in the churchyard, she wasn't sure she was ready to be a wife, least of all to a man who wasn't Jonathan Keene.

*****

"I hope you can forgive me for missing the Founders' Day celebration yesterday. I wanted to be there with you and your family but my duty called me elsewhere," Pastor Newland explained without a trace of regret.

Alice sat in the parlor across from the young pastor, without a chaperone. Her sister had been seated beside her when they welcomed the pastor with coffee and slices of apple cake, but with a smile and a wink at Alice, Louisa had made an excuse that kept her in the kitchen. James was in the fields with Will and Samuel. The children were working outside in the garden, except for Miriam, the youngest, who was at her mother's side in the kitchen.

"There is no need for forgiveness. I heard from my sister that there's been a lot of sickness in the town."

"Sickness, drought, famine, we must endure all those troubles with God's help," he said. "But I would have liked to see you when you arrived home, or at the train station after your New Mexico adventure."

She wasn't expecting that he would call Kansas *home* for her. She had only spent a few days with her sister and her old family friends, the Burkes, before she left for the territories. It was hardly enough time to set down roots in Tucker Springs, she thought silently as she poured the coffee.

"One lump or two?" she asked.

"Just one; I don't want to be greedy. White sugar is too pricey to be wasting on me."

"I'm sure my sister won't mind, after all you've done for her and her family. Thank you, by the way."

"It's a blessing I'm strong enough and have the means to help where I'm able."

Alice studied him as he spoke. He was as pleasant and kind as she remembered. It was hard to believe it had been a year since she last saw him. He hadn't changed in the slightest. He was as tall as she remembered him to be, his figure trim, his hands, sinewy from hard work. His hair was wavy and light, and his eyes shone golden brown. His voice was melodic and kind. She had forgotten how handsome he was, how much she admired him, until then. When he spoke about his work among the people of his church, he didn't brag or boast. He didn't flirt or act forward, as she had thought he was when he sent her the necklace. She was embarrassed when she recalled how she planned to return it to him. Seated across from him in the parlor, she wished she was wearing it. Could she consider settling into a life in Tucker Springs?

"I am thankful to the Lord that you were delivered safely back from that den of sin and iniquity," he said with a sternness she was not anticipating.

Alice wanted to remind him that what he was calling a den of sin, she had called home for a year. There was sin, lawlessness, and temptation of every kind, but there were also good people, kind and honest folks who were just as God fearing as anyone in Tucker Springs. Tempering her response, she said, "It wasn't entirely a Gomorrah. There were caring, Christian people in Santa Maria."

"I spoke harshly didn't I? It was not my intention to offer insult to any person you know in that town. Even in the most sinful of places, there are always a few good people around, doing the Lord's work. Allow me to explain. I know how wicked men can be far from the society of hardworking, God-fearing people. I know all too well the dark, unseemly side of the world. In my work as a pastor, I have seen suffering and vice. I only meant to say that I prayed that you would be delivered safely back to your family, far

281

from the corruption of the territories. It is my greatest relief that you have kept yourself above the reach of wickedness."

Alice was reminded rather suddenly of the abbess at Santa Maria, of her cross words and her insistence that Alice was a sinner. She was in no mood to hear a similar proclamation made by a man who knew little of her character. Nor did he know of the trials she had survived during the past year. All feelings of regard she may have had for the pastor were quickly forgotten as she remarked, "I am not a child. I am well aware of sin and vice, for I have seen the evils of it firsthand. I have been terribly judged by the abbess of the mission for saving a man's life, and I will not tolerate being deemed to be so weak of will that I could have been led to wickedness as easily as a horse is led to water."

Alice stood abruptly and slid her chair away, and left the room in a huff before she could stop herself. She felt a hand on her shoulder as she swung around. She was staring into the handsome face of Pastor Newland. Steeling herself for the inevitable sermon regarding the vice of anger, she clenched her jaw and waited as she stared at him.

"Wait, wait. Come back and sit with me. You are tired from your trip, and not yourself," he said in a calm, gentle voice.

Gazing into his eyes, she didn't see anger or reproach; she saw kindness. What if she had been wrong to presume he was judging her at all? With that realization, Alice immediately felt ashamed of her outburst.

With an enormous sigh, she returned to her chair, but she didn't know what to say. She had just unleashed a torrent of frustration on a man who had been kind to her and her family. Her cheeks flushed red from embarrassment as she stared at her hands, which were shaking.

"Alice, you have been brave for so long, but you have to understand. You're home now. You're safe, you're among friends and family who love you and care for you. I don't think you are weak-minded. On the contrary, I admire your strength and your courage. You lived through the war and did not let the horrors of it turn you into a bitter woman. You dedicated your life to making the lives of children better in a godless place. I admire your courage and your faith. Please understand, I did not mean to insult you. Far away from the eyes of the God-fearing people, you walked among sinners of every ilk. I may be a man of God but I know the sort of villainy that can be found in the territories. I know the saloons filled with drink, and cards and pleasures of an earthy kind. I know how easy it is to meet scoundrels and cheats. Some smile and appear by the light of day as honest as you and me, but they lead depraved lives. I know what evil awaits young women without chaperones and families to protect them in places like that. If I spoke harshly it was to demonstrate my relief that you remained strong, and that God protected you. No, Alice, I do not find you weak willed. I am in awe of your bravery and your independent nature, which led you to venture where no Christian woman should ever

283

go. I am relieved more than words can say that you are here, sitting in your sister's house, when you may have succumbed to corruption that could undo even the best of our spiritual defenses."

Alice closed her eyes for a minute to gather her thoughts before she opened them again to find that he was gazing at her with an expression that was warm and compassionate. She felt even worse than she had before as she sighed, her shoulders slumping in surrender. She met his gaze and said, "Pastor Newland, I don't know what came over me. I am ashamed at myself for what I said. Can you forgive me?"

"Forgive? It is I who should ask for your forgiveness. It was not my intention but I spoke cruelly to you, so badly I fear that you wanted to leave."

"No, you didn't speak cruelly. I would offer you an excuse for my behavior, but there is none. For a moment you reminded me of the abbess at the mission. The abbess was a nice woman, utterly dedicated to the children in her care, but she was convinced that I was a trollop."

Alice gasped, slapping her hand over her mouth as soon as the words were out. "Oh Pastor Newland, I forget myself. I didn't mean to say that word in your presence."

Overcome by a swift feeling of discomfort after her use of a coarse word in front of a pastor (particularly after her speech about not succumbing to the dissolute habits of the territories), Alice turned away. She didn't want to see the look in his eye or incur his ridicule. This visit was turning into a disaster and it was all her fault. She reached for her coffee cup, downed it in one long swallow like she imagined men like Jonathan did in saloons. Setting the cup on its saucer on the tray. She reached for his. "I will get your hat; I'm sure you will want to be heading back to town."

"Miss Cleary, what makes you think I have any intention of leaving?"

"Why would you stay?" she asked as she leaned towards the kitchen that was only a short distance away. She didn't know how her sister had managed not to overhear any of this embarrassing conversation, but Louisa hadn't yet reappeared. Oh, what would she say when she heard that Alice scared away the pastor with her ill temper and her course language?

"I want to stay."

"You do?"

"Yes, I do. I wouldn't be here, otherwise. Miss Cleary, you're as jumpy as a jack rabbit. Your journey must have taken a terrible toll on you. If you would come and sit still for a minute I would be obliged," he said as he gestured her back to her seat.

"This is ridiculous. I keep trying to leave, and you don't want to. I've lost my temper, and I've used foul language in your presence. You speak of Santa Maria of being a den of iniquity. I have no doubt that you must think that I fit in among the sinners. How dreadful you must think me to be!"

"There is no need for hysterics. This conversation is the most interesting one I've had in a long time. We make a fine pair, do we not? You are overwrought and I keep convincing you to remain. Besides, I have heard worse language than what you said."

"Not from a lady."

"You would be surprised," he smiled as he held out his empty cup. "If I may trouble you for another cup?"

"And what of my temper?" Alice asked as she poured the coffee, her hand was trembling but she concentrated very hard to remain steady.

"No one likes to be preached to, except on Sundays; that was my mistake. I find it far too easy to fall into the habit of thinking my position means that I know best," he smiled.

"Oh, I did say that, didn't I? Well, not in those words, but I meant it."

"You were right to say it. I may be a man of God, but I have my faults, same as the next man. You reminded me of that, when not many people would have said it. It sounds to me like your abbess was as strict as my old professor at the seminary. Did I ever tell you what he told me when I informed him I wanted to go out west?"

"No," Alice shook her head.

"He told me – let me see, how can I say this delicately – that I was casting my lot with the worst kind of people. He was convinced that I was dooming my soul for wanting to minister to cowboys and saloon girls, as he explained. I suppose he forgot about the farmers and homesteaders. As you have no doubt surmised, I ignored his censure. I am here. I'm certain God will not see it the way my professor did. Do not allow the opinion of your abbess to bother you. If you were guided by faith then you must have been guided by God. Did you say that you saved a man's life? Then that is worth any scolding you might have received; don't you think so, Miss Cleary?"

"I thought so, but the abbess was appalled that I broke every rule of the mission to do so. If I'm honest, it wasn't the first time I had broken a few rules. But even when I didn't do anything wrong, she always disapproved of me, or at least I felt like she did."

"You're in Tucker Springs now; her opinion of you doesn't matter anymore. If you want to hear mine, I would be happy to give it. Your temper is not a shortcoming, You are tired, and I had no right to speak without regard to your feelings. As a man who is tasked with the burden of easing suffering, I should have chosen my words more carefully. It was my feelings for you which led me astray."

"Pastor Newland, why are you so understanding? You should be shocked and horrified at my behavior."

"Not at all. You have spirit uncommon in a woman. You aren't afraid to speak your mind. I like that about you, I admire it. Not many women have a mind of their own and if they do, they do not share their thoughts freely with a man like me."

Louisa came into the parlor, her apron tied around her waist, and smiled at the pastor. With a gleam in her eye, she said, "Pastor, I hope you can stay for supper. We have plenty to go around."

"I'm not going to lie and say that I wouldn't welcome the invitation to stay. I've had a delightful afternoon here with your sister." He smiled at Alice. "If it would not be too much trouble," he answered.

"Not at all, I was counting on you to say yes so I made your favorite, a pecan pie."

Alice stared at her sister, but Louisa would not look in her direction. Louisa's intentions were clear, and she didn't know how she felt about it. Maybe she was tired from her trip, as the pastor suggested.

Pouring another cup of coffee for herself, she tried not to think of Jonathan as she felt the steady gaze of her sister and the pastor. Where was he, and why couldn't he be the one seated across from her in the parlor, accepting an invitation to stay for supper? She wondered where he was as she sipped the coffee and sighed once again. She had to forget about him, about that part of her life, as he undoubtedly had done the same about her.

*****

There wasn't much to see in Tucker Springs. There wasn't a town square, or a Spanish church, neither was there a single saloon, two general stores, or

Mama Rosa's. Alice already missed tortillas, spicy red chilis, and beans. Why did she have to think about Mama Rosa's? It brought back memories of good food, dear sweet Mama Rosa, and stolen moments with Jonathan. She was mad at herself for thinking about him. Since he'd left her in January, she had shed enough tears over the man, and he must have forgotten all about her by now. She promised herself that she would forget about him too, and here she was, walking down the main street of Tucker Springs thinking of him.

Tucker Springs was just as she remembered it, a small hamlet with one street going straight down the center of the tiny town. Wooden frame houses lined up neat as a row of corn near the church and the post office. Each house had a tidy garden and a clothesline with laundry fluttering in the breeze. How strange it was, to walk to town without facing the wrath of an angry abbess when she returned. In Tucker Springs she didn't have to answer to anyone. She should have felt relief to be free from so many rules, but instead she missed the mission, the regimented schedule, and her students. She thought about the letter to Joanna in her pocket, the one she planned to mail that afternoon. If she stayed in Tucker Springs she would miss Joanna, but she knew her friend would understand after the tumultuous year Alice had had at the mission.

She opened the door of the one and only general mercantile and stepped inside. The store was a narrow space, cramped and filled with farm implements and dry goods. Bolts of material and spools of ribbon were displayed behind a counter. Barrels of flour, white and brown sugar sat beside coffee and dry beans. Compared to Santa Maria, this store had a meager selection of goods, but that was to be expected. Tucker Springs was tiny, and only a few years old. It wasn't like Santa Maria with its storied past and thriving businesses.

"What can I get you?" a middle aged man asked from behind the counter.

"A small bag of candy," Alice answered.

She had come to town to look at material for a new dress but the bolts of cloth in the general mercantile were as somber and uninspiring as the rest of her own plain wardrobe. She longed for something pretty after all that she had been through, but in Tucker Springs she would have to settle for what was useful. She paid the man for the small bag a candy, an indulgence for Louisa's children. Slipping the bag into the small purse that hung from her wrist, she turned to leave the store. She smiled at the sight of someone unexpected coming in the door.

Will Cleary was standing in front of her, smiling. "What are you doing in town?"

"I was going to buy fabric, but there isn't much to choose from here. Calico and more calico if you want a work dress, I suppose. I can remember a time when I would have leapt in happiness to have new calico, but I wanted something pretty to cheer myself. But that doesn't matter. What are you doing here? I thought you would be working hard today with James."

"I am, I mean I was. The plow blade has dulled, and I went to sharpen it but the old file finally gave out.

If you aren't in a hurry, I can walk home with you. Unless you were here for some other purpose, like to meet someone," he grinned.

"Will Cleary, I don't know what you mean by that but I assure you I am not here for any special reason, though I do need to mail a letter. Why don't I meet you in front of the post office in five minutes?"

With a nod, Will went to the counter and Alice left for the post office. She had forgotten how easy it was to tease her brother and be teased by him. She'd missed him when she was in Santa Maria. If she stayed in Tucker Springs she wouldn't have to miss him anymore, she mused as she walked into the tiny, one-room post office.

Five minutes later she was standing outside in the late May sun, waiting for her brother to emerge from the general store. She looked at the church, at the houses, at the street and wondered, could she live here? Could she be happy in a place as small as this?

From across the dusty road, she saw her brother walk outside of the store, a parcel in his hand. That must be the new file, she said to herself as he joined her.

"It's a nice day for a walk," he said, fanning himself with his hat.

"Yes it is. I can't remember the last time you and I had a few minutes to ourselves," she said as they walked past the church and headed out of the town.

"Neither can I. We need to talk, don't we?"

291

"We do, but you first. What about this Millie Tucker? Are you going to marry her?"

Will blushed as he rolled his eyes. "Oh come on, not you too. Why can't I be sweet on a girl and not be thinking about marrying?"

Alice knew her brother better than anyone. She knew when he was hiding something. "Will, this is me. Remember? Your sister? We have no secrets. You can tell me the truth."

"I don't like to think about it," he said, kicking a dirt clod along the road.

"Will, I may have been gone for a year, but I'm still your sister. You can tell me anything, anything at all. What is it? What's the matter?"

"Alice, tell me the truth. Do you think I'm good enough for her?"

"I think you're good enough for any girl."

"But am I? Her father is the blacksmith, and who am I? I'm a farm hand working on my sister's farm. I don't have a farm of my own, or a trade. Why should she say yes to me, and why would her father allow me to marry his daughter?"

"*Yet*. You don't have a farm or a trade *yet*."

"Yet, or in the future, it doesn't matter. I can't marry her. What would we do? We can't live in the attic at Louisa's. I live there already and it's not a place for any wife. Maybe I might build a little cabin, but she deserves better than that. I want to build a real house, just like the ones in town, for her."

"Will, I had no idea you had grown up so much since I was away. If you love this girl so much, why didn't you mention her in your letters?"

"I wanted to tell you about her, but I was afraid you would think that I was being foolish."

"No, I don't. Before you decide not to ask her, why don't you try to talk to her? Maybe she won't mind living in a cabin until you can build her a house one day. Why should you decide for both of you? I admit that I don't know much about her, but I can tell by the way she looks at you, she's in love with you. It's as plain as day."

Will grinned. "You think so? You think she loves me?"

"Sure she does, promise me you'll talk to her. If she wants to marry, then do it. Don't wait, don't talk yourself out of it. Marry her."

"Thanks Alice, I feel better. I knew you would tell me the truth. Everyone else just plans the wedding. I will talk to her, and to her father."

"He would be a fool not to want you for his daughter. You work hard, you're honest, and you can do anything."

"What do I do if he says no? What if she says no?"

"Will, there are plenty of girls in Tucker Springs who would be happy to have you. But don't think like that. Millie Tucker is going to say yes, mark my words. When she does, you promise me you'll marry her."

"What about you? I keep hearing Louisa saying that you and the pastor will be hitched come Christmas, maybe sooner than that."

"I love our sister, don't get me wrong, but I wish she would stop meddling in my life. I've been in Tucker Springs for a week, and already she has me married and settled down with Pastor Newland!"

"Isn't that why you're here, back in Tucker Springs? To settle down and get married? I don't think she's meddling. Not when you think about it. She's older than we are, maybe she knows more about some things than we do."

"Will, not you too. Are you going to make me feel like I would be missing my only chance at happiness if I decided not to marry the pastor?" Alice groaned.

"That's what Louisa told me. I figured you must have wrote to her about Pastor Newland, because you didn't write to me about it. I don't mean to pry, but I thought there was someone else you may have liked better. Someone you met in New Mexico. Didn't you write to me about a man named Jonathan?"

"I did, didn't I?" Alice said, her voice faint as she sighed.

"You did, but you never said much about him."

"There wasn't much to tell. Will, can you be my friend *and* my brother for a moment? Can you swear not to say a word to Louisa, or James?"

"Sure. No one else has to know."

"No, they don't. That man I wrote you about, his name was Jonathan Keene. If I were going to marry anyone it would have been him."

"Then what are you doing back here in Kansas?"

Alice didn't answer her brother; she didn't want to. If she did, she knew it would make her cry. Stopping on the road, she put her face in her hands as she felt the first tears welling up in her eyes. Taking a deep breath, she wiped her eyes with her hand as she looked at horizon. The tall prairie grass moved in waves in the warm breeze of the May afternoon. It was hypnotic and beautiful and so far away from the desert of Santa Maria. How different Kansas was compared to New Mexico, she thought, in so many ways.

"I shouldn't have asked. I didn't mean to make you cry."

"No, Will, it's not your fault. I said I needed a friend. I do. I haven't told anyone about what happened in Santa Maria, except for Joanna, but she's back there and I'm here. I don't even know why I'm here, but I had to get away, to leave and never look back."

"Is it because of that fellow, Jonathan?"

"I could say it was, but it's my fault. I wanted to marry him and he didn't want to marry me. It's as plain as that. I wish it were otherwise but it isn't."

"He broke your heart?" Will asked softly.

"I broke my own heart, but he helped. He told me he wasn't the marrying kind. I didn't listen to him, I didn't want to. I didn't think he meant it. Not after all we went through together. He saved my life, more than once, Did I tell you that? I would get into trouble and he was there, getting me out of scrapes. Every time he came in like a knight to save the day, I fell in love with him a little more, even though I know I shouldn't have."

"I don't think it's your fault, how could it be? If you fell in love with him there had to be some reason. The scoundrel, making you believe he loved you. If I ever lay eyes on him, I'll make him sorry for what he's done to you."

"No, Will, it's not like that – well, not exactly. He may have said some nice things to me, he may have told me he was falling in love with me. He may have teased me that we were married. But, he never actually asked me to marry him, did he?"

"He should have, if he was a gentleman. He better hope I never see him."

"You would like him; he's a good man. He stood up for what he believed in, even if he played cards and nearly got himself hanged."

"Alice, you're not describing a good man, but a criminal. I'm glad you're safe and sound away from him. If he was as good as you claim, he would have asked you to marry him. If Louisa knew about him, she would be furious."

"Why should she be furious? I can't help who I fall in love with. I can't help it and I don't want to. But why didn't he love me? Will, why didn't he want to marry me?" Alice cried, the months of mourning and missing Jonathan pouring out of her in a torrent of tears.

Will slid the file into the pocket of his work pants and he held her. She hadn't been held by her brother in a long time. Her body wracked with sobs, the tears fell as she remembered the last time she saw Jonathan, a memory she had been trying to forget.

It had been January, just after Christmas. Joanna was back from Santa Fe; her father was on the mend. Alice remained at the mission, Sister Cecilia having convinced her to stay for the rest of the year for the sake of the children. Jonathan remained at the Garcias' ranch and made frequent visits to town to see her, whenever she could get away from the mission. It had been a wonderful blur of meetings at Mama Rosa's, of cold strolls in the square, of the occasional embrace, of passionate kisses. But soon it was all over. She remembered shivering in the cold as he told her he was leaving Santa Maria, and possibly New Mexico, for good. She remembered begging him to stay, to stay with her, but he told her as she cried that he couldn't remain, not after nearly being hanged by the sheriff. She understood, she had told him.

She remembered how Jonathan had looked at her. He was so different that day, that she questioned what she was seeing, what she was feeling. How could this man who had been so warm and caring, who had made her laugh and made her angry all at the same time, suddenly look at her so distantly? Her heart broke as he spoke to her.

"Colleen, I love you but I can't stay."

"I know you can't, and I know why. But why can't I go with you?"

"You don't want that kind of life. It's no life for a woman, for a lady," he explained.

"What if I told you I didn't care? That I loved you and nothing else mattered?" she asked him eagerly.

"It does matter. Maybe not now, but in the future you would regret leaving Santa Maria with a man like me."

"Why won't you let me decide that for myself?"

"Because, Colleen, I love you and I know you would say yes if I asked you to marry me. You would say yes, but then mark my words you would wish you hadn't. I'm not the marrying sort. I told you that, remember?"

"I do remember," she told him, "But I didn't think that mattered any more, when it came to me and you."

"It does matter. It matters to me what happens to you. I want you to have the life you deserve, not the life you would have with me. I don't have any money, not now. I can barely afford to feed myself, let alone a wife. I have to leave, to make my way in the world. I can't worry about anyone else but me for a while."

"I could work. I don't mind," she said.

"I do mind. It wouldn't be right, dragging you all over the country, never knowing if I'm going to have money to feed us or not. It's not the kind of life I want for you. I told you that."

"You did, but everything has changed," she remembered saying to him as she wept in the square that cold January.

"You've changed, but I haven't. I'm still the man you met on the train; I'm still the card player and the hired gun. That hasn't changed even if I do admit I love you. And it won't. It can't. Colleen, I don't know if we will ever see each other again, but I love you, remember that. Don't remember today. Think about the times we spent together that were happier than this. Will you do that for me?"

"Why should I do anything for you, when you're telling me you're leaving and that I'll never see you again?"

"Do it for me because you love me, and I love you. But we can't be together, don't you see that? A woman like you should have a house and a man who can give you a life of ease and contentment. There should be food on the table every night. You should never worry about how the bills are going to be paid. I can't give that life to you, not now, and I don't know if I ever will. It would be better for you, and for me, if we remember our times together and forget this day, forget that we had to part."

"Jonathan," she cried. But he was gone.

As her brother held her and she cried, the pain in her chest was a deep ache that wouldn't go away.

"What happened? Don't tell me you were the one to blame, because I don't believe it," said Will.

"It hurts so much but I don't know who else to turn to. Will, I loved Jonathan. I don't know if I will ever love again, but he didn't love me enough to change his life. That hurts me more than I can tell you."

"Your secret is safe with me, Alice, don't fear. You're here with me and your family and we all love you. I'll talk to Louisa and tell her to leave you alone about the pastor."

Alice thought about what Will said, until at last leaned back from him, wiping her face with her hand. "No, Will. Don't tell her that. I'm not going to lie. I don't love the pastor but he seems like a nice man. I may not want to marry him but he and I may be friends. I need a friend or two in this town, especially if I choose to stay."

"If you stay here with me and Louisa we could be a family again."

"I don't know. I just don't know, but until I make up my mind, there isn't any sense making any decisions I may regret."

"Like the pastor. You're still considering marrying him? You just told me you don't love him, you love this Jonathan fellow."

"I know, but I don't know what's in store for me. Maybe I'll surprise myself and find a way to love a man like the pastor. Maybe not. Oh Will, what should I do? I'm so confused. Should I stay here in Tucker Springs, or should I go back to Santa Maria?"

Her brother shook his head. "I don't know what you should do, but I want you to stay. Whether you marry the pastor or not doesn't matter to me, as long as you're happy. Do you know what would make you happy?"

Being with Jonathan would have made her happy. "I thought I did. I like teaching, and I know I want to keep doing that, but the rest of my life is a mystery. Maybe I need to stay here for a while at least until I figure that out. I don't think they will miss me at the mission for a few weeks. Really, I don't think the abbess will miss me at all."

"We could use the help around the farm. If you do decide to stay in town, you could teach here," Will said eagerly.

"I could. I'm considering staying but I don't want to make any decisions. I just need to find a way to forget about Jonathan. At least while I'm here, nothing reminds me of him," Alice answered.

As she walked beside her brother back to the Burke farm, she looked up at the clear blue sky and wondered silently whether she could live in a place like this. Could she be happy in Kansas? It was a question she was going to have to answer, but that could wait. Right now her face was still stained with tears. Even as her shoulders sagged under the weight of the decision she knew she would have to make, she felt better, better than she had in months. Talking about Jonathan to her brother helped. Replaying the last conversation she'd had with the man she loved was terribly painful, but it was necessary.

As she walked along the narrow wagon road her heart felt lighter, as if a great burden had been lifted. She still loved Jonathan, but she wasn't burdened by that feeling any more. It was true that she may never forget him or love anyone else the way she loved him, but if he could live without her, she would find a way to live without him. Maybe she would find a husband who deserved her, as he said. Maybe she could find a man who wasn't a card player and a hired gun. Stopping on the road, she turned to face the tiny town of Tucker Springs. She thought she may have already found someone. She didn't know what the future held, but maybe she knew a man who she may one day learn to love.

*****

June 15, 1877
Tucker Springs, Kansas

"It was very kind of you to recommend me for the teaching position here in town. I truly appreciate it," Alice said to Pastor Newland as he walked beside her into the church. The church was as small as the town, a one room structure built of wood and painted white. A newly erected steeple rose overhead, housing a bell, a gift from one of the Tuckers. Inside, a narrow aisle was flanked by rows of wooden pews, a podium at the other end. A woodstove sat in the back, beside a neat line of hooks for coats and hats.

"This is where I envision we will hang the blackboard, behind the altar, or should I say your desk, when I'm not using it for church services," he explained. "My house is next door, should you ever need anything – more firewood in the winter, or help with anything, anything at all."

"Pastor Newland," she began.

"Miss Cleary, if I may, why don't you call me by my first name. I like the sound of 'Pastor' well enough but I think you and I are on equal footing, especially if you take the teaching position."

"To be honest, I'm not sure what I'm going to do just yet," Alice answered as she looked at the church as though she was seeing it for the first time. In reality, she had sat here every Sunday since she'd first set foot in Tucker Springs. This time, she wasn't seeing the church as a holy place, she was seeing it as a possible schoolroom.

"This would be temporary. The town – and by that, I mean the Tuckers – want to build a schoolhouse on the other side of the churchyard. It wouldn't be very big but it would be a start."

The way he looked at her when he said the word *start* made her wonder if he was referring to something other than the proposed new building for the school. If she was going to marry him, or consider any man in Tucker Springs, she realized that sooner or later she would have to face the difference in religion. She touched the wood of the pew, feeling the sanded edges. The building had the smell of newly cut wood and smoke, not like the church in Santa Maria or the chapel at the mission. On the altar here there was no host. Nowhere inside the tiny church was there a statue of the Virgin Mary on display, or even a crucifix. There was only a simple wooden cross affixed to the wall above the altar.

Alice missed the Mass, the feeling of being inside a Catholic church. She missed the scent of incense hanging in the air, the smell of candle wax and the dark wood and stained glass. Thinking about church reminded her once again of Christmas Eve, of Jonathan appearing beside her. She shrugged that thought away as quickly as she could, and focused her attention on Pastor Newland. "You didn't tell me your name, did you?"

"No, I didn't. I was describing the plans for the future school."

"Yes, the school," she nodded.

"We'll get back to the school in good time. I wonder if you would call me by my given name. If it's too soon or too familiar, I understand. My name is Howard, Howard Newland."

"Howard," she said. The name rolled off her tongue, strange and unnatural to her ears, after she had called him Pastor for the better part of a year.

"If I may be so forward, may I call you Alice? I hold you in such high regard that I do not consider any formality remaining between us."

"Yes, you may call me Alice if you wish," she answered, watching his eyes glisten with happiness.

"Alice, I rather like your name. I tend to think of you as Alice, and not Miss Cleary."

"Then you are accustomed to it," she smiled. "Now if we may return to the subject of the school teacher position?"

"About that. I sincerely hope that you will take the position if it should be offered to you, although I have no reason to think that it will be offered to anyone else. But there is a matter which may cause some concern, and that is your current unmarried state."

"My what? What do you mean? In the teaching profession, being unmarried is requisite for the job in most places."

"That is precisely what I mean. You may marry and still teach, but surely you will give up working outside of your home when you have children of your own."

She looked at the pastor, or Howard as he preferred to be called, for a long moment. Was he, in a roundabout way, asking the same question he asked in his letter – whether or not she wished to continue teaching – or did she want to be married. What was he trying to say? Was everyone around her wrong about his intentions? Why he had recommended her for the teaching position, and then asked how long she wanted to remain teaching if she should be married? It was confusing. For a woman who was on the verge of making an important life decision, she needed facts, not speculation.

"Howard, I do wish you would answer a question for me, one that has been on my mind ever since I came back to Kansas."

"You may rely on me to answer any question you may ever have as honestly and sincerely as I can."

"That's all that I ask. Forgive me for being so bold, but why did you recommend me for the teaching position?"

He looked at her in that kind way he had, which made her feel as though he would shield her even if he had to tell her something unpleasant. Without hesitation, he replied, "I knew you would ask me this question and I am prepared to answer it. It is no surprise to you that your family did not approve of your venture in New Mexico. I knew you were bound for mission work, but I would never have permitted you to travel alone or leave the mission. But I knew you would not change your mind; I saw the fire in your eyes, the way you were convinced you were doing the Lord's work. Your family were worried about you, more than they will admit. I am breaking a confidence to tell you that, but you already know this, I'm certain."

"You recommended me to give me a reason to return to Tucker Springs?"

"Yes, I was led to do it. I saw your passion for teaching, for wanting to change the lives of children. I knew that was God's plan for you. I ask you how much better you may fulfil his plan here among your family, than among the heathens and sinners in the Godless country of the territory? It was because you were working among the poor children in the territory, that I

306

ever permitted you to go. I should have put a stop to it, but who am I to block in the path that God has chosen you to walk?"

"I'm sorry, did I hear you correctly? You permitted it?"

"Yes, you did. As the bible teaches us, a woman is to obey her father's wishes, and then her brother's, and her husband's. As you have no father who is living, and your brother is younger than you, it is my duty to see that you are protected from harm."

"You are not my husband," she said calmly, but her anger was rising. For a man of God, he had a way of making her angry – and not in the same way that Jonathan did. Pastor Newland always seemed to have an explanation and he always seemed to know better than she did what was good for her.

"No, I am not, but I would like the opportunity to earn your approval and your trust. It is no secret that I wish to marry you. If you were here in town, we could have a long courtship, which is customary for a man in my position."

"I don't love you," she said without a second thought.

"You don't have to love me. I don't love you either, but I find your qualities are ideal for the wife of a man of God. You would have to convert, there is the matter of your papist beliefs, but that can be rectified."

Alice bristled to hear her faith being called *papist*. If she recalled her history correctly, when Protestants referred to Catholics as papists, there were usually executions next. She didn't think Pastor Newland was a zealot, but she did not wish to convert from the faith that had seen her though the darkest days of the war and every trial she had endured in the territory.

Without addressing the matter of her faith, or his certainty that he was acting on God's own will, she smiled. "If you don't love me, as you have admitted, why do you find me to be an ideal wife of a man of God, as you say?"

"Alice, how can you be so blind to the truth? You were fashioned to be the wife of a man like me. Your hardships, your whole life has led you to no other fate. You know what it is to survive, to live without luxuries and niceties. You would set a fine example to the women in the community of what a godly wife should be. I have no fear that you would ever seek to adorn yourself with jewels and set yourself above your company. When I look at you I see quiet strength and faith, a testament to the mercy of God. I see you as a model of womanhood for all to aspire to who do His work."

"I was not expecting that answer. You want me to be your wife because I work hard, have been through trials, and I look the part?"

"It's more than that. I like the spark I see in you, the spirit that is unquenched by the tragedies you have endured. Louisa and your brother have told me much of the life you left behind in Georgia. It touched my heart that you had no other choice than to be strong, with God's help. When the women in our town see you they will know they are looking at a woman touched and saved by the mercy of the Lord. Together we could serve God and this town; we would lead by example. It would make me proud to have you as my wife."

"What about me? You don't love me for myself?"

"In time, I may come to love you. I admit a feeling of romantic love has begun to grow inside of me when I think of you," he said as he reached for her hand.

Her hand was resting on the corner of a church pew, and his hand came to rest on hers. She did not feel a spark pass between them. He was standing close enough to kiss, but she did not have the slightest desire to press her lips to his. He was handsome, and kind, and he was not in love with her any more than she was with him. He wanted a wife who would serve God as he did and be an example to the women of Tucker Springs. He did not want Alice, just his idealized version of her.

"What about my teaching position?"

"You can teach, while we court. You can teach afterwards if you like, but when you have children, I expect your attention to turn to home, to me, your children, and to God."

"You seem to have this all planned."

"It is not what I have planned; it what is ordained by God. Your place is in the home, caring for the family."

"You do want a family?" Alice was just curious, now.

"We should do what we must to set the example for anyone who chooses to remain unmarried. It is not the natural state of man to remain unwed, not when God commands us to go forth and multiply."

"You have given me much to think about, Howard."

"I know I have not asked you for your hand formally, but I am certain we understand each other," he replied.

Alice did not reply. She was overwhelmed by his presumption, his reasons for wanting to marry her, and much else that he said. Quietly, she explained that she was needed back home and left the church. He offered to walk her to her sister's farm, but she declined. She needed the time alone to think about all that he'd said. He didn't love her, he wanted her for a wife because of her resilience and her faith, a faith he wished to change. For a man as humble and hardworking as he was, he possessed a conceit she had never encountered before. Pastor Howard Newland was convinced without a single doubt that he was doing the work of God in everything he did, even marriage. While Alice did not have a desire to go against the word of God, she wondered how the God she knew and loved, who had stood by her throughout her entire life, would feel if she suddenly changed how she worshipped him. She questioned how she could live with a man who, when he touched her, was as cold as winter.

There was a time when she thought she might be able to love the handsome young pastor with the golden brown eyes, but now she didn't know how she had ever considered it. Walking past the empty patch of land where the future schoolhouse was going to stand, she realized with a sigh that Pastor Newland had made her decision for her. She did not want to stay in Tucker Springs. If she did, she would never be free of the man who would be a good husband to her – as long as she was content to be the plain, unassuming wife he wished her to be.

Maybe that wasn't such a bad life for some, to be with a man who followed the word of God, but she didn't know how she could live with him as her husband if she didn't love him. After listening to him explain that he didn't love her either, she was certain that the decision that had plagued her for weeks was finally made. Looking at the ground beside the churchyard, she knew she would never teach a day inside the building when it was erected.

It was a sad realization, but she could not bear to watch her life fall under someone else's control; she'd had enough of that to last a lifetime. She thought of her aunt and uncle, how they treated her as a maidservant. Would Howard Newland be any different with his orders and rules for her life? No, she did not wish for one more person telling her what she may and may not do. She was too independent to be lectured, preached to and criticized, especially when she suspected she would be trying to forget Jonathan Keene every day of her life. If she married a man as cold as the pastor, the rest of her days would be spent comparing him to the man who had left her behind in New Mexico. She did not think she could bear a lifetime of empty kisses and memories that made her cry.

It was decided; she was not staying in Tucker Springs. She did not want to go back to Santa Maria because of her memories of Jonathan, they were too painful. Yet, there was something about New Mexico, about the desert, the food, the people, that she had come to love. Pastor Newland said he admired her strength and her bravery. Maybe she was strong and brave enough to face the anguish of thinking about Jonathan every time she walked into Mama Rosa's, or when she went to Mass on Sundays in town. The more she thought about it, the more she realized that even with Sister Cecilia's stern criticisms and the rules she had to follow, she loved Santa Maria. She had fallen in love with New Mexico despite its lawlessness and its dangers. She didn't belong in Kansas, and she didn't belong anywhere else she couldn't practice her faith, listen to Spanish spoken on the streets, and see Joanna and Thomas.

Walking alone on the road that summer day, she smiled. It had taken weeks but she knew at last what she wanted to do. She wanted to remain a teacher and she wanted to keep her faith in her own way. She would become an old maid if she must, but she would never waver in her beliefs, and she would never agree to marry for anything less than love – even if that meant never marrying at all. It was devastating to think of leaving Will, but he was going to be married and then he would have Millie and children would soon follow to occupy his thoughts.

As she made her way down the dusty road, she gazed out at the prairie. It was beautiful in Tucker Springs, but her heart longed for a desolate landscape of grey mountains and flat endless desert, of cactuses and pinon trees, of desert willows and cottonwoods. New Mexico had gotten in her blood and she loved it, despite the memories that were sure to haunt her all her days. With a purposeful stride she walked back to the Burke homestead. She had news for her family and then she had some packing to do. She was going home to New Mexico.

Chapter Ten

September 21, 1877
Santa Maria, New Mexico Territory

Alice sat in Sister Cecilia's office, questioning why she had come back to the mission. She must really love New Mexico to endure the abbess's sharp tongue and disapproving glare, but here she was seated in the same chair, across from the abbess behind her desk. Only this time, Alice wasn't entirely certain what she had done to be called into the office so early in the morning after breakfast.

Sister Cecilia nodded to acknowledge Alice, but her eyes remained on a letter she held in her hand as Alice yawned as discreetly as she could.

With Jonathan gone from Santa Maria, Alice had very little reason to break the rules any more. Since her return, she had been an exemplary mission teacher, or so she had thought. Maybe this meeting was about the pretty new fabric she'd bought for a dress, the pale cream with roses and ivy that she had purchased at the Garcias' store the week she came home.

Home. Despite Sister Cecilia's cross words and her disapproval of Alice, Alice felt that New Mexico was her home now. Yet she knew it was on Sister Cecilia's approval that she remain at the mission. Alice had no choice but to be a model teacher, as Sister Cecilia cautioned her when she arrived from Kansas. Sighing, her shoulders slumping under the weight of the lecture that was certain to follow, she waited for Sister Cecilia to finish reading the missive.

The Abbess folded the letter carefully, slipping it into her desk drawer. Alice braced herself for what was coming but she did not expect a soft rapping at the door. A young novice hurried in at Sister Cecilia's command to enter. The novice slipped past Alice with her eyes downcast, but not before Alice saw that the girl was no other than Joanna's little sister, Flor. Flor offered Alice a quick smile and then she was gone, the tray of coffee left steaming on the abbess's desk.

After the adventure to save Flor from a life of corruption and sin, Alice was glad the young woman had found a place at last where she would be safe.

"I took the liberty of having coffee and cake brought in. We have much to discuss you and I," Sister Cecilia said to Alice in a pleasant voice that caught Alice off guard.

"The coffee is for me?" Alice asked as she gazed at the slices of iced spice cake on a plate beside the coffee pot.

"Yes, it is. Pour a cup and let's talk, shall we?" The abbess said as she attempted a thin lipped smile.

Alice didn't know what was coming next but the coffee smelled divine and the cake looked delicious. Not wanting to be rude when the abbess was offering her coffee and kindness, she quickly poured a cup for herself and chose the tiniest sliver of cake. As she ate the cake, she was consumed by curiosity. What was going on, and why was Sister Cecilia suddenly being nice?

"Alice Cleary, you have surprised me lately," the abbess began.

Alice wanted to groan. She was certain that nothing good was going to come out of the abbess's mouth. Sipping her coffee, she set the cup on the saucer on the desk in front of her. Brushing the crumbs from her dress, she sat up straight and rigid, ready for whatever may follow.

"Yes Sister, I know why I'm in here. I've tried to do better since I came back from Kansas. Can't you see that I have made improvements?"

"Yes, yes, there is no need for explanations in this office today," Sister Cecilia said with a smile and a raised eyebrow.

"Oh," Alice replied. "If I'm not in trouble, why am I in here?"

"You are here because I have an important matter to discuss with you, one I hope you will see as an opportunity, as I do."

The last time anyone had used the word *opportunity* in her presence, it was followed by a proposal for marriage which she did not accept. Alice braced herself yet again as she urged the abbess to continue, "Go on, I'm listening."

"I have received a letter, the letter I was just reviewing. It is from a Father Dunbar, a priest in a small town to the north of Santa Fe. It is not far from here; it's called Alamosa."

"I'm not sure I understand. Why are you telling me about this place?"

"Miss Cleary, the town of Alamosa is in desperate need of a teacher, and not just any one will do. They need someone who is intrepid, able to think for themselves and take charge."

"Are you thinking of sending Joanna? Is that why you called me into your office, to tell me that Joanna was leaving, or to ask my opinion?"

"No, no Miss Cleary. Joanna would make a fine teacher for this position but her sister is here at the mission and she has expressed interest in remaining here. She has been with us for so many years, I don't know how well our school would function without her."

"What about the other sisters? Sister Rafaela, or Gabriella?"

"They are needed here at the mission. This position is for a one-room school, serving all grades of students. There is no convent but there is a Catholic church and a priest who ministers to the town."

Alice's eyes opened in surprise. "You want me to go? You're sending me?"

"I'm not sending you exactly. I'm asking you to give the matter your full consideration."

"But I love being here in Santa Maria, with Joanna and Thomas."

"I know you do, but you would not be so far away. Alamosa is in the next county, a short distance by horse or wagon."

Alice sat perfectly still, riveted by what Sister Cecilia told her. She had so many questions but she wasn't sure she wanted to go anywhere. Sister Cecilia drank her coffee as Alice realized that this was not a request. "You say this is an opportunity, but you've already decided for me, haven't you?"

"Father Dunbar is eager to meet with you. I wrote to him that you would be an ideal candidate for the job. There will be far fewer rules in Alamosa, and less temptation. You will live in a cabin of your own on the church grounds. Your proclivity for daring ventures and sin will be curbed in a place as quiet as Alamosa. I can't think of a better situation for you."

"What if I say no?"

"Why would you say no? You will be able to put to use your independent nature to run the school and teach children of all ages. It is an ideal situation for a woman of your talents."

"You've already made arrangements for me to go, haven't you?" asked Alice.

"You leave the day after tomorrow."

Alice wanted to sulk, to be angry, but she couldn't. She was going to be close to Santa Maria but she was going to a new place, a place that had a Catholic church and a school that needed a teacher. She had to admit it did seem like a good opportunity.

"You're not saying a word. If you truly don't wish to go, I will write to Father Dunbar. He and I will both be disappointed."

"No, it's not that, I'm just taken by surprise is all. I've never had my own cabin or lived by my own rules."

"You shall have a cabin, but the rules you must abide by are similar to the ones here. No immorality, no gentleman callers, no smoking or drinking. Your behavior last year was wicked, but you seem to have made amends. I expect that you will uphold the standards you have been taught here at the mission."

"Yes, Sister Cecilia, I will," Alice said as she began to feel something she hadn't experienced in a long time, joy and anticipation. She didn't care at that moment that Sister Cecilia was sending her away, or that she was going to be alone in a new town. She was staying in New Mexico and she was going to teach in her own little schoolhouse. It was just the perfect place to forget about Jonathan and start her new life. With a grin, she reached for another slice of cake and fought the urge to hug the abbess. She was going to Alamosa.

*****

April 2, 1878
Alamosa, New Mexico Territory

Alice cleaned the blackboard as she did every day after school. In the peace and quiet of the afternoon, after the children went to their homes, she spent an hour in the schoolhouse doing all the housekeeping. The floors were swept, the stove was cleaned and wood piled ready for the next morning. Even in April, the mornings were still cold and the fire inside the tiny iron stove was a necessity, as was the pot of hot water on top for cleaning faces and hands after lunch.

As she finished her chores, she thought about the books waiting for her in the cabin. Father Dunbar believed in reading. He was always quick to lend a book to Alice or any of the older students. His books, her knitting and sewing had been her constant occupations during the winter. Now that it was spring, she looked forward to frequent visits to Santa Maria. She was thinking about what she would buy when she returned to Garcia's general store when she heard the door of the tiny schoolhouse open, its hinges creaking.

321

She was not startled by the noise. The children often forgot their mittens, or school books and lunch pails. If it wasn't one of the children it was probably Father Dunbar. The kindly old priest often stopped by to check on Alice after school to see if she needed any wood chopped or supplies. Turning to face a student or the priest, she gasped when she saw the person standing in the doorway.

"Colleen, what a fine place you have here," the man said as Alice dropped the cleaning rag on the floor, her hands raised to her mouth as she gasped, "Jonathan!"

"It's been a long time, Colleen. Aren't you going to give me a kiss?"

"I ought to slap you after what you did in Santa Maria," She said recovering from the shock of seeing him.

"I deserve that. Come on over and slap me then, but not until you give me a peck on the cheek."

"Jonathan what are you doing here?"

"I came to see you."

"I don't believe you."

"Believe me, Colleen. I tried to write to you, but you aren't at the mission anymore, now are you?"

"No, I'm not. I've been here since last autumn."

"Tucked away in a backwater, where no one could find you. Were you hiding from me?"

Alice's face turned red as she realized that she had been hiding from the memory of him, but she wasn't going to admit, not now. She was glad to see him but she was also furious. "It's been over a year since I saw you or heard from you! What in the devil do you think you're doing coming here like this?"

"I see you're the same dear, sweet girl I remember," he smiled.

Alice was enormously happy to see him; her heart leapt at the sight of him. He was the same man she remembered, from the glint in his dark eyes and the rich brocade of his vest. He was just as she imagined him to be, and he made her blood boil. "It's been taken months to forget about you and her you are. I should ask you to leave."

"You won't ask me to leave. Judging by the fact that you are a teacher, I would say you aren't married. I'm thankful for that. You aren't engaged are you?"

"Thankful you left me unable to ever love anyone else, thankful you broke my heart so badly I may never recover?"

"No, I'm thankful you are not married so I can have a chance to wed you."

"Wed me? Oh no, I'm not falling for your jokes and your teasing. You told me you were never going to marry me, remember? Back in Santa Maria, the day you left. I haven't heard from you in a year and here you stand expecting me to say yes when you don't mean a word you say. Where were you, that you couldn't come to see me, and couldn't write to me."

"Colleen, my dear, I was out in the great big world making my fortune. I traveled every river boat on the Mississippi and hit every saloon from California to Texas. I couldn't marry you back in Santa Maria because I didn't have a cent to my name, but that has all changed, I'm happy to say. I'm glad you are still free to say yes to my proposal."

"You didn't marry me because you were poor? Am I to believe that?"

"Yes, you should because it's true. I swear it on my mother's life."

"Your mother?"

"You'll get to meet her and all my family when they arrive."

"They're coming here, to new Mexico? I thought you couldn't come back here?"

"I'm not going back to Santa Maria, but I bought a place, Colleen. I want you to come see it. It's a wide open land made for cattle ranching. There's a creek and a spring and cottonwoods as pretty as you please. I plan on building two houses there, one for me and one for my mother and my family. It will be the start of new life for me here in New Mexico. I'm giving up the cards and the dice for good; I'm saying good bye to the saloons and the gun slinging."

Alice stood with her hands on her hips, and demanded, "What makes you think I want any part of this new life you have for yourself?"

"Because my dear, you love me, and I love you. That will never change. I couldn't take you with me when I left New Mexico. It was far too dangerous for you. I couldn't do that to you, not when I may have been killed in some of the places I went. Forgive me."

"You could have told me. I would have understood, you know that?"

"What if I didn't make any money, or ended up at the end of hangman's noose? I couldn't bear for you to have to see that or give up hope when I couldn't make a dime."

"Why should I forgive you? I was finished with you. I started a life without you."

"Colleen, I love you. I made a fortune for you. And I have this," he said as he held out his hand to her.

Alice should have slapped him and made him leave, but she couldn't bring herself to do that. The truth was, she did love him. She wanted to throw her arms around him as she told him that. As she held out her hand, the touch of his hand made her feel alive, like a jolt, so powerful she was sure she gasped. Trembling, she watched as he reached into his pocket and presented a golden ring that was shaped like a crown, with clasping hands holding a heart. It glistened in the afternoon light.

He held it up so she could see it, and then he kneeled down. "Alice Cleary, my own Colleen, this ring is a symbol of love that is worn by my people back in Ireland. It is made near Galway, where my people are from. It is our tradition. It is a token of my undying love

325

and my devotion, say that you will have me, that you love me and you will be my wife."

Alice couldn't breathe as she looked deep into his dark eyes. Somehow, she found the strength to say, "How can I say yes; you've been gone for a year and half."

"Alice, say yes. Say yes so we can be married. You can be mad at me as long as you want to, but marry me first." His eyes twinkled.

"I should say no. You're terrible."

"I expect you to say yes, because you love me," he said as he stood up. "Now say yes, and let me put this ring on your finger."

"No." She crossed her arms defiantly.

"You don't mean that, come and kiss me and say no again." he replied as he slipped the ring back in his pocket.

"No."

His arms embraced her gently as he gazed into her eyes. "Tell me no again," he said tenderly.

"No, I won't marry you."

"I know how to change your mind," he smiled.

She felt his arms around her, his strong, body next to hers. He knew her so well; she couldn't resist him. Not now, not when he was asking her to marry him. She closed her eyes as he kissed her, his lips pressing hard against her, the months spent apart disappearing as her legs grew weak. She wanted to marry him, she wanted to be his wife. She never wanted this kiss to end. As he held her in his arms, she felt the muscles of his broad shoulders under her fingers. He was strong and male and she wanted more of him as the passion in his kiss surged through her body like a flood of desire. She was filled with feelings she could scarcely describe. When he was through, he stepped back and said once more, "Will you marry me?"

Without a moment's hesitation, she nodded.

"Is that a yes? Tell me yes. I want to hear you say it to me."

"Yes, I will marry you. Just kiss me again," she pleaded.

"Not until you're wearing my ring," he answered as he slid the ring out of his pocket and onto her finger. "Now my dear Colleen, I will kiss you. This time I will never let you go."

His arms wrapped around her, and she surrendered once again to him. Closing her eyes, she felt tears of joy sliding down her cheeks. His lips moved to her face as he kissed the tears away, in a gesture as sweet as the promise of their new life together as man and wife.

A Note to My Readers

Thank you so much for reading my book. I hope you enjoyed the story. If you would like to leave a review, please do so where you purchased the book. You will be helping others decide on their purchase and I appreciate your efforts, so will other forthcoming readers.

If you would like to be the first to know about new releases, book promotions, and giveaways, please sign up for my mailing list on my Facebook page, http://www.facebook.com/katherinestclairauthor.

Also by Katherine St. Clair

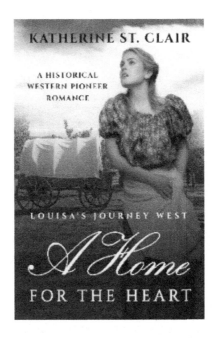

Louisa has lost her parents and her home. She is grateful for the shelter offered by her friend Sarah's family, and she works hard to show it. But they too have paid a heavy price – their son Thomas is never coming back., Matthew has lost an arm, and James…well, perhaps James will never quite recover. And the troubled times are not over. The winter has been hard, and under the new government, the taxes are more than many farmers can pay. They're going to lose the farm.

There is no future in the South. It's time to go. Samuel Burke decides to sell his farm and move his family to Kansas. What will the future bring to Louisa in Kansas?

Made in the USA
Middletown, DE
13 August 2020